THE
BEGINNING

Michael R. Nardo

ARCHWAY
PUBLISHING

Archway Publishing books may be ordered through booksellers or by contacting:

Archway Publishing
1663 Liberty Drive
Bloomington, IN 47403
www.archwaypublishing.com
1 (888) 242-5904

Because of the dynamic nature of the Internet, any web addresses or links contained in this book may have changed since publication and may no longer be valid. The views expressed in this work are solely those of the author and do not necessarily reflect the views of the publisher, and the publisher hereby disclaims any responsibility for them.

Any people depicted in stock imagery provided by Thinkstock are models, and such images are being used for illustrative purposes only.
Certain stock imagery © Thinkstock.

ISBN: 978-1-4808-1672-5 (sc)
ISBN: 978-1-4808-1673-2 (hc)
ISBN: 978-1-4808-1674-9 (e)

Library of Congress Control Number: 2015905705

Print information available on the last page.

Archway Publishing rev. date: 04/30/2015

To my wife, Mary, a beautiful person whom I both love and respect. She is largely responsible for any success I've had in my life or contribution I've made to society. For that, she earns the distinction of being my first literary dedication.

Acknowledgments

I acknowledge the works of Carl Sagan, I. S. Shklovsky, Zecharia Sitchin, Erich von Däniken, Robert Temple, Charles Darwin, and many other scholars mentioned in this book. Additionally, I used recent research conducted by SETI and NASA, including the discoveries of the Hubble Telescope, to provide evidence to support some of my conclusions. History Channel, Science Channel, and Discovery Channel documentaries also provided information on alternatives to mainstream thinking on the subject of life in the universe. These publications played a significant role in outlining some of the theories and concepts in the book.

In addition to those mentioned in this book, many more people helped shape some of the thinking in this book. My family was the first to read this book, and they offered support, encouragement and constructive criticism. They found it to be entertaining and thought-provoking science fiction. I hope that everyone else who reads *The Beginning* feels the same way.

CHAPTER 1
Close Encounter

June 23, 2012: Basra, Iraq, and the Mound of Tiamat, Southern Iraq

A sweltering afternoon sun scorched the desert floor. The sky was baby blue with a few fluffy, pearly-white clouds in the background. Even with the burning heat, it was a vibrant, beautiful day.

Basra was on the Iraq-Iran border, about one hundred miles north of Kuwait and just above the Persian Gulf. It was Iraq's second-largest and most populous city besides Baghdad. Built in 636 CE, this ancient city had played an important role in early Islamic history and was part of the historic location of Sumer, the home of Sinbad the Sailor and the Garden of Eden. Basra was one of the hottest cities on earth with summer temperatures regularly well over one hundred degrees most days.

West of Basra in Sumer, two young shepherds, a fourteen-year-old boy named Ali and his eleven-year-old sister, Shada, were tending a flock of sheep. Given the clear day and flat terrain, the two shepherds knew they were the only ones in the area for miles.

The terrain was parched, and they searched for vegetation to feed the sheep. Since fresh forage was not always available, the sheep were usually fed on stored or harvested feedstuff such as hay, silage, or green chop.

The two shepherds often traveled for miles looking for feed vegetation. However, their parents had warned them to stay out of Sumer, especially the Mound of Tiamat. There were tales of an advanced, mythical, ancient civilization that had settled in this region thousands of years ago and had a direct connection with the gods. The shepherds' parents had heard bizarre stories about this region and did not want their children exposed to such dangers. These myths were indigenous to the region around Sumer, and many locals believed them to be true.

Ali and Shada ignored their parents' warning because they wanted to go someplace different, somewhere they had never been before. Herding sheep was a boring and mundane chore, and any excitement was a welcome change.

Sitting around the nightly community campfire with the elders, Ali and Shada had heard the mythical stories of the ancient Sumerians. The two were even more intrigued by the fact that their parents had forbidden them to go to this area. Being young, they were curious to see what they would find.

Ali and Shada were on opposite sides of the herd, trying to box the herd and keep the sheep from straying. They each had a staff to keep the sheep in the herd and also to support their weight when walking for long periods of time. With serious blisters on her feet, Shada welcomed any support she could get.

Ali shouted, "How's your feet? Do the blisters still hurt?"

Shada yelled back, "Can we take a break for a few minutes?"

Ali walked to the front of the herd to stop the sheep; several of them lay down on the hot desert ground while others just stood there in anticipation of the next command.

Shada unfolded her bedroll and placed it on the ground so they had somewhere to sit. They sat and shared some water, passing a sheepskin bag back and forth until they quenched their thirst. The water had a stale taste and smelled leathery. The musty smell and rubbery flavor did not concern Shada and Ali. They needed something wet, and it did not matter if the water tasted foul. Any liquid was a relief.

The sky above the Mound of Tiamat was as spectacular as its history. Tiamat was one of the few mounds in this flat desert landscape. It protruded out of the desert floor like a pyramid against the backdrop of the level terrain. Tiamat was the largest mound in the area, and the regional tribes considered the ground sacred land. The local people deemed the Mound of Tiamat mysterious and forbidden, and they seldom talked about it.

"What a beautiful day," Shada said. "You can see across the horizon. It feels like we are the sole people on earth—us and the Mound of Tiamat."

"Yeah, it's very clear," said Ali. "I never saw it so luminous and magnificent this time of the year. It's almost too perfect."

"Why do Mom and Dad forbid us to come here?" she asked.

Ali tried to explain. "I heard the elders say Sumer and Tiamat are mystical and spiritual places, the home of the ancients who come from the heavens. I think they are our ancestors, but the elders never mentioned their name or who they were. These ancients just disappeared one day. After them, there were the Sumerians, another of our ancestors, but no one knows or will say what happened to them. It is a gigantic mystery."

Shada asked, "How do you know this?"

"I once overheard father say while breaking bread with Uncle Ali that the Sumerians were descendants from those who came from the stars. He said that the star beings settled this land thousands of years ago before the Sumerians or anyone else. Something happened here that no one wants to talk about."

Without warning, the sky turned pitch dark, and a clap of thunder roared. The clear, baby-blue sky transformed to one that was blacker than a moonless night. It was as if someone had just turned out the lights.

Thunder rumbled and crackled with streaks of lightning flashing violently. The thunder shook the ground underneath Ali and Shada like a major earthquake. As they stood up, they could barely balance themselves as the earth swayed under their feet. Rocks crashed down from the top of the mound to the desert floor.

Startled, the sheep ran off as Ali and Shada stood there dumbfounded and scared. Out of nowhere, a ray of light came directly from the sky and illuminated the top of the Mound of Tiamat. Realizing they were losing the herd, Ali backed away from the mound, still facing the beam of light. He tried to stop the herd, but it was too late.

Mesmerized, Ali and Shada did not take their eyes off the beam of light. Trumpetlike sounds blared loudly for two minutes. The ray of light got brighter, but the surrounding area remained pitch dark. When the trumpets stopped, Shada called out to Ali, and he followed her voice until they reached each other and joined hands.

A dome enclosed the mound, with the shepherds inside, and blocked all sound from outside the enclosed bubble. It was eerie but incredibly amazing.

Minutes later, a humming sound filled the air. Ali pointed to the light as two winged beings descended slowly in unison. They resembled angels and were about ten feet tall with a ten-foot wingspan. They looked strong, with large muscles and elongated, pointed heads. They were carrying an object, grasping a handle on each side. Together the two angel-like beings descended slowly down the light, glowing like spiritual figures portrayed in paintings and artifacts in museums and churches all over the world.

The angels immediately disappeared into the Mound of Tiamat. Both Ali and Shada stood there and did not move. They were both shocked and scared, trying to figure out what they had just witnessed and how the beings had disappeared into the mound.

About a few minutes later, the thunder returned for just a minute and shook the ground even harder. The winged beings appeared again and floated effortlessly above the mound for a moment, then rapidly shot up the beaming light through the tunnel and vanished into the heavens.

Within seconds, the night turned back to daylight, and the sky was clear, blue, and perfect once again.

Shada looked at Ali and asked, "Was that Mohamed, God? What was that?"

Ali turned to Shada and said, "I do not know."

He had an idea it was divine and spiritual but did not have a clue what it was. He said to Shada, "Not a word to Father and Mother, never. We must not, at any time, mention this to them or anyone else. You understand?"

With an innocent, shy, scared expression, Shada nodded to acknowledge she would not speak a word about it.

Ali stopped and wondered how many others like him and Shada throughout human history had witnessed such an amazing and deifying encounter and never mentioned it to anyone else for one reason or another. Little did he know that the most powerful and technologically advanced intelligence agency on earth was there too and had also witnessed the event.

CHAPTER 2
Military Response

June 24, 2012: National Security Agency (NSA) headquarters, Fort Meade, Maryland

It was not a normal routine day at the National Security Operations Center. The staff at the NSA was in the middle of an important secret mission in response to an elevated-threat alert, a warning of a credible terrorist threat against the United States.

Located on the grounds of Fort Meade, Maryland, the National Security Operations Center was fifteen miles southwest of Baltimore. The operations center was part of a ten-acre compound that included underground facilities that housed the greatest technology in the world, including the most powerful supercomputer ever created.

Army Tech Sergeants McGuire and Pagan were to remotely pilot two drones headed for southern Iraq where the threat originated. The drones sped toward the Mount of Tiamat, a place the sergeants knew little about. It rose two hundred feet above the surrounding plain, sloping gently downward for a radius of two and a half miles.

The drones took off from the aircraft carrier USS *John C. Stennis*, one of the top-rated nuclear ships in the US Navy. Each one was retrofitted with surveillance and high-tech, sophisticated imagery equipment. Most of the crew on the *Stennis* were on a combat training mission several hours away, leaving only three officers, four pilots, and a small unit of technicians to maintain the ship. Stationed off the Kuwait coast in the Persian Gulf, the aircraft carrier housed several drones to provide intelligence for military activities in the Middle East and Far East and performed bombing runs as necessary.

The tech sergeants used their high-tech joysticks to steer two drones over the target site. Guided by video and digital coordinates, the drones flew rapidly back and forth directly over the mound. The drones' video cameras transmitted a clear image in front of them on four fifty-five-inch, wall-mounted monitors. McGuire and Pagan could see everything, including today's target. It was like both men were sitting inside the drones thousands of miles from the National Security Operations Center.

Only a few days earlier, a satellite had been repositioned to pass directly over southern Iraq, and the intelligence and counterintelligence agency within the Department of Energy had picked up a major heat signature. It was the largest heat signature ever recorded and covered an area three miles wide and extended about four miles below the ground. The satellite had the latest video surveillance and listening and imagery technology and could zero in on any location. Deploying the same technology the National Geospatial-Intelligence Agency had used to located Osama bin Laden in Abbottabad, Pakistan, the satellites had been able to pinpoint, with precise accuracy, the source of the heat signature.

The drones had been deployed in response to pictures, audio, and live video that the satellite had recorded earlier of the blackened sky, thunder, and humming sound over Sumer. The drones were now positioned for a third run when heat-seeking ground missiles fired on them.

The captain in command yelled out, "Initiate immediate evasive action!"

The first two missiles soared past the drones and missed their targets.

Seconds later, another set of missiles were launched, and both tech sergeants began evasive action again. They quickly swerved the craft to the right, then banked to the left, but the missiles gained ground and zeroed in on the drones. It was like the drones were magnets, drawing the missiles in. The drones dived and shot up to the sky, to no avail. Both craft were hit and exploded into hundreds of fiery pieces. Smoke and flames erupted, turning the white clouds a dark ash color as the drone remnants slowly floated down from the sky.

The captain shouted, "Where did that come from?" Everyone in the room was shocked and dumbfounded and had no answers.

McGuire finally said, "Captain, nothing came up on the instruments except for those heat signatures. Those missiles came out of nowhere."

The captain asked if they had gotten the download of the surveillance information from the drones.

"That's affirmative," Pagan responded. "We forwarded the information for analysis, and we should have some results in a few hours."

The analysis of information was available three hours later, and the results were very troublesome and immediately sent to Washington. Classified as top secret, the evidence of enemy movement in the area was irrefutable. Just as concerning was the fact that the satellites registered significant seismic activity and indicated the possibility that the heat signatures could be a WMD. More concerning was the recording of an extraterrestrial event of some kind. The heat signatures were off the charts, and the intensity in the south side of the mound suggested an opening in the earth. The enemy could have already discovered the source and possibly obtained access to the opening in the mound.

The director of national intelligence (DNI) was briefed on the findings. The director called the White House and said to a top presidential aide, "It's what we thought. There is something very special buried deep in this cavern, and we need to get there quickly."

The aide said, "Move forward with Objective Hellfire at once."

CHAPTER 3
The Paradoxical Effect

July 1, 2012: Mound of Tiamat, Sumer, Iraq

A US Navy pilot fired his fighter jet's engines and throttled back, releasing blazing hot flames out the back end of the aircraft, like firecrackers on the Fourth of July. The F-15 jet inched back and forth, garnering enough power to blast off the USS *Stennis*'s narrow and short runway. The fighter jet thundered off the aircraft carrier to rendezvous with three other F-15s that had already jettisoned off.

The pilots—Cougar, Viper, Hammerhead, and Shark Tank—maneuvered their aircraft for a bombing run based upon information from a satellite positioned over southern Iraq. The four F-15 Eagles were headed for a specific predetermined target: the Mound of Tiamat in Sumer, Iraq. Given the size of the mound, the target was impossible to miss. It was the largest mound in the Iraqi desert, and the pilots could see it upon approach from several miles out. Each jet fighter was to bomb the target with four Sparrow and four Sidewinder missiles, using their Gatling guns if necessary.

The jet fighters quickly reached their target. They roared past the mound at a low altitude, circled, and rapidly returned, approaching the target from the south side. The speed and noise of the jet engines shook the ground like a tremor as they roared toward the entrance of the mound.

As squad leader, Cougar radioed the other pilots to coordinate the strike, and the first two pilots began their run. As the target became clearly visible, a stream of light burst from the entrance of the cave. Both pilots pulled up and sharply veered to the left away from the target.

"Cougar, do you see that glow at the entrance of the cave?" one of the pilots asked. "It's like the sun is inside the cave shining out. Sir, the rays are so powerful that they are blinding."

Cougar said, "Continue the strike no matter what."

"Roger that; proceeding as planned."

The pilots turned around to reposition themselves for a strike and unleashed sixteen missiles at the target. The bombs and bullets released a hailstorm, blowing smoke and dirt in all directions as the pilots plummeted downward and then quickly soared upward.

The other two jets were positioned for the second run. As they circled, they leveled the aircraft and headed directly north toward the mound, swiftly approaching the target. They launched their missiles and fired their Gatling guns. The bombs released a fiery flash that engulfed the opening and lit up the mound.

Seconds after unleashing their bombs, the F-15s soared past the mound and burst out of the flames, leaving a trail of fire behind them. The pilots had hit the target precisely, which put a huge smile on Cougar's face. As they circled around and went directly past the mound, the smile quickly turned grim when Cougar noticed the entrance of the cave remained unsealed. Instead, the bombing had produced the opposite effect: the rays from inside the cave had increased in intensity, and the size of the opening had tripled. It was a *paradoxical effect*, the term the squad used to describe not just a failed mission but one that made matters worse.

In a stressed voice, Cougar radioed back to base, "Command,

we have a positive impact but a failed objective, a paradoxical effect. Command, I repeat, a paradoxical effect; we need another option; I repeat, we need another option! The opening is now three times larger, and the beaming ray still illuminates the entrance of the cave."

"Roger that, squad leader; return to base."

All four fighter jets soared past the mound once more and headed back to the USS *Stennis*. Cougar looked at the cavern entrance as he soared past the mound and shook his head in disappointment. The result of the mission seemed both impossible and illogical.

The DNI was immediately notified of the failed mission. The DNI contacted the White House and said, "The mission failed, and it caused a paradoxical effect."

"What do you mean?"

"Sir, the bombs did not seal the mound entrance. The entrance is three times larger."

The White House representative responded, "Implement Operation Sumer immediately!"

CHAPTER 4
Operation Sumer

July 2, 2012: Mound of Tiamat

About ten hours after the F-15 jet fighters bombed their target, two MH-47E Chinook helicopters rapidly appeared on the horizon and soared over the desert terrain. With blades churning loud and fast, the helicopters immediately changed speeds and hovered overhead to position their landing. The aircraft bobbed side to side, blowing sand everywhere, which minimized visibility as the pilots struggled to find a safe landing spot.

The helicopters, armed with various attack rifles, missile launchers, and high-tech military gear, descended cautiously but quickly in unison, hovering only a few feet from the ground. The pilots struggled to stabilize the craft but managed to land safely only ten yards apart, and the fourteen Navy SEALs of Recon One swiftly jumped out of the helicopters, seven from each aircraft.

On this particular afternoon, the temperature was scalding hot. The Navy SEALs were wearing combat boots, lightweight fatigues, and hats. The colors of the uniform closely matched the area terrain. The soldiers sported tinted protective eye goggles to block the sand from blowing in their eyes.

As the helicopters departed, the American soldiers, led by Lt. Dan Colby, immediately regrouped and were only one hundred yards from the base of the large mound and the entrance to the cave. The SEALs gathered their gear and circled around Colby, awaiting their orders.

The platoon consisted of Dan Colby, Miguel Mendez, Joel Lucero, Tex Carter, Trash Thompson, Casper Pantano, Buford Bradley, "Action" Jackson Michaels, Robert "Slick" Sullivan, Joseph "Fish" Calamari, Blake Marshall, Jefferson Jacobs, Hal Collins, and Michael McDermott. Mendez was master chief petty officer and second in command to Colby. Everyone called him "Chief." The others were petty officers, first, second, or third class.

The men were the best the military had—the most physically fit, mentally sharp, mature, and resilient. The soldiers were experienced professionals who had been involved in many of the important military clandestine missions during the decade. This platoon was considered the best of the special forces in the military. The men were unique, and they had a rare blend of loyalty, bravery, and skill. These characteristics were the basic requirements of a Navy SEAL, and these men exceeded all requisites.

The platoon's orders were to recon the area to determine if there were any enemy forces in the area. As the platoon headed for the cave, Lt. Dan Colby advised the regional command center via his wireless communicator that they had landed safely and had a visual of an opening in the mound. Colby informed the command center that the platoon was about fifty feet from the entrance to the large cave with no resistance. Regional command ordered Colby to proceed with caution.

Lieutenant Colby and the Navy SEALs knew very little about this mission. The only information they had received was that enemy forces had entered the region and that there had been an air strike targeted at the mound. The platoon had been ordered to conduct a routine recon mission and was to report any suspicious activities. They had no idea what to expect and were proceeding with the utmost caution.

The Navy SEALs carefully approached the cave entrance. Using the ground for cover, they inched up closer. The soldiers crawled, stood up in a crouched position, and ran, hitting the dirt every ten feet. They repeated this method of approach several times.

As they got closer to the large mouth of the cave, they realized that the bombs from the air strike had accurately hit their target and severely damaged and destroyed anything in front of them. Lieutenant Colby directed Mendez to cover the left flank so the remaining soldiers could enter the cave. Eight men then charged the cave entrance.

The Navy SEALs took cover next to the cave's rugged carbonate rocks walls once inside. The walls were wet and damp but perfect for concealing them. Their hearts were pumping and their breathing labored as they tried to absorb the stale and humid air. They could not see in the impenetrable blackness and heard only the soft sound of water dripping off the jagged ceiling, creating a somber echo. The combination of all these factors created a mysterious backdrop.

Colby pointed to his head, then turned on the light attached to the side of his helmet. Following Colby's instructions, the men turned on their tactical helmet lights and collectively provided much-needed light in the dark cave. Colby signaled to Collins to take guard outside the cave.

The Navy SEALs could now see at least twenty yards into the cave. As they walked forward, the American soldiers discovered that the base of the cave had collapsed as a result of the F-15s' bombing. Initially, they saw twenty enemy soldiers partially buried and presumed dead.

Lieutenant Colby held up three fingers and pointed straight ahead, directing three soldiers to move forward as the remaining troops provided backup. As the soldiers went from one body to the other, they determined that the soldiers were al-Qaeda based on their clothing and were all dead.

The platoon gathered around Colby and Mendez, who tallied the dead.

"I count thirty kills," said Colby.

"I also count thirty," replied Mendez.

Fish added, "They're dead meat, Lieutenant."

"Absolutely; it looks like someone kicked their ass," Lucero interjected.

"Okay, don't get too comfortable, gentlemen," Colby said. "We need to advance!"

The Navy SEALs moved slowly into the cave, their backs to the entrance. Out of nowhere, bullets suddenly came from all directions, ricocheting off rocks and forcing the Navy SEALs to scramble for cover.

An enemy soldier, buried and presumed dead, burst out of a shallow grave. Dirt flew everywhere. Kneeling, the al-Qaeda soldier wheeled a machine gun side to side, firing hundreds of bullets. The Navy SEALs quickly found shelter behind rocks. Some simply lay down, relying only on the ground to shield them from the onslaught of enemy fire.

Gunfire was also coming from another direction. No one knew where those bullets originated until Colby spotted a sniper tucked behind a large rock inside the cave. He signaled to his men to get their attention and then pointed in the direction of the gunman.

At the same time, shots were also fired outside the cave, where Collins was stationed to provide backup. He found cover at the base of the mound but was pinned down. Without Collins covering the rear, the rests of the SEALs were vulnerable.

Colby ran over to Buford, drawing fire to himself. Side-stepping bullets, he scrambled for his life. Colby slid behind the rock next to Buford. Both were dodging bullets and pinned down. They tried to get shots off, to no avail. Colby and Buford were lying on their sides in a confined area with their heads only ten inches apart.

"Man, Buford, you got some nasty camel breath," whispered Colby.

"Sorry, Lieutenant, but I didn't get time to brush my teeth today. You know, this isn't the Hotel Ritz."

"Shit, I was afraid this would happen, a perfectly orchestrated ambush. I should have protected us better," Colby said, disappointed.

"Sir, no one could have stopped this."

As Colby looked up, bullets ricocheted off the rocks around him, and he ducked quickly. "We need to end this now before any of our men get killed," said Colby.

Colby and Buford tried to determine the best angle to retaliate. The options were limited. Realizing he had to do something quickly, Colby moved swiftly across the cave, veering left to right, again drawing enemy fire. He skirted the bullets and somehow found cover in a large indentation in the wall of the cave.

Colby signaled to Mendez and Lucero to advance. Mendez used his incredible strength to climb onto a huge boulder, pulling himself up in the midst of bullets flying everywhere. He showered the sniper with bullets, wounding him. Lucero then charged the sniper before he could refocus. As the sniper raised his weapon, Lucero pumped at least five bullets into him, dislodging the gun and immobilizing the soldier. Lucero then walked over to the wounded al-Qaeda sniper lying on the ground bleeding profusely, put his rifle directly against the man's head, and fired three times.

Lucero stood and looked down at his enemy for five seconds and whispered, "Your sorry ass will never fight again." He then kicked dirt in the soldier's face and walked away.

Seconds later, perched from the behind a boulder, Colby had a clear shot at the second gunman and pinned the enemy soldier down in a gunfight. Colby shot him squarely in the middle of the forehead. The soldier fell forward on his face; blood squirted out of his mouth when he hit the ground and splattered everywhere.

Meanwhile, outside the cave, Collins moved quickly toward the base of the mound to find cover behind a jagged rock formation. He knew where the bullets were coming from but could not get a clear shot. He tried to exchange gunfire with the enemy, but it was futile.

Collins was outnumbered and pinned down. He estimated that there were three soldiers hiding behind rocks about twenty-five yards up. He inched away from the base of the mound to look up to determine the exact location of the enemy but quickly retreated to avoid intense gunfire.

Collins then looked to his left and saw that an enemy soldier had snuck down from his hiding place, but it was too late to get a shot off. The enemy soldier fired, and Collins, shot three times, fell to his knees while trying desperately to get off a last shot at the enemy.

Collins yelled out with his final breath, "You bastard, you'll never win." He fell flat on his face and died instantly.

Now able to focus on helping Collins, McDermott and Buford quickly reached the entrance of the cave, but it was too late. Buford saw Collins on the ground and knelt down to take his pulse, quickly determining he was gone.

Without cover, the al-Qaeda soldier who had killed Collins tried desperately to retreat to his original hiding place. Buford swung around and fired thirty 7.62 mm rounds from his M60 machine gun. The enemy soldier's back looked like a dartboard with a clearly visible bull's-eye. It was too easy. As the battle intensified, Buford was distracted by enemy fire and only winged the terrorist in the leg. The terrorist's leg was shattered, disabling him. Buford dodged bullets as he raced to his enemy to finish him off. In the scuttle, the enemy soldier had lost his weapon. Lying on the ground, he looked up at Buford and said, "We will rule you American pigs and rid the world of you infidels and your wicked Western ways!"

Buford looked down at the wounded soldier and said, "You're about to meet your seventy-two virgins." Buford raised his machine gun, put it in the soldier's mouth, and said, "Take a look at the last person you'll ever see." He fired five shots, and the man's body vibrated against the ground until the bullets stopped.

Outside the cave, the remaining two al-Qaeda soldiers were on the mound ridge twenty yards up and still spraying the landscape with bullets. In a better position than Collins had been in and with reinforcement coming, the odds were now more favorable for Recon One.

McDermott was in a good position to use an explosive. He grabbed two hand grenades from his belt, tossing the first one over his head and to the left. He arched the second one up high, aiming to the right over the rocks toward the enemy. The hand grenades landed precisely in the middle of the two soldiers. Body parts flew everywhere mixed in with smoke and fire.

McDermott yelled over Buford, "Those two just met their maker, whoever that is."

Colby came running out of the cave to help his men and saw that they had already taken care of business. He looked at Buford and said, "Make sure they're dead. We don't want to make the same mistake twice."

One of the al-Qaeda was still alive, but he had lost both legs from the hand grenade. As the enemy lay there in shock, eyes opened wide, Buford looked down at him and said, "I should let you bleed out painfully, but I am a gentleman." He shot him in the head three times and casually walked toward Collins and McDermott.

Buford grabbed a body bag from his pack, and both he and McDermott knelt next to Collins, paying their last respects. Buford took the bag and rolled it out alongside Collins. They lifted him and placed him in the bag and slowly closed the zipper.

"He should not have died here," McDermott said. "He deserved better."

Buford firmly put his hand on his buddy's shoulders and asked, "What do I tell his mother and sister back in Jersey?"

McDermott said, "When we get back to the States, I'll go with you. He was one of the finest and toughest soldiers I ever served with, and they need to hear how brave he was, from people who actually knew him."

At that moment, Colby came over and saw the body bag and knew what had happened. Buford looked up at Colby and said, "We did not do enough to save our brother."

Dejected, Colby said, "I should have prevented this ambush."

Mendez joined them and looked at Colby and said, "Lieutenant, you could not have prevented this. Sometimes you just can't do enough in battle. Shit happens; it is what it is."

Still knelling next to Collins, McDermott shook his head in agony and yelled, "Why are we here?"

Mendez said, "That's a good question."

"I've had my suspicions about this mission since we got here," said Colby. "I don't understand why they would send the best special services unit in the military on a routine recon mission."

Colby ordered three Navy SEALs to recon the area outside the cave. The rest of the platoon began a search of what remained.

This part of the cave was a makeshift field operation center, hastily assembled approximately forty-eight to seventy hours ago. Usually, large tents were used for field operations, but caves offered much safer and cooler command posts. Hung to the left on the cave wall was a dusty al-Qaeda flag. In the middle of the black flag, eleven Arabic characters were written above a bright-yellow circle.

As they moved another thirty yards into the cave, the SEALs found several computers on two large tables with five chairs around each table. Small rocks and dirt covered everything in sight. Black-and-white file cabinets sat behind the tables and chairs. None of them matched, and they looked to be from old US Army surplus. In the file cabinets and on the computers they found important enemy documents and communiqués.

Radio equipment with obsolete technology sat to the right of the tables. The computers were so old they had floppy drives, and only one had a CD/RW drive. There were also five six-foot pole lights with four large 120-watt bulbs on each one and a generator.

Although there were rocks, dirt, and bodies everywhere, the air strike had caused minimal destruction to the operations center. Most of the casualties were closer to the entrance where the cave had collapsed and buried the majority of the enemy soldiers.

Colby looked around for clues to determine why the al-Qaeda platoon had been in the cave and what they had been planning. Mendez joined Colby and said, "It looks like those in the operations center were spared the brunt of the bombing. I'll bet they were the ones who ambushed us."

"Yes, it looks that way."

Mendez pointed to a place on the ground where it looked as if the dirt had recently been dug out and then filled back in. The ground was too perfectly even, as if the enemy was hiding something. "Lieutenant, did you see this?"

Colby and Mendez grabbed two shovels and started digging.

"Lieutenant, I'll do this; you don't need to dig," Mendez said.

Colby asked, "How long have you know me, Chief?"

"It's been several years now."

Smiling from ear to ear, Colby said, "Do you know me not to chip in, not to do what I ask my men to do?"

Mendez said, "No, sir, that's what I admire and respect about you."

"You too, Chief; I've witnessed how you lead by example."

Mendez laughed and with a big grin on his face said, "My only problem with you, Lieutenant, is those Dumbo-looking ears of yours."

"My wife thinks I'm handsome, and my mom's friends think I look like a blond-haired, blue-eyed Clark Gable," boasted Colby.

Laughing, Mendez said, "I got you to smile twice in less than twenty seconds. Talking about smiling, why have you had that little grin on your face since we got our orders to come to Iraq?"

"Really?" Colby said. "I hadn't noticed."

"The whole time, my man!"

Colby said, "To tell you the truth, I've always wanted to come to Iraq. It about killed me to be in Afghanistan for the past two years. You know I studied Iraqi history at Harvard?"

"You went to college!"

Colby didn't even dignify that with an answer. "We're right here, right in the middle of it. I'd give my next leave for a chance to spend a few days digging around down here."

Colby had spent a lot of his days at Harvard studying Sumerian ancient civilization. He'd decided not to pursue it because he'd been so successful in the ROTC. He'd joined the navy right after he'd graduated. A decorated officer, Colby was a rising star in the new military and was scheduled to be promoted to lieutenant commander in six months.

Lieutenant Colby was tall, extremely intelligent, athletic, and handsome. He had a large, pointed jaw with a cleft chin that was so deep you could stick a Q-tip in it. His facial features came across as odd, but the wire-rimmed silver glasses on his perfectly shaped nose made him look very distinguished for a young man.

"Lieutenant, what's important about this shit hole?" asked Mendez.

"There is much ancient history here dating back thousands of years. I studied many of the Sumerian myths."

"What do you mean?"

"Well, one myth involves the Sumerian King List. It is an ancient manuscript containing a list of all the Sumerian kings carved on cuneiform tablets. The myth says the first eight kings on the list were immortal. The story says the kings descended from the sky and ruled from the dawn of time for over two hundred thousand years up to the big flood, each king ruling for an average of twenty-five thousand years. After the flood, kings ruled for shorter time periods and were considered mortal."

"Were these eight earlier kings supernatural?"

"Maybe," said Colby. "Sumerian mythology claims that powerful supernatural gods ruled the earth for thousands of years. The Sumerians had the first human civilization, and they recorded everything on thousands of clay tablets. According to several interpretations of these tablets, the Sumerians worshipped these gods. The Sumerian civilization was organized around a social order whose primary goal was to serve these gods. The gods built a home in Mesopotamia and Sumer, Iraq, and lived here for thousands of years, just about where we are standing."

"Interpretation, what do you mean?" asked Mendez.

"There are several interpretations of the Sumerian written language. There are numerous scholars knowledgeable in interpreting the meaning of cuneiform writing and other artifacts, so there are multiple translations. Some scholars agree on what they mean, and some do not.

"The Sumerians created the first known written language. The language does not belong to any known language family and disappeared thousands of years ago. Therefore, the writings are difficult to translate because there's no basis for interpretation.

"The Sumerian language bears some similarity to Hungarian. The Sumerians disappeared from southern Iraq in 2000 BCE as a result of the military domination of their people. According to Sumerian history, Sargon of Akkad conquered the Sumerians in around 2000 BCE. The Sumerians left southern Iraq around that time and migrated through Turkey and later to Bulgaria and Romania to Hungary. Akkadian gradually replaced Sumerian as a spoken language around that same time in history."

"So the Sumerians relocated to Hungary?"

Colby said, "That's what some say. Hungarian is the only dialect that has any semblance to the Sumerian language."

Mendez shook his head and said, "Man, your parents sent you to Harvard to study this shit."

Colby looked at Mendez and said, "I think this is enough of ancient history for today."

"Yeah, Lieutenant, this is interesting, but far from anything I ever learned in East LA."

"Aren't you going back to East LA when you retire?" asked Colby.

"Yeah, I plan to coach wrestling and teach social studies. I'd like to give something back. I even have some credits toward a bachelor's degree in education at USC already. Lieutenant, I love the military. It's provided me structure and kept me out of jail. It was my ticket out of the ghetto. But I don't know how much longer soldiers like me will be around. With the work these drones are doing and the changes in warfare tactics, I'll be out of a job in a few years."

"Yeah," Colby said, "future wars will be fought by quick-striking elite forces supported by the latest technology like robotics, drones, and satellite imagery. The military will use the tactics to strike quickly and ferociously. The military tactic will focus on rapid deployment, prompt execution, and fast withdrawal with the least amount of collateral damage, minimum US casualties, and maximum enemy fatalities. The objective of tomorrow's wars will be swift in-and-out strategy with immediate closure. We will not occupy another country; it's too casualty intensive."

"Tomorrow's soldier better have an education and computer skills," Mendez said. "The military won't recruit reject jailbirds with minimum education."

"Jail? What do you mean, Chief?"

"I was arrested on several felony charges when I was seventeen. There was a gang fight, and several gang members were killed. I got caught running from the scene. I didn't kill anybody but faced prison time. They gave me two options. I was to get a GED and then enter the military or face a minimum of five years in state prison. You know the rest of the story."

"No shit," responded Colby.

"Yeah, my mom was a single parent, poor, and worked two jobs. Being unsupervised, I went to the streets and joined the Spartans. It was a tough neighborhood, and if you didn't belong to an LA gang, you were not long for this earth."

"It's remarkable that you got out of there alive."

"Believe it or not, in a small way, it prepared me for my job and has made me appreciate the military," said Mendez.

"Well, you're one hell of a soldier," said Colby.

"It's about pride in what you do, no matter what," replied Mendez.

"You know what's weird, Chief, is how different but similar we are. You grew up in poverty as a member of a violent LA gang, did not graduate from a traditional high school, and were arrested on a felony. On the other hand, I graduated from Harvard and was captain and quarterback of the football team. But we are alike in many ways, even though we came from completely different backgrounds."

Mendez asked, "How are we alike?"

"We're both loyal, strong, and generous. We have integrity and are, you know, just good, ethical individuals."

"I appreciate the compliments and the kind words. Yeah, we do have a lot in common," said Mendez. "But I never will be like you, Lieutenant; we do come from two different worlds. My background will always hinder my opportunities."

"I know you will overcome any obstacle, Chief. You're a quality person."

Suddenly, the sound of metal on metal rang throughout the cave as Colby's shovel struck something buried in the ground. Colby and Mendez worked to remove the dirt around the edges of a three-foot-long box to open and view its contents. After ten minutes of digging, Colby was able to open the box. Inside was an ancient gold relic shaped like a pyramid. Colby picked up the artifact and examined it closely.

Mendez asked if he could examine it, and Colby handed it over. Mendez asked, "Do you know what this is?"

Colby answered, "No!" and paused for a few moments. Then he put the relic in his bag and said, "We don't have time right now to examine it. We better move on."

Lieutenant Colby ordered Mendez to take three men to conceal the bodies and secure all the paper and digital files.

The three men began to remove and confiscate the computer hard drives, while Mendez started to go through the paper files. Colby told them to rejoin the rest of the platoon when they completed the assignment.

As he started to walk farther into the cave with the remainder of the platoon, Colby turned and yelled, "Shoot every last one of those bastards in the head, and make sure they are dead. Have the men thoroughly recon the perimeter to make sure we got them all." He turned and walked deeper into the cave. He did not know what to expect next.

Mendez was a rough-looking fellow with pockmarks all over his face from a serious acne problem that had gone untreated. He had black hair, a crew cut, and dark-brown eyes. His short, thick neck and large, muscular arms resembled the physique of an NFL running back. The tattoo on his left arm was a replica of a tall, strong, brave-looking Spartan soldier. The soldier had a long, pointed spear; heavy, round shield; huge, razor-sharp sword; and a large iron helmet. The colors were the same as those of his street gang. The tattoo on his right arm was a four-inch red heart with a blue anchor across it, indicating his love for the navy.

Mendez and his men shot each soldier in the head three times. They completed collecting the information and then started to inspect and conceal the bodies. Colby and the rest of the platoon were more than two miles into the cave continuing the recon.

Jacobs dug a shallow grave to bury the last body. When he finished digging, he flipped the body over to place it in the grave. He saw explosives strapped to the enemy's torso and yelled out, "Explosives!"

A nanosecond later, the explosives went off, and Jacobs's body parts flew everywhere. The moment played out in slow motion as he watched his legs, arms, and hands float in the air. His whole life flashed before him in vibrant colors. From childhood to this very moment, his life became his personal full-length movie. His body parts hit the ground, and blood splattered amid the dirt and rocks. Everything was so clear, and time was not relevant. Jacobs was in another place, another dimension.

The intensity of the blast flung the others in the air in all directions. Landing on the ground and lying flat on his stomach, Mendez first thought of his men. He looked over to see if there were any casualties while he reached down to make sure his limbs were still intact. The other two Navy SEALs were startled but were getting up and looking quickly for their weapons.

The men now knew that the explosion had come from where Jacobs had been working and proceeded cautiously in that direction. Mendez saw something on the ground mixed in a pool of blood. It was a leg and a hand. He squatted down to examine the hand. He knew it was Jacobs's because his high school ring was still on his finger, a red ruby with Reading High engraved in the silver band.

CHAPTER 5
The Cradle of Civilization

July 5, 2012: The Garden of Eden, Sumer, Iraq

It was a typical sweltering, dry day in Sumer. Bordering on the Tigris and Euphrates Rivers, Sumer was in Mesopotamia, a hotbed of ancient civilizations. Mesopotamia lay close to where the Tigris and Euphrates Rivers joined and emptied into the Persian Gulf in southern Iraq and was called the "land between two rivers."

The Tigris-Euphrates river system was part of the Palearctic alluvial salt marsh eco-region that went as far east as Russia and Siberia. Located in Western Asia, Mesopotamia was once considered an area with rich soils and abundant crops resulting from layers of silt the two rivers had deposited over the years. The Fertile Crescent served as the breadbasket of Mesopotamia where agriculture thrived in ancient times.

Sumer was a historical city believed to be the location of the Garden of Eden and the land of the gods. The city was considered one of the most famous ancient cities of all time and was considered the cradle of civilization, the beginning of man's recorded history.

Modern historians asserted that a non-Semitic people settled Sumer between 4500 and 4000 BCE and became the center of the ancient Sumerian civilization over six thousand years ago. Mesopotamia provided the first evidence of human civilization, and Sumer was the center of this ancient culture. For whatever purpose, the Navy SEALs were smack in the middle of it.

Lieutenant Colby contacted regional command to brief them on the mission's status. Command ordered Colby to proceed farther into the cave and continue to recon the area. Mendez and the two other Navy SEALs had finished securing the bodies and collecting paper and computer files and were on their way to meet up with Colby and the others.

Colby ordered the platoon to proceed in twos. The men walked cautiously down the narrow trail. Tex Carter and Lucero teamed together. A half mile into the cave, Tex heard a sound coming from the left wall.

He turned to Lucero and asked, "Do you hear that?"

"Hear what?"

"That noise. Wait a minute; there it is again. It sounds like a dripping noise inside the wall."

"It's probably water dripping off one of those stalactites."

Lucero walked over toward Tex in the direction of the rumbling noise but could not make it out.

"No, it's something else," said Tex.

Both stood there in silence, trying to determine what it was. Colby, who was about twenty yards ahead, stopped, looked back at the two men, and said into his communicator, "Gentlemen, what is the holdup?"

"Lieutenant, I hear something inside the left wall," replied Tex. Tex then turned to Lucero and asked, "Did you hear that? It's getting louder."

"Yes, I hear it clearly now," said Lucero. "It sounds like a waterfall and the flow of a river crashing down on the rocks."

"It's getting louder," said Tex.

Seconds later there was a thunderous roar like rapids hurling down a river. The ground shook, and the cave wall eroded and turned to mud in seconds. The wall collapsed suddenly, like a dam breaking apart. A rush of water burst out and knocked Tex and Lucero down hard, forcing them into a whirlpool motion about fifteen feet below the path. Both men were swirling in a circle trying to keep their heads above the water, swimming for their lives.

The water swirled like a draining bathtub. Both Tex and Lucero were hurtled and tossed around like salad in a bowl. They banged into each other several times, and it looked as if they would drown. But the water receded, and their heads suddenly popped out of the water. They were able to stand up as the water quickly drained. However, they had several bad cuts and bruises and were now twenty-five feet down below the ridge of the cave where the other men were standing.

"What the hell was that?" yelled Lucero.

"Shit, we almost drowned!" said Tex.

"You guys all right?" Colby called. "Can you climb out?"

"Not without some help, Lieutenant," replied Tex.

Both men waded through what was left of the water to the base of the ridge and looked up at the rest of the platoon. Fish Calamari threw a rope down to the men. Jackson Michaels grabbed the rope and helped Fish pull the men up one at a time.

"Thanks, guys," said Tex.

"Yeah, me too," said Lucero.

"Man, this place is a disaster waiting to happen," Colby said. "If I didn't know better, I would think the Mound of Tiamat is haunted with evil spirits and the ancient gods have cursed this place."

The water and rock had caused the cavern wall to collapse, exposing a tunnel whose trail dropped off sharply and went underground. All the men gathered around the narrow mouth of the tunnel to examine the interior of this new part of the cave. The Navy SEALs were captivated by all the colors and different rock formations. Hundreds of large, clear quartz-like pyramids twinkled in the background.

The flat terrain in the region made the interior of the cave unique.

The Navy SEALs were amazed by the massive stalactites, stalagmites, and pillars. Hundreds of stalactites hung from the ceiling of the cave like red-and-gray icicles. The stalactites resembled soda straws with water dripping from each tip. Bats hung upside down from the ceiling among the stalactites, and their dung covered the floor, looking like dark-brown rice.

"Hey, Fish, you see all those bats? There must be hundreds of them," said Michaels.

"Shit, I wonder if they're vampire bats," replied Fish.

"You watch too many of those ridiculous *True Blood*–type movies," said Michaels.

"Don't be surprised if one of your ancestors is a vampire," Fish said.

"Fish, you're out of your mind. Get real! Those shows are as thought provoking as watching paint dry."

As the team of Navy SEALs went farther into the cave, the path got wider and steeper as it went straight into what seemed to be a pit of hell. The air in the cave was damp, musty, and moldy and had a foul odor that made the cave eerie, mysterious, and mystical. Numerous pointed stalagmites, too many to count, pointed up from the floor like earth-colored spears. The various gray-and-rust-colored rock formations and pillars were dotted with gold specks, like the colors of leaves on a fall day.

Buford caught up with Colby and said, "Do you think the bombing and the water unearthed an underground hollow that has possibly been here for years?"

"I don't know," said Colby. "It's possible."

"This place is incredible. The farther we go, the more amazing it becomes," said Buford.

"Yeah, and the farther we go, the steeper and darker it gets and the harder it is to see. Let the men know to increase the lighting."

The soldiers were equipped with excellent fluorescent lighting, and cameras mounted on the sides of their helmets recorded and transmitted video back to Colonel Christopher at the regional command center on a secure line, the video streaming on a high-resolution seventy-inch HDTV in the control room.

Lieutenant Colby said, "We better find out the status of Mendez and the rest of the platoon. I told them to bear left at the opening of this tunnel."

Lieutenant Colby ordered his troops to take a knee while they waited for Mendez and the other Navy SEALs left behind to clean up and gather intelligence. Colby requested Jackson Michaels and Fish stand watch. The men removed their backpacks, secured their weapons, and found comfortable places to sit. Many replenished themselves with energy drinks, and most ate beef jerky for nourishment. Tex Carter and Buford took a piss.

Lieutenant Colby called Mendez on the wireless. "Chief, come in. Is everything all right? This is Recon One to Cleanup Crew; come in."

"This is Cleanup Crew; come in, Recon One."

"Chief, what's your location and status?"

Mendez replied, "All the enemy soldiers are dead and the bodies secured. To hide the bodies, we dug half graves and covered them with dirt. We also secured all the al-Qaeda's military files, including their plans to retake the region." Mendez paused and said, "There is some bad news, sir."

Colby asked anxiously, "What?"

"The enemy set a booby trap, fastening explosives to a dead al-Qaeda. The explosives detonated and killed Jacobs immediately. There is not much of him remaining except a few body parts and his ID. We were able to find a leg, hand, his high school ring, and parts of his torso."

Colby's face turned white, and he shook his head. Hundreds of thoughts raced through his mind. At least fifteen seconds went by, and then Colby asked, "Did you secure the hard drives?"

"Yes, we secured all six of them," replied Mendez.

"Good! Bring up the rear. I want to be at full force as we recon the rest of the cave," Colby ordered.

"Sir, there is one more thing. The documents we discovered included a partial map of Iraq that seemed to be a blueprint for recapturing southern Iraqi territories. There was also some communiqués that talked of a major event. Something big happened here."

Colby asked, "What do you mean by something big?"

Mendez responded, "I have it right here."

Mendez pulled out a set of documents from his backpack and referred to a section of the communiqué and said, "The documents indicate that the al-Qaeda knew something significant was hidden in the Mound of Tiamat that would help them take back southern Iraq. I could not make it all out, but it seems to indicate that someone left something in the cave that could drastically tip the scale of the war."

"Maybe it's that gold pyramid we dug up."

"Could be."

"But I don't really think that's it. If it was, they would not have buried it," said Colby.

Mendez then asked, "Do you want me to leave some men to cover the entrance of the cave?"

"No, with the loss of Collins and now Jacobs, I need every man to help us recon this cave. There is something down here, and it is not at the entrance of the cave. Bring the patrol back. I need everyone here."

"Roger that, Lieutenant. We'll be there soon."

Lucero came over to Colby and said, "Sir, I'm sorry. Jacobs was one of the best men in the entire military, and I know he was your good buddy."

Dejected, Colby said, "That's two of my brothers gone. I was responsible for them. We walked into a shit storm. A routine recon mission, bullshit! I can't wait to see what's next."

Lucero said, "Roger that."

Thirty-five minutes into the break, Mendez and his men finally caught up with the rest of Recon One. When the Navy SEALs stood up to greet the patrol, Mendez yelled, "You guys are lit up like a Christmas tree. What the hell is on your pants and boots?"

Lieutenant Colby and the rest of the soldiers looked down at their pants and quickly dusted off the gold sparkles, but traces of the shiny substance remained. Some of the men kicked their heels together to remove the gold substance from their boots.

Lieutenant Colby yelled out, "What the hell is this?"

"It looks like fluorescent gold dust!" said Mendez.

Colby said, "We better move on."

Fish said, "This place gives me the willies."

"We got our orders; let's move out," Colby instructed.

The twelve remaining men gathered their belongings. Many of the men were still dusting off their pants as they walked away.

Lieutenant Colby signaled to two soldiers to proceed, one on the left flank and one on the right flank. He then signaled the remaining soldiers to proceed forward. As they went deep into the subterraneous earth, it got darker. If not for their helmet lights, they wouldn't have been able to see one inch in front of them.

Fish called out to Lieutenant Colby, "Sir, why are we still here in this godforsaken shit hole?"

Lieutenant Colby said, "You shouldn't even ask."

Fish said, "Whatever was here is dead. This place even smells like death."

Ten minutes later and another two hundred yards into the cavern, a bright gold glitter appeared in front of them for about twenty yards. The gold sparkle was so intense it glowed almost as brightly as the sun, lighting up the cavern. Lieutenant Colby ordered everyone to turn off their lights to reduce the glare. Mendez quickly joined Lieutenant Colby at the front of the platoon, and they both could not believe their eyes.

"Holy shit, Dan! What is that?"

Lieutenant Colby blurted out, "Command, can you see this?"

Command replied, "Yes, we can!"

Mendez looked at Lieutenant Colby with concern and asked, "Are we falling into a trap? I've never seen anything like this. The light is getting brighter every minute."

Command told Colby to move cautiously.

As the Navy SEALs proceeded carefully toward the light, Lieutenant Colby was surprised to notice that the walls of the cave had transformed from a rough, rocky surface to a flat, smooth, and shiny one, like marble. The cave now looked too perfect to be formed by nature.

"Check this out, Lieutenant," said Buford. "These walls are as smooth as a baby's ass."

Five yards farther into the cave, strange symbols were deeply carved on numerous marble tablets about five feet by three feet in size. The tablets were stacked in a grid. Colby recalled seeing such writing in his studies of Sumerian texts at Harvard. He had enough knowledge of this antediluvian culture to recognize what the tables were.

"Lieutenant, what are these objects?" Mendez asked.

"It's Sumerian writing," responded Colby.

"You studied Sumerian culture in college," said Mendez.

"Yes, I did, but it's something I don't necessarily want all these grunts to know."

Mendez stopped and stood next to Colby as he inspected the tablets. "Lieutenant, what does this mean?"

"They remind me of the Seven Tablets of Creation."

Mendez asked, "So what do the tablets mean?"

Both men continued to walk as Colby said, "The Seven Tablets contains the ancient Sumerian creation story. Some scholars believe the tablets explain the birth of the gods and the origin of humanity and the universe. Amazingly, the tablets describe our solar system in detail. Now we are talking thousands of years ago. Interpretations also reference celestial collisions and the gods Anu, Marduk, and Tiamat."

"Hold up there, Lieutenant," said Mendez. "Can you give me the short, simple version?"

"Chief, Sumerian methodology does not have a short, simple version," replied Colby. "The Seven Tablets of Creation were discovered around 1851 by Henry Layard in Nineveh in northern Iraq. The tablets were buried among the ruins in what is believed to be the library of King Ashurbanipal, the ruler of ancient Assyria. The tablets, each with one hundred fifteen to one hundred seventy lines, tell of Tiamat, the mother of everything associated with the development of the universe. Depicted as a ferocious monster with scales and terrible claws, Tiamat often took the form of a huge serpent and represented all that was physically terrifying and evil.

"One interpretation of the tablets tells a story of a group of younger gods who kills Tiamat's husband, Abzu. Tiamat becomes outraged, and a major battle between Tiamat and one of the younger gods, Marduk, ensues. Marduk triumphs over Tiamat and then becomes the king of kings. Those who joined Tiamat are forced into hard labor. Then from Tiamat's body, Marduk creates the heaven and the earth. Along the way Marduk also slays Kingu, Tiamat's champion. Marduk ordains that giant human creatures are to be created out of Kingu's blood."

"Why did the younger gods kill Tiamat's husband?" Mendez asked.

Colby stopped and looked back at the men and shouted, "Stop lollygagging and be alert!"

"I think the men are getting tired," said Mendez.

As they continued to walk, Colby answered Mendez's question. "I think the myth means that Tiamat and Kingu were annoyed that the younger gods challenged and threatened their power. On the other hand, the younger gods did not like what was happening on earth."

"Do you mean power and control?" Mendez asked.

"Isn't that the root of most conflict?" Colby said. "My thinking is that the young gods rebelled. Maybe they were tired of performing labor. The translation of the myth is a matter of interpretation. There are several translations; thus there are several versions of the stories."

"This sounds like a big-ass fairy tale," Mendez said.

"Could be."

"One more thing, Lieutenant … Was the Tiamat in the creation story the same god that this mound is named after?"

Colby replied, "I'm not sure, but it seems logical given that the myth originated from this region."

Mendez said, "This is all too coincidental."

"We need to get back to our mission," replied Colby.

Regional command ordered the platoon to document as much as they could. Lieutenant Colby ordered two of his men to video the area with writing on the walls. Minutes later, Colby asked command if the platoon could camp here for the night. Command approved the request. Lieutenant Colby told his men they would rest here tonight and directed them to set up camp.

Mendez approached Lieutenant Colby and said, "Lieutenant, I've seen some crazy things in my day, but the gold particles and the tablets ... Man, what are these symbols, and what do they mean?"

Lieutenant Colby said, "Well, Chief, they are Sumerian cuneiform writing, like wedge-shaped symbols or pictures used for writing. They used these pictograph symbols six thousand years ago to write scriptures, stories, and poems; document the planets and the stars; and record history, births, and many other important events. The Sumerians developed the first written language. They were very advanced for their time, and their spiritual beliefs influenced all successive Near Eastern religions, including Judaism, Christianity, and Islam."

Mendez said, "I thought that the Egyptians or the Romans were the first civilization to use a form of writing."

"That's the popular belief. However, the Sumerian civilization began in 4500 BCE and was ahead of its time, almost one thousand years before the Babylonians, whose empire began around 3500 BCE. The Egyptian civilization started in 3100 BCE, so the Sumerians were 1,400 years older.

"The timeline of history has changed dramatically since the turn of the twentieth century because thousands of clay tablets with Sumerian writing were found and translated only a few hundred years ago. It has taken one hundred sixty or so years to interpret the tablets Layard discovered. Most of the archaeological work was done in the late nineteenth century from 1877–1930, starting just one hundred and thirty-seven years ago. Kramer's Sumerian mythology appeared in 1944, only sixty-seven years ago.

"Samuel Noah Kramer spent most of his life studying this literature, by piecing together clay tablets in far-flung museums. His work included an extensive body of literature, among the oldest in the world. He translated most of the important Sumerian myths. To this day, scholars are still trying to determine what they mean.

"According to some interpretations of the writings, the Sumerians were the first to have schools, libraries, laws, cataloguing, agriculture, architecture, art, music, proverbs, medicine, doctors, health clinics, astronomy, jobs, government, and even a farmers' almanac. We are talking about 4500 BCE, six thousand years ago."

"Historically, it seems out of whack," Mendez said. "How did the Sumerians get this knowledge? If it weren't for the seriousness of this situation, I would think you're putting me on, Lieutenant."

"No, Chief, I'm not putting you on. It's puzzling how the Sumerians obtained all this knowledge so early on in human cultural evolution."

"This is some heavy stuff, but I'm not buying into it," Mendez said.

Historically, Colby knew that there was little consensus among scholars on the interpretation of the Sumerian texts, since there was little documentation of the Sumerian language and the Sumerian people, who seemed to have disappeared overnight. It was not until recently with the development of a Sumerian dictionary at the University of Pennsylvania in Philadelphia that scholars had collaborated more closely on the interpretation of the Sumerian writings and language.

Sullivan interrupted Mendez and Lieutenant Colby. "Lieutenant, command is on the communication link. It's Colonel Christopher."

Lieutenant Colby walked over to the radio, picked up the headset, and said, "Sir."

Colonel Christopher asked, "What's the status?"

Lieutenant Colby said, "Sir, it looks like those F-15 fighter jets unearthed a possible important archaeological find, the kind that archaeologists live for. This is something, but I'm not sure what it is just yet. The cave turned into a deep subterranean cavern. In some places, it resembles a grotto."

Colonel Christopher asked Lieutenant Colby to not draw any conclusions until they investigated further. Lieutenant Colby acknowledged he understood.

Lieutenant Colby walked over to Mendez and said, "They want us to examine the area further and gather more evidence."

Mendez asked, "What are we investigating?"

Lieutenant Colby said, "Regional command is checking to see if there is any record of an archaeological site at this location. We unearthed something that was either buried here on purpose or by accident. They will be contacting Hitchens at United States Central Command."

Central Command also had an interest in the writings. They were aware of the significance of the archaeological find and wanted to make sure it was all documented thoroughly. Central Command intercepted Recon One's video stream and sent it to Washington and a team of experts at Andrews Air Force Base.

Colby was intrigued by what his team had discovered. He was now more interested in the archaeological find than the recon mission, and so was command. However, he knew his first responsibility was to his men and their safety.

Lieutenant Colby got the attention of his men and told them to get some grub and some rest.

CHAPTER 6
United States Command Center

July 5, 2012: Central Command, Kabul, Afghanistan

Secretly located in Afghanistan, Central Command was the military headquarters for the Middle and Far East, including Iraq and Iran. Responsible for all military operations, the Central Command was under the command of General Hitchens. Central Command was relocated to Afghanistan at the end of the Iraq War. Since the United States and its allies had withdrawn, there had been only handful of military and civilian consultants in Iraq remaining to train and assist the Iraqi military and police. Most of the US soldiers stationed in Iraq had either been sent home or redeployed to Afghanistan.

After the US troops had withdrawn, the al-Qaeda had developed a strong presence in the area around Basra. The al-Qaeda soldiers were Sunni Muslim who had been forced out of the region at the height of the second Iraq War. It was not until their resurgence that the US military had become concerned with the growing strength of al-Qaeda in southern Iraq.

Alarmed about the increasing numbers of al-Qaeda, Washington had ordered an air strike based on military intelligence from the area. The directive for the air strike had come straight from the National Security Council (NSC) with the approval of the director of national intelligence. Besides the DNI, the NSC, the pilots, the chairman of the Joint Chiefs of Staff, and a very few high-ranking military officers, no one else knew of the planned air strike against targets in Iraq.

After learning that the al-Qaeda had resurfaced, the White House had become anxious and uneasy, worrying that the public would now perceive the decision to pull out of Iraq as a bad one. There had been some political opposition from those who felt that the United States had left Iraq prematurely and that enemy factions would return to the region and become a threat to the area. Given the fact that the start of the presidential campaign was less than four months away, everyone in the administration was sensitive to any bad press, especially of this magnitude.

Some said the Iraq War had severely tarnished the previous administration, and the new president did not want any negative perception of his presidency so close to the election. The war had lasted nine years. American forces had withdrawn from Iraq in December 2011, only six months ago.

Recent polls suggested that the majority of Americans tired of war. More importantly, people felt the Iraq War had been a mistake and a failure. However, that had occurred on the past president's watch, not the current one. The current president had just been trying to get out of Iraq before the election, but in reality, he'd only changed the address of the war. His people were crafty in massaging the spin to their advantage.

Concerned about Recon One, Colonel Christopher decided to contact General Hitchens at Central Command. General Hitches was the commander of the United States military special operations and in charge of all forces in the region, including Iraq and Afghanistan. Hitchens had a direct link to the Pentagon, which gave him access to the White House. Typically, the colonel would not bother the general with such detail, but given the turn of events, he thought a personal update in lieu of a routine written report was appropriate and in line with protocol. Colonel Christopher contacted General Hitchens, but Lieutenant Colonel Brock, the general's aide, who everyone called Brocky, answered the video link.

"Hey, Chris, how's it going down there?" Brock asked.

"Shit, Brocky," Colonel Christopher said. "I think we are in a real quagmire. It's a real cluster fuck … There is a platoon of Navy SEALs conducting a recon mission in Iraq, in a cave in Sumer about fifty miles south of Basra. They stumbled into something very unusual and remarkable. There are Sumerian writings all over the walls of the cave. Lieutenant Colby, who is leading the platoon, studied ancient Mesopotamia and Sumerian culture in college, and he's sure that the geometric shapes etched on some tablets are ancient Sumerian writing. From the little I know about history and anthropology, we've unearthed something pretty fantastic, extraordinary, and possibly six thousand years old. I think the general needs to know before we do anything else."

Lieutenant Colonel Brock said, "Your call is timely; the general said that he was going to call you as soon as he gets off the phone with someone in Washington. He has been following the platoon activities on satellite. The old man is real interested in this for some reason. The best I can ascertain is that it has something to do with the NSC, the DNI, and I think the White House. I believe they call it Operation Sumer."

"Operation Sumer, what is that?"

Lieutenant Colonel Brock said, "I just heard the name and assumed that it had to do with Lieutenant Colby's recon mission."

"That's news to me."

Lieutenant Colonel Brock caught himself and realized he should be more careful in what he said. Due to his personal friendship with Colonel Christopher, Brock felt comfortable talking to him. They both trusted each other.

Brock didn't want Chris to think he was bullshitting him, so he leveled with him. "Look, Chris, I don't know that much about what is going on. However, I did hear enough to know that there are some people, both military and civilian, who are real interested in what's down in that cavern. I can tell you that."

"Thanks, Brocky, I can always count on you for being a straight shooter."

Colonel Christopher was a highly decorated officer of the First Iraq War where he had led one of the platoons that had fought and beaten the Iraqi National Guard, Iraq's elite fighting force that the United States and its allies had defeated in less than a day. That victory had marked the end of any real resistance in the first Iraq invasion.

A graduate of the United States Naval Academy, Christopher also had a master's degree from Yale in international affairs and was studying part-time for his law degree. Chris, as all his friends and fellow officers called him, was ambitious with major career aspirations. He had his sights on joining the State Department after he completed his twenty years in the military. Since he would be only forty-two years old at retirement, he thought this could be a great second career for him.

Chris was about five feet nine, stockily built, about 195 pounds, fit, athletic, and handsome. He had brown hair and brown eyes, broad shoulders, and a sculpted chest and abs that were more like a twelve pack than a six pack. Christopher had Italian heritage that gave him olive skin, a long nose, and a peanut-shaped head.

Chris grew up in a poor middle-class family and had lived in a traditional row home in Detroit, Michigan, while growing up. Many of his neighbors had worked for GM, Ford, and Atlas Oil Company as either assembly-line or blue-collar workers. At the center of the neighborhood had been the Catholic church and parochial school where most of the community worshiped and went to school.

The neighborhood had had an equal mix of good and bad influences. Drugs had been prevalent, and friends had become divided as some used and some did not. All things considered, there had been positive role models that one could emulate.

Chris's father had been bedridden for two years and had died of cancer when Chris was fifteen. His mother had been a clerk, barely making more than minimum wage, but she had made it work. He'd received a good education and never been denied the necessities of life.

However, Chris probably would not have gone to college immediately after high school had he not gotten into the Naval Academy. A senator from Michigan had recommended Chris for the academy appointment, and Chris had graduated with honors. After graduation, Chris had married Mary, a beautiful, smart, and educated woman from a small suburb just outside of Detroit in Dearborn, Michigan. They had met one night at a club that neither frequented. But by chance, they had seen each other across the crowded room, met, and gotten married a year later. They now had three beautiful daughters.

Chris and Mary both came from similar backgrounds and had a lot in common. He not only loved her but also respected her and how she raised their children and managed their family. Chris thought Mary was especially remarkable since he was often away on assignments in all parts of the world. When he was home, he was always studying or working in the Pentagon.

Chris was now a decorated war hero in charge of a battalion of men in Iraq. He had made a successful career in the military and was astutely preparing himself for a second career upon retirement. But little did Chris know what was next in store for him and Recon One that would impact their lives forever.

After reconnecting on the video link, Lieutenant Colonel Brock informed General Hitchens that Colonel Christopher was on the video link requesting to speak to him.

"Good, thanks, Brocky. Colonel Christopher, I'm glad you called; it saved me a videoconference call to you. You know how this technology is sometimes. It works most of the time, but when it doesn't, it just pisses me off."

The colonel asked, "Sir, what is Operation Sumer? Command said the assignment was only a routine recon and that we may engage enemy troops, but this sounds like something bigger."

General Hitchens said, "Oh, shit, son, they call missions anything to give them a name; you know that. I understand your surprise, but maybe it didn't filter down to either you or Colby. Speaking of Colby, make sure he understands this is a top-secret mission; nobody outside the platoon and Central Command is to know. No word about either the al-Qaeda or the contents of the cavern. The mission is to be carry out with the strictest secrecy. Need-to-know basis, son, need to know. Understood?"

"Yes, sir," Colonel Christopher said.

"Chris, according to the information I received, Lieutenant Colby said there was Sumerian cuneiform text all over the walls down there in that cave."

"Yes, sir, that is correct."

In a polite voice and cajoling manner, General Hitchens said, "Colonel, let's keep all this on the hush-hush. I will get back to you and make sure you record all activities. We do not know what you will encounter down there. Hell, it could be just gold deposits or dust; who know what we unearthed. It could also be a trap by the enemy."

"Understood, General."

As General Hitchens clicked the mouse to end the video transmission, he turned to Brocky and said, "You too, Brock, not another word."

Lieutenant Colonel Brock said, "Yes, sir, General!"

General Harvey Hitchens was the oldest officer in the Marine Corps and was two years away from retiring. He'd risen up through the ranks from a platoon sergeant. He had been part of the program to replenish the ranks with officers after the Vietnam War. Many officers had left the military after the war, leaving a deficit in the ranks five years later. The

Vietnam War had tarnished the military's reputation, and it had been difficult to recruit qualified personnel. The military had needed officers and had selected exceptional platoon sergeants with excellent military records to go to Officer Training School. Hitchens had been one of them.

Hitchens was a big man—six feet four, 220 pounds, and massive shoulders. He had a long neck, green eyes, and very pale skin common to redheads. Now fifty-seven years old, he was in great shape for his age and tried to work out three days a week when he could. His gray hair was closely cropped in a crew cut that barely covered his unusually large head and was in severe contrast to his long, bushy, red eyebrows. Coupled with tattoos on both arms, his look was a definite throwback from the fifties.

A few minutes after the general finished his videoconference with Colonel Christopher, precisely at 8:30 a.m., Lieutenant Colonel Brock said, "General Hitchens, the children!" The general had instructed Brock to interrupt him at this precise time every Wednesday so he could Vox, Skype, or FaceTime his grandchildren, Sienna and Ella.

"All right, Brocky, hold on to your jockstrap."

The aides knew how the general loved his family and how they were a big part of his life. The soldiers respected him for that. In spite of all that hard-ass gruffness, he always showed a real sensitive side to his granddaughters and family that he did not show as a Marine. It made him seem genuine to his men, and they admired him for that.

Sienna and Ella would sneak into their mother's room a bit before eight o'clock pacific time every Tuesday and take her cell phone from the charger on the nightstand where their mother left it each night.

Since his grandchildren lived in California, Kabul was about twelve hours ahead. It was Wednesday morning in Afghanistan and Tuesday evening on the west coast.

On this Tuesday, at about seven forty-five, the girls slowly and quietly snuck up, inch by inch, to their mother's nightstand, so no one would hear them. Then Ella grabbed their mother's iPhone and crawled as swiftly and silently as possible back to their room. When they passed their mother's bedroom door, they ran down the hallway as fast as they could and jumped into bed and hid under the covers.

"Let's Vox Pop Pop tonight. FaceTime doesn't always work," said Sienna.

Ella slid her index finger across the bottom of the iPhone to unlock it, looked up at Sienna, and said, "I don't see the Vox icon."

"Oh, just give me the phone."

Sienna grabbed it, but Ella pulled it away and said, "You called Pop Pop the last two times. It's my turn."

"Mom is going to hear us, and then we are both going to be in big trouble."

"I'll be quiet. Where do I find the Vox icon?"

"Okay, this is the last time I will show you. You need to swipe right to turn the page. Then you'll see the Vox icon at the bottom."

Ella and Sienna loved their pop pop and looked forward to Tuesday nights.

"Pop Pop, are you there? It's Sienna and Ella calling. Pop Pop, are you there? Come in, sir."

The general said, "Roger that. I'm here. How's my Little Si and Little El?" The general always used those nicknames for his granddaughters.

"We're just great, Pop Pop!" said Ella.

Sienna grabbed the iPhone and said, "Let me talk!"

Sienna and Ella struggled to get control of the iPhone; Sienna pulled the phone away and almost disconnected the call.

"We almost got caught by mom, but mission accomplished," said Sienna.

"Good girls. We don't want your mom or dad to know about our secret rendezvous. You are good soldiers. Now tell me about your week. I will just listen."

Sienna gave Ella back the phone and said, "There you go"buddy bud head."

Ella yelled out, "Don't call me "buddy bud head. Mom told you not to call me that."

"You're going to get us in trouble if you keep yelling like that." whispered Siena.

The general sat in his private lounge chair brought from the States with his feet propped up. He sipped an iced tea that Brocky had just brought him.

Ella said, "Siena and I got in trouble. Daddy is really mad."

"What happened?" the general asked.

"Remember the garden Sienna and I helped Daddy plant? Dad said we could pick the tomatoes once they were ripe. They started to grow, and we wanted to pick them, so we filled up a whole bucket with twenty tomatoes."

"So what is he mad about?" asked the general.

"Well, those tomatoes were green, and most of them were little. We tried to put them back on the plants with duct tape, but that didn't work. It just broke the branches, and Daddy got even madder."

The general could not stop from laughing. "Well, girls, that's not good, not good at all. You know how your dad loves that garden."

Ella said, "We told him we were sorry. We just could not wait to pick those dumb tomatoes."

Sienna gently elbowed Ella and took the smartphone. "Johnny and Joey—you know, those two bad boys in the white house two houses over—well, they chased me and El all the way down the street with that gigantic dog of theirs, but we were too fast for them."

"That's those great Hitchens genes. You girls are fast like your mother."

"Pop Pop, what are genes?" said Ella.

"That's a complicated question for such a little girl. Genes are things passed down at birth from your mommy, daddy, and grandparents that make you what you are. It's what you come from."

"Johnny and Joey said we came from the bogeyman," said Sienna. "Where did we come from?"

"No, you did not come from the bogeyman. There is no such thing."

"Then where did we come from?" Sienna asked.

"That is the biggest mystery since the beginning of time," replied the general.

"So where, Pop Pop? Where did we come from?" asked Sienna.

"You and Ella came from your mommy, daddy, and the great creator."

"Who is the great creator?" asked Ella.

"Some call him God."

Sienna asked, "Who's God, and where does he live?"

"Some say he lives in heaven."

Ella quickly asked, "Then where do the others say he lives?"

"Many cultures have different gods, but in many instances their stories of creation are the same."

"What are their names?" Ella asked.

"Well, some are named Anu, Apollo, Brahma, Atum, Allah, Pangu, and Phanes. These are gods and creators from several ancient cultures from different parts of the world."

Just then the call was disconnected. The general banged his fist on the armchair and said, "Oh balls, all this technology is bullshit. It never works. It's infested with bugs, you know, cockroaches."

Sgt. Clinton Branch, the tech sergeant, was responsible for the technology at the camp. Branch was called "Two-Way" for two-way radio. He hated Wednesdays because he knew that the general would complain and give him shit. When the general would connect back home, there were often problems, and Two-Way would always have an excuse.

"General, it's not on our end; it's the bandwidth at your daughter's house," he would say. "She needs to get a new Internet provider."

The general would always say, "You're full of crap, Two-Way, and your technology is full of bugs. You are always blaming someone other than yourself."

All the aides in the room would smile and just shake their heads, just another Wednesday. They loved it.

Later that day, General Hitchens ordered Two-Way to contact the NSC headquarters. Hitchens had just received some information about an American archaeological expedition around Basra and needed to inform the NSC. Washington had ordered Hitchens to report any unusual activity in the area around Basra and Sumer.

Unfortunately for Two-Way, there was some problem with the technology. A few minutes later, Branch looked over to the general and said, "Sir, we have a problem with the connection to Washington."

The general barked back, "What's the excuse this time, Two-Way?"

Everyone in the room started to laugh and in unison shouted, "It's those damn cockroaches again."

CHAPTER 7
The Archaeological Expedition

July 5, 2012: Archaeological Site, Basra, Iraq

South of Sumer, a team of American archaeologists were digging for ancient artifacts. Professor Anderson Ashe and his team were excavating a site just outside of Basra, about fifty miles north of Sumer. This area had been excavated for hundreds of years, and numerous well-known archaeologists had found ancient relics, tablets, and many other artifacts of the ancient Sumerians.

Abdul, a member of the expedition dig team, was carefully brushing a stone object wedged between two small rocks. He noticed that it had an engraving, and as he brushed some more, he realized it was an artifact of a strange-looking humanoid with a pointed hat and face mask.

He called over to another team member, Natalie, and she asked, "What is it?"

"I found something of importance. It reminds me of something found in another archaeological dig years ago. Please come, Miss Natalie."

She knelt down next to Abdul, took his brush, and slowly stroked the object until the image became clearer. She took a wedging device from her tool belt and carefully pried the object out of the ground. Natalie placed it in her hand and brought it closer to her face to examine it.

"Holy shit! Do you know what this is? Come; we have to show the professor."

She rushed over to Dr. Ashe, holding the artifact carefully. "Professor, look what Abdul found."

Natalie handed the artifact to the professor, who pulled a small but powerful magnifying glass from his shirt pocket and carefully studied the object.

"This looks like a humanoid figure riding in a vehicle that resembles a rocket or small spaceship. I saw one like this in a museum several years ago. It was a Sumerian artifact. I don't want to jump to any conclusions just yet, but this is evidence that this site may have other important ancient artifacts."

"What does it mean?" asked Natalie.

"Sumerian, Indian, Chinese, Mayan, and Egyptian cultures have numerous statues, figurines, paintings, and other artifacts depicting humanoids in what some have interpreted as spacecraft or flying chariots. There are cultures all over the world that have similar artifacts. Some artifacts have what looks like fire spewing from a rocket. They also depict winged humanoids descending from the heavens. They are convincing, but mainstream scholars say they are only mortal kings or nobles dressed in costumes."

Natalie said, "I'd heard before that Indian culture has similar ancient artifacts, but I've never seen any in person. I've been told the artifacts are very interesting and authentic replicas of spaceships."

Professor Ashe replied, "I've seen them and can understand why many believe them to be credible models of space vehicles of some type. In Hindu mythology, the gods and their avatars travel from place to place in flying vehicles. They were called *flying chariots, flying cars,* or *vimanas.* There are numerous stories of these flying machines in the Ramayana, which dates to the fifth or fourth century BCE. Lord Rama is the seventh avatar, which means the deliberate descent of a deity or of the Supreme Being to the earth. There is a painting that depicts Rama being welcomed upon his return riding in a flying vehicle. In book 6, canto, "The Magic Car" is a poem that describes flying vehicles as chariots flying to earth."

"Many of the artifacts I've seen are often clear and precise and cannot be mistaken for anything else, but there are those that can be explained in many different ways," said Natalie.

"Have Charlie deploy the Finder around this area," said the professor. The Finder was a device equipped with intensified image technology used to find just about anything buried in the ground. "I am sure we will locate more artifacts in the area where you found this one. Let's get back to work."

This particular archaeological expedition was not sanctioned by any government and not protected by international law. They were in Iraq illegally. The expedition team was lucky that al-Qaeda had not yet discovered their camp.

Sponsored by the Premier Oil Company, the expedition was equipped with a small security force and amply funded from a substantial grant. The oil company was interested in using the Finder for commercial purposes to help quickly find both gas and oil deposits. The intensified image technology in the Finder went well beyond any tool of its kind, and the benefits could be astronomical to any oil company that owned the technology. The Finder had dollar signs written all over it, and the oil company knew it.

Professor Ashe had invented the Finder and owned the copyright, and he did not want to see this technology exploited and used for commercial means, especially since he was an environmentalist. He knew he was a hypocrite, but he needed the funding for his expedition. Funding was scarce for these types of expeditions. He realized Premier Oil's commitment would require some payback, but he thought the risk was worth the funding.

Professor Ashe was an expert and noted scholar in archaeology and anthropology with a focus on Sumerian culture. Ashe was also famous for the use of technology in these fields, specifically in transcribing Sumerian writing and finding artifacts underground in the most difficult places.

In his late '50s, Professor Ashe was overweight. He was only five feet seven but weighed about 250 pounds and was out of shape. His belly stuck out and drooped over his belt, and sometimes he looked like a pregnant woman. Given the fact the professor always worked eighty hours a week, he never ate properly, never eating three square meals a day. He often fasted and binged.

His hair was completely white and occasionally groomed. He had brown eyes and bushy eyebrows, and one eye was visible crossed. He had a round, puffy face and short neck, and his wire-rimmed glasses sat awkwardly on his small, pudgy nose. His lips were thin and his teeth crooked.

The archaeological expedition consisted of three archaeologists, a nine-member security force, and six Sunni Iraqis that made up the dig team. Besides Ashe, the two other archaeologists were his two graduate student assistants, Natalie Duval and Charles Babbitt. They both had undergraduate and master's degrees from Stanford University. Charlie and Natalie were pursuing their doctorates and were extremely knowledgeable in Sumerian culture, archaeology, and anthropology.

The security force consisted of freedom fighters from the First Iraq War, mercenaries, and professional soldiers all recruited by the Premier Oil Company. The security team was there to protect the oil company's investment and those working in the expedition from al-Qaeda and rebel tribesmen in the region.

Premier Oil was not worried about interference from the Iraqi government because it had connections with those in power due to its investments in the oil fields in the Middle and Far East. However, Premier Oil wanted the security force there to protect the expedition and the Finder from al-Qaeda. Premier Oil had obtained intelligence indicating that large numbers of al-Qaeda had recently returned to the region, and so there was a risk terrorists would discover the expedition team.

Rocky Savin was the chief of security for Premier Oil and leader of the security team. His job required him to travel all over the world. Rocky was single and liked traveling, so he enjoyed that part of the job. He had thick, blond hair and blue eyes. He was tall, about six feet two, of medium build with long legs and broad shoulders. He weighed about 185 pounds and was athletic, lean, and in good physical shape. Rocky wore fitted shirts that accentuated his well-defined chest and bicep muscles. He always left the two top buttons of his shirt undone to heighten his sexiness further. Rocky was educated, mild mannered, smart, and a real womanizer.

Rocky never had any problem getting woman, and that was one of the reasons he'd never gotten married. Regardless, he knew no woman would put up with him, always traveling and never home with his family. More importantly, he liked the freedom to do what he wanted.

Rocky had been in a few scrimmages in his day. When he had been a CIA operative, he had fought in Nicaragua and Central Africa in the '80s and '90s. In his twenties he had been a Green Beret sniper whose job had been to assassinate enemy officers, foreign politicians, or any other person who had stood in the way of an American military or political objective.

Back at the expedition camp, Rocky met briefly with the professor to give him his daily briefing. Rocky also had a message from the Premier Oil executive management team to give to the professor. The management team was always raising the ante on the price it was willing to pay for the Finder. Ashe looked down at the offer sheet and just shook his head.

He paused for a moment to process the buy offer. Ashe yelled over to Rocky, "Do you believe they tripled the offer?" Ashe could live like a king the rest of his life. He looked at Rocky and said, "These guys are persistent; they don't play."

Ashe completed the briefing with Rocky and walked one hundred yards toward the dig site. It had been incredibly hot all day, and the professor told the dig team to call it a day. The crew headed to the camp for food, water, and rest after a hard day's work. Although modest, the site had several amenities that were probably not available at home to members of the dig team. One thing about Premier, they did things right and never spared any expense. With gas at almost four dollars a gallon, the cost of the expedition was pocket change to them.

The six members of the dig team quickly entered camp, cleaned up, and grabbed trays and eating instruments. They filled their trays with rice, corn, and a local fish called Masgûf. A carp fish indigenous to the regions near the Tigris-Euphrates Basin, Masgûf was a famous traditional dish going all the way back to the Sumerians and the Babylonians.

The chef prepared the Masgûf with a marinade of salt, olive oil, turmeric, and tamarind. The chef cooked the fish until it was crispy and served it with limes, lemons, and onions. Tonight's dessert was carrot cake. Both were camp favorites, especially with the dig team.

The chef, Hormuzd Bashir, was well known for traditional cuisine in Basra, where he worked at several restaurants. Employees of the oil company who had frequented the restaurants in the area had recommended the chef to Premier's vice president of operations responsible for planning this expedition. The oil company wanted to make sure that the professor and the expedition team had good food and accommodations. Management paid the chef more than he would receive at any restaurant in Basra to entice him to join the expedition. The dig team loved the chef's cooking and looked forward to eating three great meals daily.

The six Iraqis on the dig team were Sunnis from Basra. All six were Islamic, hardworking, and righteous men. They received a small sum for their toil, but it was still more than they would receive doing comparable work in the area. When they were not working, they lived with their families in Basra, the capital of Basra Governorate, which was only fifteen miles from the expedition site.

Abdu had organized the labor for the expedition and was the leader of the dig team. He handpicked each of the five men, including his son Kamal. Abdul had worked on at least fifty expeditions in the past thirty years. He was an expert in excavating a dig site and knew the history of many of the sites around Basra and Sumer. Abdul was sought out by many archaeologists and was very valuable to the expedition.

Abdul was strong but, as a holy man, did not believe in fighting. He was able to stay out of both Iraq wars and would have resisted if forced. He was very religious.

Abdul had three sons and one daughter. The family lived together in a modest 1,200-square-foot apartment in Basra. It had only three bedrooms. The three boys shared a bedroom and gave their sister the small bedroom, leaving the other for the parents.

After Abdul finished his Masgûf, Natalie joined him to discuss the status of the day's work. Under the direct supervision of Professor Ashe, Natalie coordinated much of the dig activities. She worked closely with Abdul and was responsible for recording the day's work and reporting it to Professor Ashe.

"How far did you go today?" Natalie asked Abdul.

"We excavated about five tons of earth today," Abdul said.

"The professor will be real happy if we keep up this pace," Natalie said.

Kamal interjected, "Miss Natalie, please do not forget our day of prayer. We do not work on our day of prayer."

Annoyed that Kamal kept mentioning the holy day, Natalie told Kamal she had calculated that into her projection. "Your father and I have everything under control. I respect your holiday, but if we fall behind, everybody will work on the holy day."

"I will handle the business with Miss Natalie," Abdul said in a slightly raised voice. "Now, go back and join the others."

Abdul was a little upset with Kamal for speaking out of turn and said to Natalie, "I am sorry; please excuse my son. Such matters should only be between you and me and not Kamal. He displayed a sign of disrespect."

"Don't worry," Natalie said.

Mildly upset, Abdul said, "Unfortunately, the younger generation does not believe in all the traditions of Iraqi culture. The two wars have had an impact on our young. They have become rebellious and resentful of the American aggression and how the American presence has disrupted both their education and the little freedom they did have. Many do not like how their people quickly surrendered and became subservient to the Western armies."

"You are the leader of the dig team, and I will always respect that." Natalie quickly reached out and put her hand on Abdul's shoulder to assure him. "I understand, Abdul; do not worry. All is on schedule."

Natalie Duval was the only woman in the expedition. Any other woman would feel threatened around all these men, but not Natalie. She was an expert kickboxer and had won several amateur competitions all over the world. An avid runner, she also had competed in numerous marathons, duathlons, and triathlons. She could take care of herself, and everyone knew it.

She was from a wealthy New York family. Her grandfather had pioneered software applications for mainframe computers. As the use of mainframes had become less prevalent in businesses, the company had reorganized and developed voice recognition software used in cell phones, navigation systems, and personal computers. The family estate was worth billions of dollars.

Natalie did not need to be out in these harsh desert conditions because she didn't need this job. However, she had a real interest in ancient mythology and the ancient-astronaut theory. Natalie used her knowledge in anthropology and archaeology to search for evidence to either support or refute various theories she explored. Her only goal was to discover the true origin of humanity and unlock the mystery of human life. She was continually in pursuit of the answers ... Where did humans come from? What was humanity's beginning? Natalie referred to it as "the search for the beginning."

Her studies of traditional Western religion and modern archaeology had weakened her belief in the more-traditional teachings and mainstream thinking on the subject of religion and science. Natalie though scholars focused too much time on minute details, proving little pieces of science to support their theories or ambitions. Although essential to science, Natalie felt that scholars lost sight of answering the bigger questions, like determining the origin of humanity.

Natalie believed that humans had already discovered and most likely hidden or destroyed evidence of humanity's origin to maintain the status quo. She believed religions and governments made sure that any credible evidence that contradicted the more traditional and mainstream thinking was hidden from the masses to keep them in check and to further political and religious institutions. Natalie Duval was interested in finding the truth. In fact, she was obsessed in her pursuit of the beginning.

Natalie walked over to visit Charlie Babbitt. They both played important roles in the expedition.

Natalie said, "We should be ready for the Finder in a couple days. Has it been recalibrated? Just a heads-up; you know the professor is going to ask."

"It will be ready. I need to finish some last-minute programming—you know, some tweaking."

It was Charlie's job to run the Finder. He documented the terrain, soil, and temperature and used that data to program the Finder. The Finder was nothing more than a state-of-the-art imagery machine that could see solids, liquids, and gases in all depths of the earth. There was nothing like it on the planet.

"And don't forget to reset the imagery services in the computer," reminded Natalie.

"It's good to go," said Charlie.

Charlie was only on the expedition was to further his career. His goal was to get his doctorate and become tenured at one of the most prestigious universities in the United States, preferably Stanford University.

The professor was Charlie's ticket to reaching his goals, and he did everything he could to stay in Ashe's good graces. Since Charlie was a good kiss ass, his relationship with Professor Ashe was extremely good. Professor Ashe did not like confrontation, so Charlie's amiable personality provided a comfortable relationship for Professor Ashe.

Charlie was plain, scrawny, and nerdy looking. On his large, pointed nose, he wore black plastic-frame eyeglasses with thick lenses that resembled Coke bottles. Growing up, everyone called him "Coke Bottle Charlie." He dressed awkwardly, and usually nothing matched. He stored his pencil case, which always had four to five writing instruments, in his shirt pocket. His long, blond hair was always dirty, oily, and seldom washed; it usually hung down over his dark-brown eyes. He had visible white specks of dandruff in his hair. He was not clean shaven, and his beard was thin and spotty.

Rocky Savin had a real interest in the expedition and Professor Ashe. He would talk to the professor every opportunity he got to learn more about various ancient cultures and all the expeditions Ashe had participated in over the years. They both enjoyed each other's company and talked for hours about archaeology as well as Savin's numerous travels and adventures. It almost seemed they both would like to trade lives. Ashe hungered for adventure; Savin hungered for knowledge. When they talked to each other, they were able to quench their thirst for those things missing from their lives.

The professor and Rocky Savin were about to begin one of their evening discussions after dinner when Natalie and Charlie showed up.

"Professor, can you sign these forms for me? Just initial here and on the next page," said Natalie.

"Natalie, stay a while," said the professor. "I believe Rocky has forty questions, and I could use your help. You too Charlie; I'm sure you'll have something to say."

"So, Professor, what is so significant about this godforsaken place?" asked Rocky.

"Godforsaken; you don't know how appropriate that statement is."

Rocky asked, "What do you mean?"

"Well, do you want the long or short version of the story?"

"I'll take the bottom line."

"Well, there is no bottom line when talking about the Sumerians. We are in Basra, but the region is popularly known as the ancient city of Sumer to historians. Sumer is a famous city rich in the history of humanity. It is the cradle of civilization, home of the ancient Sumerians, and the birthplace of math, writing, science, technology, and medicine.

"The Sumerians were the first known civilization on earth and the first to have a written language. They invented a writing system by using a cuneiform script on clay tablets. Over twenty-two thousand of these tablets were discovered in Nineveh in the nineteenth century. According to some interpretations of the tablets, the Sumerians believed that an alien race came from the heavens to occupy earth.

"The evidence to support this claim is found in the Sumerian creation myth. The legend is written on cuneiform tablets found in Nippur, an ancient city in Mesopotamian settled in 5000 BCE. Sumerian mythology claims that in the beginning, humanoids of extraterrestrial origin ruled over the earth. They traveled through the sky in flying vehicles resembling rockets."

"So where is the proof?" asked Rocky.

Natalie interjected, "Let me read something to you." She pulled a laminated card out of her knapsack and said, "This card contains an excerpt from Enuma Elish, the Babylonian epic of creation. It was originally written in Sumerian."

"You're kidding me; you carry this around with you?" said Rocky.

"I'm not kidding you," said Natalie. "The creation story is one of the most important Sumerian stories of our time and was written on seven clay tablets and has several different translations. This is just one translation of a verse from one of the tablets."

"What does it say?" asked Rocky.

Natalie said, "According to the writing on the tablets, man was created in the Garden of Eden. It says:

> "When Marduk heard the words of the gods,
> His heart prompted him to fashion artful works.
> Opening his mouth, he addressed Ea
> To impart the plan he had conceived in his heart:
> I will take blood and fashion bone.
> I will establish a savage, 'man' shall be his name.
> Truly, savage-man I will create.
> He shall be charged with the service of the gods
> That they might be at ease!
> The ways of the gods I will artfully alter.

"The story says humanlike beings of extraterrestrial origin ruled earth. They needed gold for their survival. The gods built a habitat on earth and began mining gold and other minerals. The gods grew tired of labor, and Anu, the god of gods, agreed. His son Enki recommended that they create man in the likeness of the gods to do the work."

Rocky asked, "Are Enki and Ea the same person?"

"Yes," replied Natalie. "Enki is later known as Ea in Akkadian and Babylonian mythology. The Sumerian myth goes on to say that the body and blood of a god were mixed in with the clay of the earth to create the first humans. Humans were later modified to be independent and capable of reproduction, and the first such human was called 'Adapa.' These events caused a conflict between Enki and his brother Enlil. To obtain revenge, Enlil treated humans harshly and experienced much hardship."

Rocky leaned over and looked directly at Natalie and said, "Now that is one hell of a tale. So these Sumerian stories primarily address the beginning, like Genesis in the Bible?"

Natalie responded, "No! First of all, there are hundreds of tablets that address other myths, knowledge, and recorded history. Secondly, let's not be parochial in our thinking. There are similar creation stories in almost all cultures, such as Hindu, Chinese, Japanese, and American Indian, to name a few. They may not call the first humans Adam and Eve or Adapa, but the stories are similar."

"Come on, Natalie; this story resembles Genesis," said Rocky.

"Yes, it does, but this is a Sumerian myth, not Judeo-Christian scriptures," Professor Ashe said. "The Sumerian myths were written in 4500 BCE. Genesis was written in 1447 BCE. So I think we can conclude that the Sumerian creation story was written long before the Bible's Genesis story."

"Professor, why do you think they created humans?" asked Rocky.

"Based upon this interpretation, they needed someone to perform labor. The story goes that the extraterrestrials came to earth in need of resources for their planet, particularly gold. The planet was losing its protective shield, and they needed gold to reflect heat in their atmosphere. Many gods grew tired of mining the resources and sustaining a habitat, so they rebelled. The resolution was to create man to perform the labor," Professor Ashe said.

Then he added, "You know, traditional historians and archaeologist insist these stories are myths and are not to be taken seriously. Mainstream scholars just discount them. Some of the interpretations of the Sumerian texts are so contrary to what the mainstream scientists and scholars hold to be true that they characterize them as radical or off the wall."

"Do you believe this to be true, Professor?" Rocky asked.

"I don't know what I believe; that's why I'm here: to find out the truth. It's my job to gather facts and evidence and then make conclusions."

"No shit! That's real wacky, Doc. No wonder the mainstream scholars discount these interpretations."

Charlie Babbitt said, "I told you that last night, Rocky. Most people can't handle anything that is against the norm. The traditional scholars hold to what they've been taught over the years, so they are not about to change their thinking over some wild-ass theory. Many scholars believe the translations of myths are based upon too many assumptions."

"Shit, I agree with them. What do you believe, Professor?" asked Rocky.

Professor Ashe said, "I think we are still in the Dark Ages when it comes to the origin and history of humanity, God, the universe, alien life, and even religion. The notion that the sun was the center of the universe was first introduced as early as the third century but was not accepted by most astronomers until Kepler and Galileo proposed it in the 1600s. Christ, we just discovered Pluto in 1930, and then just recently scientists now say it's not a planet, all in the span of eighty-two years."

"So what does this have to do with the Sumerians?" asked Rocky.

The professor said, "According to some interpretations of ancient writings and artifacts, the Sumerians knew the sun was the center of our solar system. They also knew the earth was round and that Pluto was part of our solar system. Some interpretations of the Sumerian tablets say there is a twelfth planet that enters our solar system every three thousand six hundred years." To emphasize his point, the professor stood up and walked over to Rocky. "We're talking six thousand years ago! Compare the Sumerian knowledge of the universe six thousand years ago to our knowledge just five hundred years ago when more modern man thought earth was the center of the universe."

"Again, Professor, this is only one interpretation," said Rocky.

"How could the Sumerians have possessed this knowledge six thousand years ago?" asked Charlie. "Did they just discover this, or did someone give them this knowledge?"

Natalie said, "Some scholars believe that someone more intelligent and not from this earth gave them that knowledge."

"This is ridiculous!" Rocky said.

Professor Ashe said, "Rocky, there are several well-known scholars who believe alien civilizations visited earth long before man walked the earth. Many believe these aliens had a significant influence on our history. The number of well-known scholars who believe keep growing every day. There are several other respected scholars who have studied and written about such theories."

"Nobody believes this stuff," Rocky said.

"There are three scientists sitting here who entertain the possibility, Rocky. We do not ignore or discredit it," said Professor Ashe.

"I cannot believe the three of you think this is possible," said Rocky.

"Look," said Professor Ashe, "don't be so fast to write this off as rubbish. It is possible. There are over a billion stars in the Milky Way alone and an estimated average of at least three planets revolving around each star. Couple that with the fact that there are a billion galaxies, each one with a billion stars, and each one with an average of three planets. Now do you think there is no intelligent life out there in the universe with an older, wiser, more intelligent, and more advanced culture than ours? What is the probability? I say it's huge."

The professor got up and said, "I'm starving, and I've been waiting all day for the chef's famous fish dish."

Charlie quickly responded, "Me too; that fish is awesome."

Rocky said, "You guys are just going to drop all this Sumerian mythology on me and just walk away?"

"Relax," replied the professor. "We have many more nights to talk about this, and we haven't even gotten to the good stuff."

"Boy, I can't wait," Rocky said half jokingly.

The professor and Charlie walked one hundred yards toward the dining area to get some food and call it a day, while Natalie and Rocky continued to converse.

CHAPTER 8
The Wall between
Information Sharing

July 5, 2012: Central Intelligence Agency headquarters; George W. Bush Center of Intelligence, Langley, Virginia

Patty, a professionally dressed and attractive young woman, walked down the hall toward the break room. She had two immediate assignments. The first task was to get the CIA director a cup of coffee, and the second one was to advise Assistant Director Brown that the director would like to meet with him at 11:00 a.m. today. These were mundane tasks for such an intelligent and sophisticated young woman, but she took them seriously and performed them well.

Patty could have sent the assistant director an e-mail or calendar invite, but his office was only twenty feet from hers. She liked to use the fifteen minutes before the start of her workday to socialize and get the office chatter. Even in the CIA, the most secretive organization in the world, there was gossip and rumors in the halls of the headquarters building just like any other workplace.

Patty Deichert had been the director's appointment secretary for the past two years. A graduate of Georgetown University, Patty had studied prelaw and Mandarin. She'd had the opportunity to attend law school at Columbia University in New York City but had been unsure she wanted a career in law like her dad, who was a famous and influential lawyer in Washington, DC. Patty had wanted to work for a few years before she decided on a career path and specific field of graduate studies. The CIA intrigued her, and she'd wanted to learn more about what they did.

Jim Brown walked into Patty Deichert's office, and Patty said, "The director will be with you shortly. He's on the phone with the president and his chief of staff. He'll finish in a minute."

Given her awesome figure, beautiful hair, and gorgeous looks, Jim could not keep his eyes off of Patty as he stood outside the door to let the director know he was there. The director waved Jim in and pointed politely to a chair for Jim to sit down.

The director completed the conference call by saying, "Yes, sir, Mr. President, I am on it, and I will keep the chief of staff updated per your request. I understand the importance of this matter."

The president had appointed Nathan Stiles as director of the CIA in January 2009. Stiles had been a member of the House of Representatives and then become the majority leader in the US Senate. Altogether he'd served thirty years in Congress and was a well-connected career politician who had become a millionaire on a government salary.

Nathan was sixty-eight years old and was overweight at 295 pounds. He had ragged, poorly trimmed gray hair that made him look older than he was. His face was rough and had brown spots from years of overexposure to the sun. Even though he wore $1,000 suits, they did not fit him, and he still looked sloppy. His clothes looked as if he'd borrowed them from his older brother. His tie was loose because he could not button the collar of his shirt.

Nathan Stiles hung up the phone and greeted Jim with his classic big smile and pleasant personality that endeared him to everyone.

"Hi, Nate, how are you doing?" Jim asked.

"Shit, I've seen better days. The president is upset about the presence of al-Qaeda in southern Iraq in some godforsaken place called Sumer."

"Why is he upset?"

"That's why I wanted to meet with you today. We need to discuss the emergence of al-Qaeda in this region. The president and the Joint Chiefs are concerned about the al-Qaeda reappearance in the region around Basra. They want us to gather some intelligence in the area. We need to know why they are there and what their intentions are—you know, the routine questions."

"Well, to be blunt, the answer to the first question is simple: it's their land, and they want it back. They want to control the region again for both religious and political reasons. They are Sunni Muslims, and you know the history."

"I need more information. Get our contacts in the area to provide us with some answers. What else do you have for me?"

"Believe it or not, it's about the same region. I attended an NSC briefing today at nine. According to NSC, they sent some Navy SEALs into Sumer yesterday to recon the area outside Basra."

"The president didn't say anything to me about that. I would assume he knows that the military had sent the Navy SEALs to gather intelligence."

"We also picked up some chatter from video link between General Hitchens and Colonel Christopher, who is overseeing the mission and the platoon's activities. The mission is called Operation Sumer."

The director raised his voice. "Operation Sumer? What the hell is that?"

"It gets even better," said Jim. "They found about thirty dead al-Qaeda soldiers, some of the same ones the White House is concerned about. They got caught up in an F-15 bombing raid. The Navy SEALs found most of them dead and then killed the rest."

"What's puzzling is why the president didn't tell me any of this."

"I also don't understand why only some of this information was available to us at the NSC briefing today."

"There must be a reason," said the director. "This president is all about sharing intelligence information, but here we are again, banging our heads together to find out what the other sixteen intelligence agencies know."

"Maybe the NSC is waiting for confirmation," said Jim.

"Damn it, we are the CIA, and another US intelligence agency is keeping information from us! We need to get some people on this, ASAP."

"You know, nothing has changed. Shit, do you remember what I told you when you took over as CIA director? The reason we have sixteen intelligence agencies with over sixty thousand federal employees and private contractors is so we can spy on each other and not share information. No single agency knows where all the bodies are buried, and that's the way they want it."

"Yeah, you may be right. Why else would you have sixteen intelligence agencies? It's not cost effective," said the director.

"I saw a figure the other day that we spend sixty billion on intelligence, and that only includes what is published in the budget. You and I know that there are clandestine operations supported by secret funds."

"No one wants any of our dirty laundry getting out to the public or the rest of the world."

"Before I forget, there was another quick item," said Jim.

"What's that?" asked the director.

"Well, there is an American archaeological expedition in this same area."

"How did that happen? I thought archaeological expeditions were forbidden by the Iraqi government, and given the presence of al-Qaeda, why would anyone chance being captured, kidnapped, or killed? An unauthorized expedition in this region truly amazes me."

"It's Professor Ashe's expedition, and Premier Oil is funding it. The oil company provided a security force of nine mercenaries, led by, of all people, Rocky Savin."

"Now I can see how they got there and why they're still alive. Rocky is a good soldier and has connections with both the Iraqi government and the rebels. I'm sure he will protect them well."

"Ashe probably sold his soul to the devil to get the funding and protection for that expedition."

"I'll bet he did," replied the director.

"There is one final thing, sir. Regarding the chatter heard earlier, there was some dialogue about heat signatures and weapons of mass destruction."

"I thought the administration wanted nothing to do with any talk of WMDs. That was something pinned on the prior administration."

Jim said, "The administration is concerned about how it will look if al-Qaeda returns to Iraq and these weapons turn out to be real."

"Okay, Jim, thanks for the briefing. I'll meet with you again tomorrow at 11:00 a.m. Send Patty in, please."

Jim left the director's office thinking about the previous administration's obsession with WMDs. So far, all efforts to produce concrete evidence of WMDs had been futile. The previous administration's failure to link WMDs to the Iraqis concerned the new president and military. WMDs were the primary justification for invading Iraq in 2003. Consequently, the reason for the Iraq War had shifted from the search for WMDs to eradication of al-Qaeda forces and the capture of the 9/11 mastermind Osama bin Laden.

When the new president had taken over, he'd wanted to distance his administration from WMDs. Therefore, the new administration had further shifted the focus of the war to defeating al-Qaeda, capturing bin Laden and anyone associated with 9/11, and disabling al-Qaeda's ability to attack the United States again.

After the US forces had begun pulling out of Iraq, the al-Qaeda had returned to Mesopotamia. The redeployment of US military forces from Iraq to Afghanistan in 2011 had provided an opportunity for al-Qaeda to reenter the area and exert some influence over the southern region.

Al-Qaeda was a Sunni Muslim extremist group whose main purpose was to create civil unrest and take control and power over the southern territories. Iraq was a big part of their strategy to rid the region of US occupation and Western ways. Al-Qaeda's ultimate goal was to establish a caliphate, an Islamic state base, and propagate Islam religion worldwide.

CHAPTER 9
Passing Time

July 5, 2012: Mound of Tiamat

It had been a long day for the Navy SEALs, but they were familiar with fourteen-hour days, harsh conditions, and minimal food and water. The platoon's day had begun at five in the morning, and it was now seven in the evening. Lieutenant Colby knew he'd pushed the men to the point of exhaustion, so he called it a day and told the platoon to set up camp for the night, get some chow, and sleep.

Assigned guard duty, Jackson Michaels and Blake Marshall were on both ends of the path to protect the front and the rear. The rest of the men set up pole lights and opened their ration packs and mess kits. Tonight's supper was chicken pesto, crackers, soup, and a fruit or energy drink.

Lucero called over to Petty Officer Carter and Master Chief Petty Officer Mendez and asked, "Are you gentlemen interested in some poker?"

Mendez said, "I'm always ready to take your money. Who else is in?"

"Count me in," Tex Carter said.

Casper Pantano also indicated he wanted to play. Casper always lost at cards. He was easy to read, and everyone knew when he was bluffing and when he had a good hand. It was a big joke in the platoon.

Back at the base camp, several members of the platoon would play Texas Hold'em every Tuesday night till dawn. The winner typically took home an average of $3,000. Lucero usually was the biggest winner.

The men finished eating, and the rest of the platoon lay down or sat on their sleeping bags while the others played poker. Lieutenant Colby began writing in his journal, something the men always kidded him about. Robert "Slick" Sullivan was reading Robert Taylor's novel *The Revenge*, an action-packed espionage thriller that had been on the *New York Times* best-seller list for ten weeks. Buford Bradley loved his *Playboy* and would always boast about the "vivacious, smoking hotties," as he called them, in the centerfold.

Joseph "Fish" Calamari and Michael McDermott were both sharing fantasy baseball magazines, passing back and forth the latest editions. The baseball season was nearing midseason and the All-Star break. Both men were looking for free-agent sleepers to add to their teams for the rest of the season. They were passionate about fantasy baseball, and they were in the same league, so there was a friendly competition each week, especially when they went head-to-head.

The men played cards for hours. Mendez was red hot and won five hands in a row. Lucero lost all his money.

"Hey, Lucero, you look a little piqued," Tex said. "Is it because you lost your ass tonight, or is this cave a little too tight for you? I know you get claustrophobia. Looking a little sweaty over there, amigo."

"Up yours," Lucero said.

"Remember that sniper assignment?" Tex asked. "The one where we were to assassinate a Guatemalan general. Shit, I even forget his name. We were in this tight underground enclosure with hardly any room, and you freaked out. If it weren't for me popping the general and his five aides, we would be in a Guatemalan jail right now."

"Fuck off, Tex; you're full of shit," Lucero said.

Mendez shouted, "All right, you assholes, cut the shit. We're trying to play cards, and I'm about to take this turkey down. Can you give a man a little space please?"

Trash looked at Mendez, trying to gauge his hand. Thinking that Mendez had no possibilities on the board other than three of a kind, Trash saw the $200 and raised another $200. Mendez looked surprised at the bet. Apparently Trash had not kept track of the cards and all the possibilities. Running out of cash, Trash was sweating and decided to call. Mendez, cool as a cucumber, knew he had Trash beat.

Trash had ace-high spades flush, but unfortunately for him, Mendez had four kings. Mendez slowly put his cards on the table, reached across the table to scoop up the pot, and said, "Now that's what I'm talking about."

Lucero turned to Mendez and said, "Nice."

Tex blurted out, "Horrible, just horrible!"

The rest of the men cheered loudly.

Lieutenant Colby stood up from reading his book and told the men to settle down. "Gentlemen, that's it for tonight; it's time to turn the lights out and get some shut-eye."

The men all groaned, and Trash said, "Shit, Lieutenant, I lost my ass, and you're not giving me any time to break even."

All the men got silent. They were kind of taken aback by the way Trash barked at Lieutenant Colby. Although they were some of the toughest men in the military, they all knew their place and respected and admired Lieutenant Colby.

The lieutenant fired back, "Well, shit, Trash, you just earned yourself some extra guard duty, so go and relieve Buford. Slick, you take over for Blake so they can eat before lights out."

Thompson was called Trash because of his momma's food. She would send him soul food about once a week when he was at the base. She was not the greatest cook, at least according to others in the platoon. Everyone in the platoon had tried Momma's soul food, and it was the worst soul food they'd ever eaten. But Trash loved it, and he could not wait till it arrived on Fridays each week, tightly packed in hot ice. Everyone called his food package "the trash bag." The men loved soul food, and the smell of Momma's food was great. But shit, when they bit into it, the food had such a sour taste nobody could stomach it except for Trash. He would wolf it down in fifteen minutes.

Everyone thought the food was horrible, but Trash couldn't get enough of it. After eating his mom's soul food, Trash would always say, "Wee doggy, now that is good eating." Everybody in the platoon, even Colby and Mendez, would just shake their heads. That was how Trash had gotten his name, and it had just stuck.

With Trash and Slick on watch duty, Lieutenant Colby ordered the platoon to get some rest till morning. When Colby would say, "Lights out," the platoon would always say, "Good night, Chesty, wherever you are," in reference to Chesty Puller. Chesty Puller had received five Navy Crosses. He was the most decorated man in naval history. Chesty was known as the bravest man ever in the navy. He was a legend.

Trash took his position for watch duty as instructed. He looked over at Slick and whispered, "You know, Slick, the one thing I hate in this military is standing watch. Shit, I thought when I joined the Navy SEALs I wouldn't have to stand watch anymore."

Slick said, "Stop complaining. Christ, you sound more like a little old lady than a Navy SEAL! I don't want to hear you bitch the rest of the night."

"You tellin' me you like this shit?"

Slick responded by changing the subject. "Hey, do you think that Chesty Puller really got five Navy Crosses?"

"Yes, I reckon so. They say Chesty was the epitome of *A Few Good Men*—you know: Duty, Honor, Country," Trash said. "Chesty was the man!"

"You can say that again, brother."

Trash looked up at the ceiling of the cavern and said, "Good night, Chesty, wherever you are. I hope it isn't hell, like this godforsaken shit hole."

CHAPTER 10
The Cavern of Hell

July 6, 2012: Mound of Tiamat

It was dawn, and Master Chief Petty Officer Mendez was the first one up. When he first opened his eyes, he lay there for a moment thinking about how the cave was so eerie and damp but mystical and extraordinary at the same time. He had to take a minute to adjust to the creepy, dark, bizarre, and dreary surroundings.

As he focused his eyes, he looked down and saw the large head of a snake three inches from his feet. The red snake with black bands slithered around the toes of his boots, undulating slowly upward, parallel to Mendez's legs, about four inches from his body. Sliding along in an accordion-like movement, the large snake hissed, showing its grooved, hollow fangs used to inject lethal venom into its victims. Mendez knew it was a deadly reptile.

As the long, scaly, tapered body moved past his waist, Mendez lay there lifeless, trying desperately not to startle the noxious creature. Peering through the corner of his eye, Mendez saw the snake change direction toward his stomach, only inches away. The snake stopped as it sensed prey, and its pitchfork tongue hung in the air, warming up for a deadly strike.

Already grasping his knife that he always kept next to him when he slept, Mendez knew he needed a set of incredible moves to escape the venomous bite that was seconds from striking his body. In what seemed like a nanosecond, Mendez quickly rolled away from the snake, and at the same moment, the snake reared up, flashing its tongue and darting forward at its prey. Mendez swiftly grabbed the snake just below the head and swung his knife, cutting the snake in half and miraculously escaping the lethal bite.

Taking his time to collect himself, Mendez decided he did not want the others to know what had just happened. He thought there was no need to alarm the others, since the snake was not indigenous to the area. Mendez lay there wondering how a snake from the swamps of South America had ended up in a cave in Sumer, Iraq.

With everyone still sleeping, Mendez quietly got up and buried the snake about five yards from the campsite.

Making his rounds and not knowing what had just gone down, Jackson Michaels appeared and asked, "Chief, is everything okay?"

"Of course. I just took a dump, and I'm burying the remains," Mendez said.

Mendez returned to his bedroll nonchalantly and reached into his backpack to get his rations as if nothing had happened. He took out muesli, powdered milk, a fruit energy drink, and a coffee pouch. He also grabbed a pint of bottled water and a small pot from his mess kit to heat water for hot cereal and his coffee.

As the rest of the platoon began waking up, they started to fold and put away their sleeping bags. The men removed their rations from their backpacks and helped themselves to fruit cocktail, fruit bars, energy drinks, hot chocolate, tea, and coffee. The coffee aroma was strong and masked the musty smell in the cavern.

The selection of rations had improved significantly over the decades. The soldiers now had some input into the type of food. From peas and pork to pasta and pesto chicken, the selection of rations had come a long way since the first two world wars.

As the platoon finished up their chow, Lieutenant Colby advised the men to clean up their mess kits and get ready to move out. While the men prepared for another day of recon, Colby called Mendez over for their daily meeting to go over the assignments.

Mendez asked, "What's the plan?"

"About an hour ago, I spoke with Colonel Christopher at regional command, and his orders are for us to keep our guard up and continue to recon the cavern. I've decided to have you remain with me toward the front of the platoon. Tex Carter will take the point, and Lucero will cover us from behind."

"Lieutenant, I think you should know that I encountered a large, venomous snake just before dawn when everyone was sleeping. It was close, but I was able to kill it before it could bite me," reported Mendez.

"Are you kidding me?" Colby replied in shock.

"No, I'm not; it was a South American aquatic coral snake," said Mendez.

"I thought you only found those in South America."

"So did I," Mendez said.

"Why didn't you wake me?"

"I didn't want to bother you or alarm the others. I took care of it."

"Chief, you are the epitome of a Navy SEAL."

With a mild smile, Mendez said, "Just doing what you would, sir."

Picking up his gear, Colby said, "You know, Chief, this is one of the strangest places I've ever encountered. How does a South American aquatic coral snake end up in a desert in Iraq?"

Mendez said, "I can't imagine what's next."

"Yeah, we'd better move out."

The Navy SEALs quickly resumed their recon. Tex and Joel were the third and fourth in the platoon's chain of command behind Colby and Mendez. Tex Carter was an experienced point man. The platoon trusted his abilities to handle this important assignment.

Tex's birth name was Clay Bruno Carter. However, from his first day of boot camp, everyone had called him Tex, even though he was from Chicago. Carter had gotten the name because he'd been a nationally known football player at the University of Texas. Tex had run for over 2,500 yards and twenty-five touchdowns his freshman year, but unfortunately, he'd flunked out of college at the end of his first semester.

Tex was six feet two and weighed 240 pounds, but it was all muscle. He worked out religiously and did at least three sets of one hundred push-ups and sit-ups every morning. Tex was a strong black man, well groomed, with closely cropped black hair, brown eyes, a thick neck, and a large nose that spread across his face. His charcoal-black skin highlighted the whites of his eyes and his pearly teeth.

There was a large three-inch scar on Tex's right check that he'd received in a knife fight with a Taliban rebel in Afghanistan. The rest of Tex's face was rough and blemished. There was some wear and tear on his body, but he was one hell of an athlete and one tough son of a bitch.

Tex had had over three thousand all-purpose yards and twenty-five touchdowns his senior year in high school and had been the most highly recruited athlete in the country. Being such a huge man, it was incredible that he had been able to run a forty-yard dash in 4.33 seconds. Tex had been the top running back in the country coming out of high school, and he'd received a football scholarship to the University of Texas right out of Grover Wilson High School in South Chicago.

Tex's accomplishments as an athlete were quite amazing given his early life history. He had been a crack baby, and his mother had died at age nineteen from an overdose when he was only two years old. The Illinois Child Protective Services had discovered his mother's dead body in a public housing project building located in the Bronzeville section of South Chicago. The same day they had found Tex alone in a bathtub full of water. He'd never known his father and had been raised by his grandmother. He had a very low IQ, and he'd struggled in school, barely avoiding being put in special education classes.

Tex was a product of his environment, and one year in college was not going to change that. He had not maintained the grades needed to comply with NCAA standards. His grades had been so bad that even the coach and the alumni could not get him another chance. So fifteen days after flunking out, Tex had joined the navy. He planned to stay in the navy for four years, and after that, he planned to turn pro.

When qualifying to be a Navy SEAL, Tex's physical prowess and his ability as a sharpshooter had prevailed over his mental-aptitude shortcomings. He could hit a quarter squarely in the center from twenty yards out with an automatic rifle. Tex had been the winner of the 2010 and 2011 National Open Championship sponsored by the National Shooting Association. He was the best sharpshooter and sniper the navy had and had been assigned to several secrets missions with the highest need-to-know classification. It was rumored he'd registered numerous kills of foreign high officials and military officers, but nobody knew for sure, because Tex never talked about it. Lieutenant Colby was grateful to have Tex and often positioned him as the point man to take advantage of Tex's strength, great instincts, and sharpshooting ability.

The deeper the platoon went into the cavern, the steeper it got. At the same time, the width of the path got narrower and more treacherous as they advanced. The tapered pathway forced the Navy SEALs to walk carefully and in single file.

A mile into the cavern, Lieutenant Colby tried to contact regional command and Colonel Christopher. For whatever reason, the transmission was now garbled and unintelligible. The radio transmission problems were quite unusual given the fact that the military recently had deployed a new state-of-the-art communications system. However, the contractor was still working out some of the bugs in the system.

Ground communication had improved tremendously with the launching of a new communication satellite. Developed by Comtech Industries, the communication satellite was the first of its kind to provide significantly improved data, voice, 4G wireless, and video services.

The military knew good communication was essential to military combat and could be the difference between victory and defeat.

Turning to Mendez, Lieutenant Colby said, "Do you have any ideas why we are having communications issues?"

"I think we are experiencing some interference," Mendez said.

"Let's keep trying to contact command," ordered Colby. "As we change position, maybe the communications will improve."

"Sounds like a plan," said Mendez.

Lieutenant Colby signaled to Tex to move forward.

The Navy SEALs went a mile more into the cavern. Colby stopped and turned around to Mendez and asked, "Chief, did you notice the gold substance has disappeared? We better stop for a moment and try to communicate with command again."

Mendez signaled to the men to take a knee. After a fifteen-minute break and no luck reestablishing communications with command, Colby ordered the platoon to continue their recon. As the platoon went forward, there were no longer ancient writings on the walls of the cave, and it became darker. Lieutenant Colby signaled to the platoon to turn on their helmet lights. Tex and some of the men also pulled out flashlights from their backpacks.

As they went yet deeper into the cavern, the temperature became cooler, dropping to sixty-five degrees, while the temperature outside the cave averaged around a hundred degrees. The cooler temperature was the only consolation for being in the dark and dreary cave.

As the Navy SEALs traveled onward, the flashlights filled the cave like spotlights painting the angular columns. The reflection of the flashlights highlighted the red, gray, and gold limestone formations and underscored the stalactites, the earth-toned, cylindrical needles that hung from the ceiling. Rectangular quartz crystals crisscrossed each other horizontally and vertically, creating an interesting backdrop to the stalactites and hollow columns. The combination of all these factors made for an incredible sight so beautiful and bright it was breathtaking.

As they moved to the left, Tex noticed a sharp curve in the passageway ahead. The pathway began to slope downward into the cavern. Tex was concerned that the turn was so sharp that they could not see what was around the bend. Also, the footpath got narrower, and the fissure in the rock formation created an enormous hole that dropped off into the earth just to the side of the path, making conditions dangerous.

Tex stopped, and Lieutenant Colby carefully moved forward to join him.

Tex turned to Colby and said, "Sir, I have a bad feeling about this. We don't know what's on the other side. It could be a trap."

Colby said, "This is definably a quandary. Let's try to contact regional command again."

Each time Colby tried to contact Bravo Company, there was considerable static and noise on the line. Ironically, the communications between the platoon members was very clear. Lieutenant Colby concluded that the communication problem was within the frequency between regional command and Recon One, most likely caused by something in the cave.

Trying to decide whether to move forward or turn back, Colby carefully surveyed the area. One of his responsibilities was to minimize danger to members of his platoon. Without communication, Colby knew they were at a significant disadvantage, almost blind.

Suddenly and out of nowhere, a swirling, circular wind resembling a tornado appeared about fifteen yards ahead. Churning like a black hole in a bottomless abyss, the phenomenon was so dense that they could barely see anything three feet below. Colby could not believe his eyes and froze in his tracks.

Realizing he had to react immediately, Lieutenant Colby carefully changed places with Tex to take the lead. Colby waved his hand forward to direct the platoon to continue. The footpath was still getting narrower as they approached the sharp bend. It became too treacherous to proceed.

Each soldier walked cautiously, taking small steps. The phenomenon continued to spin wildly out of control. The Navy SEALs correctly gauged the impact of the black hole–type wind against their chances to navigate past it.

Standing still, Lieutenant Colby carefully thought through all the possibilities. Should they move forward or turn back? The situation caused Colby a serious dilemma. Given the dangerous conditions and their inability to communicate with regional command, Lieutenant Colby realized moving forward was too dangerous at this time. He decided to turn around and go back fifty yards; they would sit tight and send someone from the platoon back to reestablish communication with regional command.

The lieutenant knew he needed to brief Colonel Christopher on the situation and obtain further orders. He decided to send Lucero, one of his best men, to contact the superiors, brief them on Recon One's status, and receive specific orders on how to proceed.

Petty Officer Joel Lucero was not your typical Navy SEAL. Overall, Joel exceeded all the requirements of a special forces soldier but lacked some of the rough, stereotypical characteristics of a Navy SEAL. He was extremely mild mannered and was the most skilled and intelligent soldier in the platoon. His aptitude test had placed him at the top, and he had one of the highest ASVAB scores ever.

Although physically not intimidating, Joel was the strongest and best hand-to-hand combat soldier in the navy. He'd won the navy weight-lifting competition two years in a row, even though he weighed only 190 pounds and was only five feet nine. Lucero had a medium, stubby build that was firm and lean, and he had brown eyes, black hair, and a round, tan face. He possessed a rare mix of both Hawaiian and Filipino features.

Lieutenant Colby called Lucero over to the side so they could speak privately. Colby knew he could always count on Lucero, and Colby leaned heavily on him, Mendez, Tex, and Buford. But Colby knew Lucero was best fitted for this assignment.

"Yes, sir, what's up, Lieutenant?"

"Joel, we need to communicate with regional command and give them a status. I want you to go back toward the entrance of the cave, contact Colonel Christopher, and wait for orders."

"What should I tell them?" asked Lucero.

Colby thought for a minute, then said, "Just tell them that we have encountered enemy resistance and incurred casualties. However, there have been no signs of the enemy in the past twelve hours. Let them know that the cave is extremely dangerous and that I'm concerned we're putting the men unnecessarily in harm's way. We need orders on how to proceed."

Lucero grabbed his gear and an extra flashlight and some batteries. Fish tossed Lucero an extra quart of water and nodded as he said good luck.

Knowing how Joel loved cherry licorices, Tex said, "Take these Twizzlers with you." Tex patted Joel on the shoulder and said, "See you soon, big guy."

Joel grabbed his gear and headed back toward the cave entrance.

CHAPTER 11
The Sumerians and the Search for the Truth

July 6, 2012: Archaeological Site, Basra, Iraq

After enjoying an excellent dinner, Professor Ashe and Rocky Savin were sitting alone by the fire swapping stories and drinking coffee. Rocky looked forward to smoking a cigar every evening after dinner and making conversation. He pulled out a Cuban cigar and a disposable lighter from his shirt pocket and rubbed his thumb across the cylindrical striker to ignite the flame. Looking directly into the blue flame, he puffed three times to make sure he lit his cigar. The smoke from the cigar mixed with the smell of the campfire and resulted in a pleasant aroma.

Rocky leaned back in his chair, adjusting to be more comfortable. He looked over and noticed that Professor Ashe was also enjoying the aroma. Rocky offered Professor Ashe one of the Cuban cigars. Ashe had quit smoking years ago, but surprisingly, he accepted one along with Rocky's lighter. Ashe said thanks and lit the cigar.

The professor turned to Rocky and said, "Shit, I forgot how awesome these were. There is nothing like a cigar, coffee, and a fire to make you appreciate the small things in life."

Rocky nodded in agreement. Professor Ashe and Rocky got along famously. They enjoyed conversing about Savin's adventures, and Rocky especially liked to listen to Professor Ashe's stories about ancient history and archaeology. Rocky always had twenty questions.

Carrying a cup of coffee carefully to make sure she didn't spill any, Natalie Duval slowly approached the two men and asked politely if she could join them. Given her beauty and pleasant but purposeful personality, neither one objected. Both men extended their hands as an invitation to her to sit down. They admired her toughness but, at the same time, thought she was incredibly feminine. What a raw combination.

"Please, take a seat," Professor Ashe told her.

"Yes, always a pleasure to be in your company," added Rocky.

"Thank you, gentlemen. It's a beautiful night. You can see all the stars so clearly."

Charlie Babbitt also joined them.

Savin was always messing with Charlie, and tonight was no different. Rocky said, "Hi, Charlie, where did you get those glasses? Man, they're thicker than a magnifying glass. No wonder everyone calls you Coke Bottle Charlie." Rocky was the only one laughing.

"Rocky, leave Charlie alone; you know he's sensitive," said Ashe.

Natalie looked over at Rocky and asked him if she could have a cigar. Surprised, he reached into his pocket and pulled out his last one, passed it to Natalie, and lit it for her. Savin thought there was something very sexy about a beautiful woman with long, black hair and blue eyes smoking a cigar.

Suddenly, Joey Bags yelled, "Duval, you look great puffing on that stogie, but you would look better sucking my dick."

Rocky shouted back, "Hey, shithead, watch your mouth. I'm not putting up with that crap. Just keep it up, and you're going to be in the unemployment line!"

Bags just looked away and snickered.

Rocky looked back at Natalie to see her reaction. Calm, Natalie brushed it off quickly and was only mildly irritated by Bags's behavior. Rocky thought that Bags was a smartass, and he needed to bring the man down a peg when the security team returned to corporate headquarters. But for now, they needed every man.

"I apologize for his behavior," Rocky said to Natalie.

"Can't you do something about your man? He's a pig," said Charlie.

"Don't worry. He's just a social dinosaur with no class or respect. I'm sure his mother is very proud of him," Natalie said sarcastically.

Bags had harassed Natalie since he'd joined the expedition. Rocky was getting concerned that she could file a sexual harassment complaint that would reflect negatively on the security team and the company. But he knew she was not the type. He admired and respected Natalie for not only her beauty but also for her brains and athletic prowess. He thought Natalie was equal to and better than most men he knew.

"Can I ask you a question?" Rocky asked Natalie.

"Sure," she replied.

"Why would such a beautiful, wealthy, and strong-willed woman like you be in the hottest place on earth with us jarheads, when you could be anywhere else or have whatever you wanted?"

"You're referring to my dad's wealth, not mine. I'll make my own way."

"But you could be anywhere; why here?" asked Rocky.

Natalie said, "I want to know the truth about the origin of humanity. I don't care how long it takes or if I have to devote my entire life to it. All that other stuff like lustrous clothes and exciting vacations is okay, but it's superficial and eventually gets old. It's like my dad says: 'If you eat too much filet mignon, it starts to taste like bologna.'"

Charlie looked over at Natalie and said laughing, "I'd like to try some of that filet mignon. I'm tired of eating bologna."

Laughing, Rocky shouted, "Charlie, you're full of bologna, like that bullshit you tried to give me the other night about Sumerians. Man, that was some heavy stuff."

Charlie stood there with a stupid look on his face, not knowing what to say. Rocky and the professor were laughing so hard tears were running down their checks. Like Charlie, Natalie did not think it was amusing. Gaining his composure, Rocky knew he'd better act more seriously before he insulted Charlie and Natalie any further.

"Okay, I'm only kidding. Lighten up, you two," Rocky said.

"I don't think that was funny," said Natalie.

Trying to change the subject, Rocky said, "So, Natalie, you seem driven about your work."

"There's a quote from Thomas Wolff that best represents my passion about my work," said Natalie. "It goes like this: 'We are made to persist. That's how we find out who we are.' I am persistent about getting the answers to the mysteries of humanity. It's my life's passion. That's how I roll."

Professor Ashe said, "Let me tell you, Natalie is one of the most persistent people I know. I remember one time we needed some test results back quickly from a lab at the University of Oregon. We uncovered artifacts of Sumerian gods and needed to determine their age. Natalie called the lab five times a day for four days. It almost always went to voice mail, and when she did get to someone, she got some vague answer on the status of the test. On the fifth day, Natalie got in her car and drove five hundred sixty miles in eight hours and sat outside the lab till they gave her the results. The lab staff was so impressed with her persistence they expedited the request while she waited. Once she got the results, Natalie got back into the car and drove all the way back to Stanford."

"Wow, Natalie, you're determined," said Rocky.

Natalie took a puff of the cigar and changed the subject. "So what are you gentlemen discussing tonight?"

The professor quickly said, "Well, Rocky wants to learn more about the Sumerians. He keeps asking me so many questions. You're also an expert in this area. Can you help?"

"What do you want to know, Rocky?" asked Natalie.

"From the little I learned about the Sumerians since being here, it's a fascinating culture, but I'm skeptical about some of the claims. I want to know more."

"Like what?"

"Who were the Sumerians? What's written in the Sumerian text on those tablets Charlie was telling me about? I want to know how they obtained so much knowledge of science and technology so early in the development of humanity."

Natalie smiled because she was delighted that they respected her knowledge on the subject. As she took another puff of the cigar, Natalie thought about how to organize the information. There was so much material on the Sumerian civilization. Natalie knew she could not address it all in a one-hour conversation.

"That's a tall order. Let's start at the beginning," said Natalie. "The Sumerians were the first recorded human civilization dating back to 4500 BCE. According to the tablets found in 1800, the Sumerians invented the wheel, plows, cuneiform writing, arithmetic, geometry, irrigation systems, bronze, leather, saws, chisels, hammers, braces, nails, pins, rings, hoes, axes, knives, arrowheads, swords, glue, waterskins, bags, harnesses, armor, quivers, scabbards, boots, sandals, harpoons, beer, and boats. They were the first civilization to have laws, courts, schools, government, medicine, libraries, copper tools, bronze weapons, jewelry, sun-dried bricks, the pottery wheel, mythology, and a lunar calendar with twelve months."

The professor interrupted Natalie and said, "The Sumerians had this knowledge six thousand years ago. That's pretty incredible."

"Yes," said Natalie. "Besides inventing the first written language, one of the most fascinating Sumerian achievements was the establishment of laws to govern their society. The Code of Ur-Nammu is, as yet, the oldest known code of law. It was found on a cuneiform tablet in Nippur, Iraq, and Samuel Kramer translated it in 1952. Forty additional Sumerian laws were later found in Ur and deciphered in 1965.

"The Sumerian laws protected the weak, poor, orphans, and widows from those who would prey upon them. There were also laws against abuse of official powers, overcharging for goods and property, and unfair use of power. The Sumerians promoted a sense of justice, equality, and freedom before any other known civilization, and they were the first to have a recorded social conscience."

"Big deal; someone had to be the first to have laws," said Rocky.

Natalie said, "The Sumerians also had a sophisticated social order. Priests governed, and the majority of the people were servant-slaves of the temple god. Based on the city-state political structure, the communities were organized around the temple. The communities were comprised of priests, craftsmen, servant-slaves, and soldiers.

"The priests ruled in the Sumerian society, and the people believed them to be human representatives and communicators with the gods. The priests served in government and practiced medicine in addition to their religious duties. The craftsmen dedicated their lives to producing goods, constructing buildings, and providing other skilled services needed for the temples, priests, or soldiers. The soldiers protected the city, while the slaves did the hard labor."

Rocky interrupted. "So how did the Sumerians get so advanced?"

Natalie said, "Many scholars believe someone intervened and gave them this knowledge. The Sumerians couldn't have obtained this knowledge on their own."

"Who intervened?" asked Rocky.

"Let's just say an advanced, intelligent civilization," Natalie said.

"Charlie already told me that they were extraterrestrials," said Rocky.

"Okay, that's one translation of the ancient Sumerian mythology," replied Natalie.

"Come on; that's bullshit. It's this kind of claim that hurts your credibility. Give me an example that can be supported by fact," Rocky said.

Professor Ashe turned toward Natalie and nodded to indicate he had something to say. Natalie returned the nod and said, "Please do, Professor."

"Okay," the professor said. "How did the Sumerians get so much knowledge of astronomy? Their knowledge included cataloging and documenting the stars and movement of the planets and the sun and moon. They invented the zodiac constellations. The Sumerians had prodigious knowledge of the planetary bodies in our solar system, and according to some interpretations of their ancient tablets, extraterrestrials gave them this knowledge."

"Man, this is getting deeper every minute. You amaze me, Professor, how you continually entertain me every evening," said Rocky.

"Try to keep an open mind," said the professor.

"Do you have any tangible evidence?" asked Rocky.

"Zecharia Sitchin points to a Sumerian cylinder seal, referenced as VA 243 and now in the Vorderasiatisches Museum in Berlin, Germany, to support this theory. According to this famed scholar and author, the inscription on the seal depicts twelve planets revolving around the sun and provides proof that the Sumerians had advanced astronomical knowledge of the planetary bodies in our solar system."

"Who is Zecharia Sitchin?" asked Rocky.

"He's a Russian-born scholar who studied Sumerian culture and their writings for thirty years. He theorized that the cylinder seal shows twelve planets: Earth, Mars, Uranus, Jupiter, Saturn, Pluto, Mercury, Neptune, Venus, the moon, Tiamat, and Nibiru, the so-called twelfth planet.

"According to Sitchin, the planet Nibiru had a three-thousand-six-hundred-year orbit around our solar system. Nibiru collided with Tiamat, which was located between Mars and Jupiter. When the two celestial bodies crashed into each other, Tiamat split into two halves. The half toward the sun split off and became earth. Tiamat's principal satellite became our moon. The other half of Tiamat smashed into bits and pieces and formed into the asteroid belt."

Rocky interrupted the professor. "I thought Tiamat was a goddess in the Sumerian creation story. In Sumerian mythology, didn't Marduk and Tiamat do battle, and Marduk won and became king and ruler?"

"Yes, that's one interpretation; Sitchin has another," the professor said.

Natalie said, "Professor I'd like to comment on the Sumerian cylinder seal in Sitchin's book. There are other varying translations of the seal. For example, the German Mesopotamian scholar Anton Moortgat translates the seal as a depiction of a deity, not an illustration of twelve planets as Zecharia Sitchin claims in his book *The 12ᵗʰ Planet*. According to Moortgat, nothing in the inscription suggests anything remotely to do with astronomy or planets."

Rocky said, "It sounds like you can interpret these stories several ways. It seems to depend on who's translating. One story talks about a war in the universe, pitting Tiamat and Marduk in a drag-out battle, and the other depicts them as celestial bodies colliding into each other and creating earth. Maybe the ancients were trying to record a story of how our solar system was created?"

"Yes," said Ashe. "Regardless of assorted interpretations, the fact remains that there are a growing number of scholars who now believe that the Sumerians could not have obtained all this knowledge without some help. Some scholars believe help came from smarter beings from another place in the galaxy."

"Your evidence is ambiguous. Give me something more convincing," said Rocky.

"Sure!" said Natalie. "The Sumerians' knowledge of astronomy was exceptional, and to some degree, the Sumerians knew as much as astronomers in the nineteenth century.

"For example, the Seven Tablets of Creation show that the Sumerians had incredible knowledge of our universe. The tablets tell of twelve planets in our solar system rotating around our sun and detail each planet thoroughly. They call earth the seventh planet."

"What a minute!" Rocky said. "The earth is the third planet."

Professor Ashe said, "That's how we classify earth if you are counting the planets from the sun. However, if you approach earth from the outer edges of space, we are the seventh planet."

Natalie asked, "How did the Sumerians have this knowledge of the universe thousands of years ago? Did they have telescopes or some device that could track the planets' movement around the solar system?"

Rocky said, "You're the expert; you tell me."

"There is no evidence the Sumerians had telescopes," said Natalie. "Without telescopes, there is only one way they could have known that the earth was the seventh planet."

Rocky asked, "How's that?"

"They traveled to earth from outer space."

"So you're saying that someone more advanced had to give them the information or they had to have witnessed the alignment of the planets from space?"

Natalie said, "Both are possibilities."

"This is bullshit! I'd like some other evidence of the existence of extraterrestrials on earth," said Rocky.

"Okay," the professor said. "All over the earth, paintings, sculptures, artifacts, and ancient writings depict and describe extraterrestrials descending from the heaven in fiery chariots, rocket ships, and other space vehicles. Some scholars call them ancient astronauts.

"There are several Sumerian artifacts that illustrate helpers of gods or Watchers who resemble modern-day descriptions of Grays. Numerous petroglyphs found in caves all over the world suggest aliens have visited earth. From ancient Japan, scholars have speculated the Dog to be an ancient astronaut who visited earth. Also, there are six similar one-thousand-year-old artifacts in the Chicago Field Museum of Natural History that represent models of high-speed aircraft piloted by ancient spacemen. These are just a small sample of artifacts and writings that claim ancient astronauts visited earth."

"I'm still not convinced that any of this has any validity," said Rocky.

Natalie thought for a moment. She looked at Rocky and the professor and chose her words carefully. "Many theorize that someone or something intervened in human development, providing the bridge from a primitive species to *Homo sapiens* and modern man."

Rocky asked, "You mean God, right?"

Natalie said, "Yes, that's one way to look at it. But let's think out of the box a little. Many cultures all over the world have similar creation stories in scriptures and ancient text. These texts refer to gods descending from the heavens, and many civilizations also reference heavenly hybrids."

Natalie continued, "Some scholars say that the Hebrew and Judeo-Christian writings have several books, some that are in the Bible and some not, that support these theories. For example, Apocrypha and Pseudepigrapha reference Watchers and giants who had intimate relations with beings from earth."

"What! Give me a valid example of one scripture or ancient text," said Rocky.

Natalie said, "The book of Enoch."

"What is the book of Enoch?" asked Rocky.

Natalie said, "The book of Enoch and the Dead Sea Scrolls were discovered in a cave around 1773. Richard Laurence interpreted them in 1821, and later R. H. Charles did so in 1912. According to the translations of the book of Enoch, Hebraic scriptures, and other legends, there was a race of giants and superheroes who did acts of great evil. Their great size and power likely came from the mixture of demonic DNA with human genetics.

"According to the book of Enoch, the Watchers were angels dispatched to earth to watch over the humans. They soon began to lust for human women. Then fallen angels mated with earth women and taught them forbidden knowledge, such as art, weaponry, cosmetics, mirrors, sorcery, and technologies. The offspring of these unions were the Nephilim, savage giants who pillaged the earth and endangered humanity. The story ends when God created the great flood to clean the world of all humans except Noah."

Rocky asked, "Where is this written?"

Professor Ashe said, "Rocky, pass me my pack lying next to you."

Rocky passed the pack over, and the professor pulled out a manuscript. He scanned the pages for a specific section and said, "Here it is." He looked over to Rocky and the group and asked, "May I read this section from the book of Enoch?"

Rocky said, "Please do."

The professor read:

> And it came to pass when the children of men had multiplied that in those days were born unto them beautiful and comely daughters. And the angels, the children of the heaven, saw and lusted after them, and said to one another: "Come, let us choose us wives from among the children of men and beget us children."

> And all the others together with them took unto themselves wives, and each chose for himself one, and they began to go in unto them and to defile themselves with them, and they taught them charms and enchantments, and the cutting of roots, and made them acquainted with plants. And they became pregnant, and they bare great giants, whose height was three thousand ells: Who consumed all the acquisitions of men. And when men could no longer sustain them, the giants turned against them and devoured mankind.

Rocky said, "I've never heard of this book of Enoch. Is it scripture?"

Professor Ashe said, "The book of Enoch was Jewish scripture but was excluded from Christian and Jewish canon, and now only a few religions recognize it as scripture. It is banned from the Christian Bible. It was written by Enoch, who was the seventh from Adam and the great-grandfather of Noah."

"You interpret this scripture literally?" asked Rocky.

"I think the meaning is incredibly clear," replied Ashe.

Natalie said, "There is another story similar to Enoch in the Bible. According to Genesis 6, the sons of God took female humans and created superhumans: 'And it came to pass, when men began to multiply on the face of the earth, and daughters were born unto them. That the sons of God saw the daughters of men that they were fair; and they took them wives of all that they chose. And the LORD said, There were giants on the earth in those days; and also after that, when the sons of God came in unto the daughters of men, and they bore children to them, the same became mighty men which were of old, men of renown.'"

"So what does this prove? It could mean a lot of things," said Rocky.

Natalie responded, "Whether right or wrong, this is one interpretation. There are references throughout human history and in many cultures of men of prominence, giants who had great powers and lived for hundreds of years."

"So you are saying that these giants could be some form of extraterrestrial or gods from heaven?" asked Rocky.

"Yes! Almost every civilization has similar stories," said Natalie.

"Like what?" asked Rocky.

Natalie said, "Another example of why some scholars believe extraterrestrials interceded in man's origin is in Native American culture. According to their mythology, extraterrestrials called Star People had sex with Native American women and impregnated them. The legend goes that after six years the Star People returned to earth and took the children up to heaven to live with their fathers."

"Could these just be made-up stories? Or their meanings just interpreted incorrectly?" asked Rocky.

"Come on!" bellowed Natalie. "How could so many prominent civilizations misinterpret the same stories?"

"You tell me," said Rocky.

"Look, throughout history, writings, scriptures, and artifacts have often been misinterpreted. We have been told many things that have turned out to be untrue," Natalie said.

"Natalie, no offence, but you're jumping around now. So where are you going with this?" Rocky asked.

"What I'm saying is that there is so much we do not know, and what we do know many in our society take as gospel. As scientists, the professor and I must question things and should not always accept mainstream theories. That is what a good scientist does. Unfortunately, some scientists are caught up in minute detail trying to support one hypothesis or theory their whole lives. As a result, they do not look at all the evidence collectively, and they miss the big picture. I must keep an open mind and not disregard anything out of the ordinary."

"So why is this information regarding the Sumerians just now coming into play?" asked Rocky.

"Well," the professor said, "there was no credible written account to indicate that the Sumerians existed till the Sumerian tablets were discovered in the sixteenth and seventeenth centuries. It took another two hundred years or more to interpret the writings in any significant manner. We're just now beginning to put the pieces together in the past one hundred or so years."

The professor continued, "I think there are other buried tablets, artifacts, and technology we have not found yet that will shed more light on humankind's history. I am also sure there is other evidence that has been purposely hidden or destroyed all over the earth. Many believe countless documents, tablets, and artifacts are hidden in the basement of the Vatican in Rome or concealed by the US government in places like Area 54 or the town of Dulce."

"So there is more evidence out there? Where is it?" asked Rocky.

"Shit, Rocky, this is why Natalie and I are on this expedition," Ashe said. "To find more history, more knowledge; to determine where we came from; to uncover the mysteries of human life."

Professor Ashe stood up and said, "I think that is enough for tonight. It's getting late; we can continue this tomorrow. We'd better get some shut-eye."

"Yeah," Rocky said. "Man, my mind is racing like the Dover 500."

The professor, Rocky, and Natalie all laughed, finished their cigars, and called it a night. As Rocky and Ashe went their separate ways, Natalie and Charlie passed by the security team to get to their quarters.

Bags shouted over to Natalie, "Hey, Duval, it's chilly tonight. Need a real man to keep you warm?"

Ed Paradee, one of the members of the security team, yelled over to Bags, "You'd better be careful. Natalie is one tough cookie, and she's not the kind of women you want to trash-talk."

Bags said, "Man, she's just another chick."

"Don't underestimate her," Paradee said.

As usual, Natalie shrugged off Bags's rude behavior.

Charlie said, "Why doesn't Savin do something about that asshole?"

"Forget about him. I can't stop thinking about the discussion tonight. Why does the book of Enoch have so many references to fallen angels who came to earth and had so much impact on humanity? Why did they exclude this book from Jewish canon and the Bible?"

"Those are great questions," said Charlie. "Something historic happened back then, and Enoch was smack in the middle of it. I think someone purposely hid the original Aramaic version that was found as part of the Dead Sea Scrolls."

"Yeah, I also think something spectacular happened back then."

Charlie walked toward his quarters and said, "Good night, Natalie."

Natalie lay in her bunk thinking of the few references to Enoch in the Bible. Genesis mentioned Enoch only twice. According to Genesis 5:23–24, Enoch lived only 365 years, far less than other patriarchs in the period before the flood. Enoch walked with God; then he was no more, for God took him. Enoch was taken to heaven, where he learned the secrets of the universe and of the coming judgment.

Natalie lay there thinking about what happened to Enoch and why his writings were not part of Jewish and Christian canon. Could the fallen angels be extraterrestrial beings? Could they be ancient astronauts?

CHAPTER 12
Loss of Communications

July 7, 2012: Regional Command Center, Outskirts of Baghdad, Iraq

Not hearing from Lieutenant Colby and Recon One, Colonel Christopher was concerned. He told his communications tech sergeant to check the wireless connection and continue to troubleshoot the communication problems. Tech Sergeant Peters tried to tell the colonel that something external was causing the problems, but Christopher was not buying it.

"Colonel, sir, there's something interfering with our signal, and it's not on our end of the transmission. Wherever Lieutenant Colby's platoon is at this moment, they may be near some type of electrical charge that is so powerful it's interfering with our signal."

"Keep trying, Sergeant," ordered Christopher.

After several failed attempts to communicate, Colonel Christopher became more concerned and decided to contact Central Command in Afghanistan to let them know of this new development. Given the failure to troubleshoot the problem, the colonel asked the tech sergeant to get Lieutenant Colonel Brock on a secure line.

"Sir, I have Lieutenant Colonel Brock on the line."

"Hey, Brock, Chris here; we have a situation that the general should know about."

"What's that?" asked Brock.

"Well, we lost contact with the Navy SEALs in Sumer," said Christopher.

"How long ago did you lose communication?" asked Brock.

"About twelve hours ago. We've been working to fix it, but according to my technical team, there's some kind of electrical interference jamming the signal."

"I will pass this on to the general. He just finished lunch and will be back from the mess in a few minutes," said Brock.

As the lieutenant colonel hung up, the general walked into his office. Brock immediately walked over and said, "Sir, we have a situation."

"Well, spit it out, Brocky. It can't be as bad as Cooky's taco surprise I just had for lunch. Shit, I should have never eaten that stuff. Tell Cooky to take it off the menu."

"We have a situation with Recon One of Bravo Company. Colonel Christopher just called and said that they've lost communication with Recon One—you know, the Navy SEALs that went into Iraq on Operation Sumer."

"Shit, I know who they are. What's the problem?"

"Some type of electrical interference," reported Brock.

"There are those cockroaches again. Keep me posted and advise me the minute you hear something. Also, bring me yesterday's casualty reports. Also write a report to the chiefs asking them to put the vendor's feet to the fire to fix these bugs in the new communication system."

"Yes, sir."

"Brocky, one more thing: tell the tech sergeant to set up a videoconference with Washington at 3:00 p.m. and make sure it is a secure line. Hopefully it will work this time."

As the general leaned over a large regional deployment map, he noticed that Recon One's location was not on the map. He turned to Brock and asked, "Why isn't Operation Sumer on the map?"

"I wasn't informed about the mission till yesterday; that's why. I thought it was a need-to-know special mission kept from the public."

General Hitchens replied, "Nevertheless, put it on the map so I can see the locations of other platoons in their surrounding area. You never know when that information will come in handy. Just color-code it purple; no one will know."

"But the press, sir, they might start asking questions," Brock said.

"Tell the press that it's a security training mission with Iraq allied forces. We are not to mention the true purpose of this mission. If any information is leaked, we will deny it, and if pressed, we will say our secrecy is in the best interest of national security."

"Will do, sir!"

"Brocky, we need to get the communication fixed. I'm really getting concerned about Recon One. You know how important communication is to any military activity. Without it, we are blind."

CHAPTER 13
The Run for Help

July 7, 2012: Mound of Tiamat

Lucero was halfway to the entrance of the cave in his quest to reconnect with command. He'd been walking for several hours and stopped to rest. He drank some water and put the canteen back into his backpack.

Lucero got up, brushed the gold dust off his pants, and walked quickly, almost jogging, toward the entrance of the cave. After barely going thirty yards, he saw a dim light ahead. Initially, he thought it was the reflection of the gold substance.

He slowed down and cautiously took six steps forward. At that moment, he heard muffled voices. He immediately stopped, stood completely still, and listened intently. At first, he could hear only the beating of his heart and the dripping water from the rock formations all around him. Minutes later, the voices got louder and became clearer.

Lucero quickly placed his back firmly against the wall of the cave and walked sideways in the other direction, trying to hide from whatever was coming. The voices got closer, and he was able to make them out. Joel was no expert, but he knew enough to determine they were speaking

Arabic. Before he'd been deployed to the region, his orientation training had included lessons in Arabic.

Back about ten yards, Lucero remembered seeing a small opening in the cavern wall just big enough to crawl in and hide. He turned around and ran back to the opening as swiftly as possible. He tossed his backpack and his rifle into the hiding place. He immediately fell to his knees, lunged forward, and crawled through the narrow, egg-shaped opening, squeezing and forcing all of his body parts inside.

He was barely able to move around but somehow rolled over on his back. Using his feet, he leveraged himself against the wall and ceiling of the cavern to turn his body around. Now lying on his stomach, Lucero could see the soldiers, twelve of them, passing by through a small horizontal crack between two rocks.

Lucero had an excellent visual of the soldiers and counted them as they passed. He noticed that a number of the soldiers had unkempt facial hair with streaks of gray mixed in their dark beards. They wore dishdashas, full-length white garments with long sleeves; some of them had colorful embroidery. They wore colored *ghutra* or white *yashmagh* on their heads that were held on by *egals*, a sort of headband. One of them was carrying an al-Qaeda flag, so Lucero knew they were terrorists.

The al-Qaeda soldiers carried automatic rifles. They looked tired, so they must have traveled a long distance. Two of the ten soldiers appeared to be the leaders. The two leaders seemed out of place and were probably from another part of the region or a surrounding Arabic country, maybe Saudi Arabia.

The total number of al-Qaeda soldiers the Navy SEALs had encountered in two days was now over forty. That was a lot considering the US military had publically proclaimed they had purged the region of the enemy when they had left southern Iraq for Afghanistan. But apparently the al-Qaeda had returned and possibly in bigger numbers.

When all but one soldier had passed Lucero's hiding place, one of the leaders ordered the patrol to stop and take a break. Surprised, Lucero whispered softly to himself, "Oh shit." Slowly and quietly he flipped his body over so he could lie on his back, trying desperately to better conceal himself.

Lucero was relieved when the leader indicated that the break would be only ten minutes. The position of his body was so contorted that the pressure on his back pushed against his bladder, and he had a sudden urge to urinate. He could not help but think that this may be the longest ten minutes of his life.

Most of the soldiers in the patrol sat down, reached into their backpacks, and pulled out containers of water, flatbread, fruits, and dates. The officer at the end of the line was sitting down with his back against the wall of the cave, in full view of Lucero's hiding place. The al-Qaeda soldier's glossy eyes were staring directly at the small opening that served as Lucero's hiding place.

A few minutes passed before the soldier facing Lucero suddenly got up and walked straight for Lucero's hiding place. From his position on his back, Lucero could barely see the soldier out of the corner of his eye, but he knew he was close enough to be discovered. Lucero prepared himself for battle.

The soldier stopped directly in front of the opening to Lucero's hiding place. Unexpectedly, he pulled down his pants and urinated all over the bottom of the egg-shaped opening. After relieving himself, the terrorist slowly returned to his previous position, still directly facing Lucero.

Lucero too was relieved. However, the urine had a strong odor. It reminded Lucero of the smell of bathrooms at airports and sporting events. The enemy soldier still could not see Lucero but had left him with a real smelly mess.

While hiding, Lucero thought about how the al-Qaeda could cause so much destruction and kill so many Americans on US soil. During training, he had learned that al-Qaeda was an international Islamic fundamentalist organization associated with several terrorist incidents, including the attack on New York's World Trade Center.

He remembered September 11, 2001, as if it were yesterday. It was etched in his mind forever. He had been only thirteen at the time of the attack but still clearly recalled the events of the day. He remembered coming home from school and seeing his mother sitting on the floor in the middle of the family room dumbfounded and glued to the TV coverage of the 9/11 attack on CNN. To this day, he could still see the smoke, soot, and ash everywhere like black snow falling from the sky.

He still had flashbacks of thousands of innocent people, firemen, police officers, and many other first responders trapped in the towers with no way out. The impact of the moment had become even more emotional when Joel had seen tears streaming down his mother's face as she sobbed hysterically. At that moment, Joel had pledged that he would never take his freedom for granted and that he would do his part to protect his country and all Americans' freedom.

Osama bin Laden had established al-Qaeda in 1989 to further traditional Muslim ways and rid the region of Western culture. Osama bin Laden wanted a new world order ruled under Muslim law. One of al-Qaeda's objectives was to purge Americans and their influence out of Muslim states and bring down pro-Western forms of autocracy in the Middle Eastern and global economy.

Lucero could never understand their purpose or their objective. But it was simple: al-Qaeda hated Americans and wanted to destroy their culture and way of life. They sought a world under sharia law, Islamic rule, and Muslim religion.

Petty Officer Lucero's thoughts then shifted to his confined surroundings and his claustrophobia. The dimensions of his hiding place were less than six feet in length and two feet wide. The distance between the floor and the ceiling was a little more than three feet. With the back of his head propped up on a rock, he could see his boots and the sides of his egg-shaped enclosure. Looking straight up at the ceiling of his enclave, he knew now what it must be like to be buried alive.

Lucero had flashbacks of the Guatemalan sniper mission and feared he would freak out like before. He grew faint and started to sweat profusely. He gritted his teeth, hoping this feeling would subside. Freaking out would surely give up his hiding place and most likely result in his death.

Further compounding his problems, Lucero's urge to urinate was growing stronger. He thought about the movie *The Right Stuff*, which he had seen as a child, and how astronaut Alan Shepard had relieved himself in his space suit before liftoff. Lucero thought how embarrassing it would be for a Navy SEAL to piss himself, but the urge was getting worse by the minute.

At that moment, the Navy SEAL saw something out of the corner of his eye. As he quickly looked down, Lucero noticed something crawling on his boot. Due to poor lighting, he could barely make it out. As the object moved slowly to the right, it came into the light from the crack in the two rocks. It was a spider—a camel spider!

There were horrible stories all over the Internet of bloodthirsty camel spiders attacking American soldiers in the Iraqi desert. The stories said that these spiders were huge and fast. Although terrified, Lucero's first reaction was not to panic, so he froze and did not make a move.

The spider was the size of a softball. Bronze in color, it had two distinguishing camel-like bumps on its back. Camel spiders were carnivores, predators that preyed on their victims by turning them into pulp using a chopping or sawing motion with their jaws and digestive fluids to liquefy the victim's flesh.

Lucero knew the Internet stories were bogus. Camel spiders only ate rodents, lizards, and small birds. Although humans were not one of their prey, the spiders had been known to bite humans with their powerful jaws, and although not deadly, the bite was extremely painful.

The spider crawled from his boot to his pant leg. A bite from this spider could evoke a response that would give him and his location away to the enemy, so Lucero knew he had to do something quickly. However, given the confined area restricting his movement, his options for a swift response were minimal.

Taking a deep breath, he suddenly swung his leg to the right, catapulting the spider against the wall. When the spider bounced off the wall, it hit the ground, and Lucero smashed it with the heel of his boot. He slowly lifted his boot enough to see the pesky insect's yellow guts splattered on the ground. It was dead and no longer a threat.

Lucero took a deep breath and sighed in relief. He thought, *What else?* In ten minutes, he had been almost captured by the enemy, buried alive, pissed on, nearly bitten by a camel spider, nearly pissed his pants, and twisted into a pretzel. His intuition was right; it was the longest ten minutes of his life.

Lying quietly, Lucero finally heard the commander of the enemy patrol order his men to their feet. The soldiers stood up, gathered their belongings, and began walking. In a few minutes, the soldiers' voices and footsteps faded off in the distance, and Lucero knew he was in the clear. He rolled over on his stomach, lifting his left leg up two inches to make sure he did not get any spider goo on his pants.

Lucero looked through the crack between the two rocks so he could have a better view of the soldiers as they walked away. He had to make a decision whether to ambush the enemy patrol from behind or continue back to the entrance of the cave to update regional command as Colby had ordered.

Given the number of enemy soldiers, Lucero realized it would be futile to try a sneak attack. An unsuccessful attack would most likely alert the enemy that US combat forces were in the cave. He concluded that it was no time for foolish heroics and that the best decision would be to continue his mission to contact Colonel Christopher at the regional command center.

He lay there waiting for another ten minutes, then squeezed his body through the small opening, trying desperately to avoid the urine and the spider remains. Once cleared, Lucero grabbed his rifle and backpack and rose to his feet. As he got up, he became lightheaded and dizzy. Being in the same tight position so long had restricted his blood flow, and the sudden movement to his feet caused him to stumble.

Lucero hurriedly pulled down his zipper as fast as he could and relieved himself. After he finished urinating on the cave wall, the lightheadedness eventually subsided. Lucero then quickly grabbed his backpack and rifle and again began walking toward the cave entrance.

Fifty yards ahead, the cavern got extremely dark again, so Lucero pulled out one of his military flashlights. As he got closer to the entrance of the cave, he tried to call regional command. Lucero knew he had to do something to notify both command and Recon One of the trouble ahead. Walking swiftly, Lucero called regional command repeatedly: "Command, this is Recon One; Command, come in. Recon One reporting; Command, this is Recon One, over …"

There was no response other than the disappointing sound of white noise. He proceeded hurriedly to the mouth of the cave. As Lucero got further along, he could see a beam of sunlight shining ahead at the mouth of the cave. Lucero whispered, "Now what? This is unbelievable!"

CHAPTER 14
The Black-Hole Decision

July 7, 2012: Mound of Tiamat

In spite of the danger posed by the treacherous trail, Lieutenant Colby decided to move forward about fifty yards till they got to the sharp bend in the trail. There was a high probability that something had happened to Lucero. Too much time had passed without word from Lucero or regional command, so Colby decided to continue the recon mission.

Moving forward, the path was narrow, unstable, and dangerous, and the earth was soft and crumbling in places. The cavern below was an endless dark pit with no bottom. It was extremely unsafe and too hazardous to continue. Nevertheless, they were Navy SEALs and had their orders.

Tex was in front and led the platoon as Colby and Mendez lined up behind him. As he approached the bend and peered to the other side, Tex could see the swirling, cone-shaped object that seemed like a black hole. The vortex spun rapidly out of control so fast it appeared to swallow up anything in its path, further compounding the treacherous, hell-like conditions.

Tex stopped and looked back again for direction from Lieutenant Colby. Unsure, Colby looked at Mendez to get his opinion of whether to go forward or not. Colby was always confident in his decisions, but given the extraordinary conditions, he wanted to get a second opinion. Mendez nodded to indicate yes, and Colby waved his hand to continue.

Just as Mendez took a step forward, the earth underneath him collapsed. In a second, his body plunged down toward the endless abyss. Mendez quickly reacted and grabbed onto a ledge just eighteen inches below the ridge. Swinging side to side, Mendez hung desperately from the ledge as he tried to secure himself to avoid falling.

As Mendez swayed back and forth, debris flew everywhere. Small pieces of rock and dirt struck his head, back, and shoulders. It was something just short of a miracle that Mendez did not fall straight down into the abyss.

From a kneeling position, Lieutenant Colby swiftly reached down for Mendez, who was hanging on for dear life. Tex Carter and Buford Bradley also reacted quickly. On one side, Tex grabbed on to one of Lieutenant Colby's legs, while Buford grabbed the lieutenant's shoulder. Both men tried everything to keep Colby from falling.

In a split second, Lieutenant Colby plunged downward and grabbed one of Mendez's wrists. As Mendez swung from one hand, Lieutenant Colby started to pull Mendez up, and Tex quickly reached down and grabbed Mendez's other wrist. The two men pulled Mendez up to the ledge. The excessive force caused Tex to loss his helmet, and it fell into the spinning black hole.

Mendez knelt on the ridge with Tex and Colby grasping his shoulders to secure him. All three men were breathing heavily and gasping for air.

Colby stood up carefully from his kneeling position and said, "Man, this is nuts!" Colby asked Mendez if he was okay, and Mendez nodded. He patted Mendez on the back to signify his relief that his good friend was okay. Mendez reached for and latched onto Colby's arm. He looked him in the eye, wordlessly saying thanks for saving his life.

Mendez stood up with Buford Bradley's help, and both men were now on their feet ready to proceed in either direction. After all the commotion, the black hole suddenly stopped spinning and disappeared without a trace. Colby was puzzled how it could turn itself on and off in seconds.

Given what had just happened, Colby had to make a quick decision about whether to move ahead or not. He was fearful for what was on the other side of the sharp bend. His gut told him that the conditions were probably more of the same or possibly worse.

"Lieutenant, man, this place is treacherous," Mendez said. "Did you see how that swirling tunnel almost sucked me in?"

"What the hell was that?" Tex asked.

Colby replied, "It resembled a black hole—you know, the ones scholars say serve as a gateway to others parts of the universe, like a wormhole. But it just disappeared, like someone just turned it off."

"I bet it comes back if we try to move forward," said Tex.

"Yeah, I agree," replied Colby. He turned to Mendez. "Shit, Chief, we don't know what's on the other side, and the ground is so soft and brittle. The situation is a real quandary."

Mendez said, "Yeah, Lieutenant, between that and the black hole, who knows what's next?"

Colby raced through all the possible scenarios. "Do we go forward? Is the path around the bend even more treacherous? Is it secure enough to walk on? What's on the other side?"

"It's your call, Lieutenant. Go with your gut," advised Mendez.

Colby assessed all the possibilities and the ramifications of each option. He was weary that he had not heard from Lucero, and that too weighed into his decision. Then he remembered command's last order, which was to continue the reconnaissance of the cavern. With his decision made, he signaled to Tex and then to his men to move forward.

Even though the men did not like the decision, they trusted Colby. They were Navy SEALs and were familiar with this type of danger. They too were getting impatient and were fearful something had happened to Lucero. But they were all in.

Tex turned off the safety on his rifle and moved forward very slowly. Pushing his back firmly against the wall, Tex carefully walked sideways, inch by inch, until he reached the sharp turn at the bend in the trail. Thinking the worst, Tex froze for a few seconds and looked back at Lieutenant Colby, who nodded to continue.

Tex carefully took two shuffle steps and moved his head slowly around the bend. He peered out of the corner of his left eye to focus on what was around the other side. He saw a large landing only 150 feet in front of him that was safe and perfect for setting up camp. Tex turned to Lieutenant Colby, and with that classic smile he lifted his right hand and gave the okay sign. They were clear and good to go.

Colby and the rest of the troops were relieved and curious about what was on the other side. As Tex turned and looked down, he noticed the golden substance under his feet and on his boots. The material provided some light and got brighter and more luminous as the platoon traveled farther into the cave, just like yesterday.

"Why is this gold substance is some places and not in others, Lieutenant?" asked Tex.

"Good question!" Colby said. "I'm not sure, but this substance had a texture similar to baby powder."

The Navy SEALs still had one hundred feet of treacherous terrain to navigate to reach more steady ground. Lieutenant Colby and the rest of the platoon were about twenty-one feet behind Tex. The men moved cautiously, repeating every move Tex and Colby made until they reached safer ground.

To secure himself, Tex dragged his hand across the wall of the cavern that was smooth as marble. Curious, Tex turned to face the wall and saw objects and pictures that continued along the wall as far as he could see. Tex looked back at Lieutenant Colby and pointed to the writing on the cavern wall. He carefully went another ten feet, and the path got wider and safer with each step.

Tex yelled over to Lieutenant Colby, "Sir, did you see the symbols and pictures on the wall?"

Colby acknowledged and said, "They were pictographs." Colby pointed to the wall and yelled to Mendez, "Do you see the tablets?"

Mendez responded, "Yes, sir, and did you see the gold dust? It's all over our shoes and pants again, just like the other day."

"Yes, it's the weirdest thing I've ever seen," said Colby.

"Lieutenant, can you interpret the writing on the wall?" asked Mendez.

Colby said, "Yes, enough to be dangerous."

Tex asked, "Did you guys notice that the gold particles always precede the stone tablets?"

"It seems that way," said Mendez.

Colby said, "It could be just a coincidence."

As the last man reached the other side to safer ground, Tex and Mendez were already inspecting the area for the best campsite. Lieutenant Colby looked at the pictographs as he walked to the end of the landing. Colby signaled to the men that they would camp here tonight. Everyone was relieved and welcomed the rest.

When the men settled in, they refreshed themselves with food, water, and energy drinks. Slick Sullivan asked if anyone had any spare energy drink. Blake Marshall reached into his backpack and pulled out an extra one and tossed it over to Slick, who nonchalantly saluted Blake in appreciation of his kindness.

Once all the men were settled in, Lieutenant Colby tried to contact command and Colonel Christopher. Again, there was static and white noise. Lieutenant Colby looked at Mendez and just shook his head. Mendez gave Colby a look to assure him that it would get better. Lieutenant Colby stood up to brief his men.

"Listen up! I like to commend you all for how you have handled all this today. I guess you already know that we have been unsuccessful in communicating with regional command. We will stay here tonight and see what tomorrow brings. There will be three three-hour watch duties.

First watch is Marshall; second watch is Buford; third watch is Pantano. Relax, refresh yourselves, and get some chow and some shut-eye. Lights out in three hours."

Joey "Fish" Calamari started to light the gas stove used for cooking.

Pantano looked over at Fish and jokingly said, "Hey, moron, don't blow up the place."

Fish just laughed and said, "You're no Einstein either, asshole. You know, Pantano, I'm tired of your dumbass negativity. You can say whatever about me, but at end of the day, I am the man."

McDermott chimed in, "There he goes again, telling everyone he's the man. Christ, you both have a severe case of cellular debris."

Fish asked, "What the hell is that?"

McDermott said, "When normal people sleep at night, our brain flushes all the bad cells from our body. Unfortunately, you two are not normal, and the only thing that flushes is the toilet that gets rid of the shit in your brains."

"You know, McDermott, that's real intelligent. Is that the best you got?" replied Fish.

Mike McDermott turned away and started to set up some lighting, and the other men settled in for the night. Lieutenant Colby ordered McDermott to assemble only half the lights and to set them on dim. McDermott always went a little overboard because he needed enough light to read his fantasy baseball magazines and his books. However, Colby was concerned that too much light may draw attention.

When they finished their chow, the men began to relax. Casper Pantano and Buford Bradley engaged in a knife game. Both men stood about ten feet from the wall and took turns throwing their army knives. Whoever got the closest to the wall without touching it won. It was best of nine.

Several of the men played cards. Trash Thompson and Tex Carter sat around the campfire and read. They both were reading *Fifty Shades of Grey*. Everyone in the platoon busted on both men for reading an erotic chick novel.

"Why in the hell are you two reading that book?" Mike McDermott asked. "It's for old horny chicks. Are you two gay for each other? Man, that is weird!"

"Up yours, McDermott!" said Tex. "If you had any class or sophistication, you'd know that this novel has sold over seventy million copies, and it wasn't just chicks buying it. Trust me; millions of men are reading this book to find out what makes females tick and what makes them hot. The book is the number one best seller of all time. Shit, it even surpassed Harry Potter."

Fish chimed in, "Tex, you need all the education you can get. You couldn't get a one-legged prostitute to have sex with your sorry ass, even if you paid her five thousand bucks."

Tex responded sarcastically, "That's real bright, Fish, real clever, shit brain!"

Laughing, Trash said, "Gentlemen, calm down. All this fuss over this book is a lot of bullshit for nothing. The book is just plain hot, and I mean *hot*. Christian Grey just does a job on Ana Steele. I mean, wee doggy! Man, she is just sizzling. I feel the steam! Lord, I feel the steam!"

Lieutenant Colby was distracted by the ruckus and looked over at the men. "Gentlemen, calm the hell down. It's only a book. Maybe if some of you jarheads read anything except comic books, you might be dangerous."

Away from his men, Lieutenant Colby sat next to the Sumerian cuneiform tablets and examined the pictographs. He was busy taking notes, documenting the artifacts and the day's activities in his journal. While looking at the pictographs and the gold powder, Lieutenant Colby thought that this was a unique find, something truly amazing.

This time there was more gold material than before. Lieutenant Colby scooped up the shiny material and rubbed his thumb and index figure back and forth over the powder. The substance was silky smooth and glowed, giving it a very rich appearance. It was truly remarkable. Unfortunately, he could not communicate with the outside world to tell anyone about their unique discovery.

CHAPTER 15
Interpretation of Faith

July 7, 2012: Mound of Tiamat

Just as Lieutenant Colby stood up, Mendez walked over to join him. At night, both men often swapped life stories or talked about the daily activities and plans for the next day.

"Did you eat something, Lieutenant?" asked Mendez.

"No, I just finished up my report. I was just about to grab some peanut butter crackers and a drink from my backpack."

As Colby went past Mendez, Chief firmly grabbed Colby's arm and said, "Sir, I just want to thank you for saving my life today."

"I appreciate it, Chief, but that's not necessary. That's what we do, watch each other's backs."

"I know that, Lieutenant, but I want you to know that I am grateful."

"Chief, you don't need to say any more on the subject; you would have done the same for me."

Both men respected each other, and without thinking, they would put their lives on the line for each other. It was an unspoken bond among the members of the platoon.

Colby and Mendez rolled out their sleeping bags and sat down. Colby pulled out his journal, and Mendez started cleaning his rifle. After discussing the plan for the next day, their conversation switched quickly to the tablets, the gold substance, and the Sumerians.

Mendez was fascinated with the ancient Sumerian tablets. The gold substance and the cuneiform writing was everywhere, which further increased his excitement and anticipation of their meaning. He was hopeful that Colby could interpret the writing and obtain a clue of its meaning and why they were in the cave.

Mendez asked Colby, "What do the tablets mean?"

"Chief, that is a lot to chew over. I'm not a scholar in this area, but I can tell this new set of tablets seems more sophisticated than those we saw yesterday. According to many of the books I've read, there are many contrasting interpretations of Sumerian cuneiform writings," said Colby.

"You keep mentioning different interpretations," said Mendez.

Colby said, "There is still disagreement over what the tablets mean. Many say the writing on the Sumerian tablets is myths, made-up stories and legends and not fact. Some say they represent major celestial events; other think they document human creation, culture, and history. There are many known scholars who believe that the tablets say we are descendants of an extraterrestrial alien race that visited this planet and gave us tremendous knowledge before they disappeared. Others say that such claims are embellished and misinterpreted."

Mendez asked, "Who interpreted these tablets and came up with those observations and conclusions?"

"In the past, there were only a handful of real experts who could translate the Sumerian tablets. More recently, the numbers have grown. In fact, the University of Pennsylvania is working on a Sumerian dictionary with collaboration with other scholars in the field."

"How many scholars believe that we are descendants of extraterrestrials?" asked Mendez.

"There are many now who believe that the Sumerian tablets and artifacts provide evidence that extraterrestrials created us to be slaves to perform hard labor they didn't want to do."

"This sounds absurd! Are these theories widely accepted in the mainstream scientific community?"

"Not really," said Colby. "Some of the scholars who believe in these interpretations are called ancient-astronaut theorists, and some mainstream scholars consider them radicals."

Mendez responded sarcastically, "Come on, ancient-astronaut theorists! What is that?"

"Many people believe in the ancient-astronaut theory. Scholars such as Erich von Däniken, Zecharia Sitchin, and Robert Taylor pioneered the theory. These scholars claim that early man could not have progressed as quickly as he did without the assistance of extraterrestrial being. They now have many disciples who continue to search for evidence to prove that humanity was shaped by astronauts from the heavens.

"Erich von Däniken's *Chariot of the Gods* was the first popular book on the subject of ancient astronauts. His book sold millions of copies, and it has been translated in several languages. Von Däniken believes that there is evidence of ancient astronauts in scriptures, paintings, statues, structures, and other artifacts and writing all over the world. Given the number of books sold, the theory received much interest and even acceptance by a significant portion of the public.

"Erich von Däniken supposes that extraterrestrial aliens from other planets had a major impact on human history. He professes that ancient astronauts came to earth thousands of years ago and gave humans knowledge of science, technology, and social structure that is still with us today. He points to many wonders of the world—such as the pyramids in Egypt, Mexico, and South America and monoliths and other stone objects in England, Easter Island, Sri Lanka, China, and Costa Rica—as evidence of ancient astronauts. Erich von Däniken theorizes that early man did not have the knowledge or tools to accomplish these major feats of construction without help from a more advanced intelligent being."

Mendez said, "I heard of Erich von Däniken's books. An officer I knew read all his books and believes in his theories. Who's Sitchin?"

"Zecharia Sitchin was truly a pioneer of the ancient-astronaut theory. He was different than Erich von Däniken because his focus was solely on the Sumerians. Sitchin's books are based upon thirty years of linguistic and archaeological research of the Sumerian culture in and around Sumer. He documented his findings in several books, including the popular *The 12th Planet*, from the Earth Chronicles. In these books, he claims an extraterrestrial alien race called the Anunnaki created man through genetic engineering. He too suggests that these ancient astronauts influenced man's early development by providing them with knowledge of agriculture, education, astronomy, construction, mathematics, medicine, and more.

"Robert Temple also had similar theories. He believes that an alien race from the star system Sirius created the Sumerian, Egyptian, and Dogon civilizations and is now ready to return. In his book *The Sirius Mystery*, Robert Temple says that five thousand years ago, the people of Dogon, Africa, had incredible knowledge of astronomy. The Dogon knew of the rings of Saturn and the existence of four moons around Jupiter as well as companion stars around Sirius. He theorizes these discoveries could not have happened without a telescope.

"Temple also indicates that the Dogon knew of an invisible companion star that circles Sirius every fifty years. More recently astronomers have confirmed that such an object does exist and is called Sirius B. The Dogon had such accurate, detailed knowledge of Sirius, like that the companion star was small and extremely heavy, that could only be detected with sophisticated technology that the Dogon could not have obtained without help."

Colby added, "Temple based this information on the work of two French anthropologists. Part of the evidence included a representation of the Sirius system drawn by a blind Dogon, who had knowledge of folklore that was imparted only to the tribal elders. According to the Dogon priests, this astronomical knowledge had been imparted by the Nommo, a fish-like water species, who landed on earth thousands years ago.

"The question remains: How could a five-thousand-year-old civilization in Africa with no known telescope obtain such detailed knowledge of the universe. Temple claims that primitive humanoids could not have possessed this knowledge without help from intelligent extraterrestrial beings such as ancient astronauts."

"The officer I mentioned earlier told me that Temple based his findings upon incorrect information," Mendez said.

"It depends on who you talk to about it."

Mendez looked up at the lieutenant and said, "Dan, I learned that several mainstream scholars look upon the claims as a joke. According to them, the evidence is based upon bad archaeology and anthropology and twisted interpretations. Temple bases his findings on folklore passed down through generations, a drawing by a blind man, and two scholars' findings that have been severely criticized. Come on, Lieutenant; I might have grown up in the slums of East LA and didn't finish traditional high school, but you expect me to believe this crap?"

"No, I don't," replied Colby.

Mendez said, "I tend to agree with the critics. The little evidence you present is weak, based upon too many assumptions and individual interpretations. Theories like ancient astronauts sound great and are fun, but let's get serious. Where is the evidence? Where are the bodies buried?"

"Don't get me wrong, Chief; there are many critics of the ancient-astronaut theory. Erich von Däniken has been the focus of criticism for years. Scholars, journalists, and even governments have tried to discredit both his work and his character.

"For example, in their book *Intelligent Life in the Universe*, astrophysicists Carl Sagan and I. S. Shklovsky say that scholars should be open-minded about the possibility of extraterrestrial aliens visiting earth throughout its history. However, in this same book, and in Sagan's later book *Broca's Brain*, both authors seriously question von Däniken and conclusions other ancient-astronaut theorists have drawn. Sagan and Shklovsky state that von Däniken's theories lack scientific evidence and traditional scientific methods to support his findings."

"Why do you think they are viewed with criticism?" asked Mendez.

"Well, in defense of the ancient-astronaut theory, it is only about forty-five years old. There is always a period of speculation with any new theory. Look throughout history, some great scholars were severely criticized and even jailed and persecuted, and then honored as great scholars hundreds of years later.

Mendez asked, "Like who?"

Colby responded, "For example, Galileo Galilei was convicted in 1633 for publishing his evidence in support of Copernican theory that the Earth revolves around the Sun. Galileo was tried and sentenced to house arrest for nine years for heresy by the Holy Office in the Vatican. Giordano Bruno, an Italian Dominican friar, philosopher, mathematician, poet, and astrologein, went beyond Copernican theories by proposing that the stars were just distant suns surrounded by planets that could even foster life of their own. Bruno also professed that the Universe is infinite, thus having no celestial body at its "center". Pope Clement VIII sentenced Bruno to death, and burned alive as an impenitent and pertinacious heretic.

All throughout human history, the Vatican has silenced anything that is not centric to the Catholic Church. Galileo said the earth is not the center of the earth and Bruno proposed the existence of extraterrestrial life. This is contradictory to the Vatican's belief that the Church is the center of everything. It took over one hundred years to recognize Bruno's and Galileo's as two of the greatest scholars of modern science. Religions and mainstream scholars want to hang on to the traditional principles of science. New ideas, concepts, and discoveries were seldom immediately accepted."

Colby stopped for a minute and said, "I think I am digressing from the topic."

Mendez responded, "No, it all relevant."

"Yes, I guess it is pertinent. Chief, did you know they gaged Bruno before they burned him alive?"

"No, please continue Lieutenant."

"Let's go back to the Sumerians. First of all, the majority of the Sumerian tablets were discovered a little less than three hundred years ago. Since there is no language to serve as a base for understanding these writings, Zecharia Sitchin spent thirty years studying and interpreting the Sumerian writings and putting together a language based upon the artifacts left behind. Scholars have used ancient pictographs, drawings, paintings, statues, and other artifacts to form a base for translating the Sumerian tablets."

"So why is there little agreement between mainstream scholars and ancient-astronaut theorists?" Mendez asked.

Colby replied, "Many mainstream scholars think a lot of the ancient-astronaut interpretations of monoliths, artifacts, and writings are incorrect, full of assumptions, and lacking real scientific proof. They also believe some of their conclusions are fabricated to prove their points. The real problem is with who interprets the writings and how. Words have different meanings to different people, and thus they are interpreted differently. Also, many of these stories, poems, and myths have been passed down from generation to generation. Thus, the meaning is sometimes lost in the interpretation and even embellished or twisted to make a point or support a conclusion."

Mendez asked, "So there is no consensus on the interpretation of the Sumerian written language and the ancient-astronaut theories?"

Colby said, "No, there are several different interpretations of Sumerian writing. Additionally, numerous mainstreams scholars discredit these ancient-astronaut theories because their conclusions contain too many assumptions, possible misrepresentations, and speculations in their findings. Mainstream scholars criticize these theorists for trying to make the material fit their conclusions."

"Lieutenant, in my opinion, the problem with the ancient-astronaut theory is there is no substantial evidence to support their claims," Mendez said.

Colby replied, "I would not be so quick to disregard these theories.

Do we have any real evidence that the story of Adam and Eve is about an apple and original sin. Ancient astronauts interpret the tree of knowledge to be a metaphor for the human DNA sequence. They also say Adam and Eve ate the forbidden fruit in order to be godlike and that this represents the first step in human evolution."

Mendez responded, "So ancient-astronaut theorists believe the traditional interpretation of the Adam and Eve story and the apple is wrong?"

"Again it is a matter of interpretation," Colby said. "Religion asks us to accept scriptures that lack scientific evidence. Let me give you a concrete example. Religions require us to have faith when events are questionable, seemingly impossible, and difficult to believe. You know, like the parting of the Red Sea, the virgin birth, the fish that magically fed thousands of starving people, miraculous healings, and resurrections."

Mendez laughingly asked, "Could these acts have been performed by extraterrestrials?"

"Come on, Chief; don't be a smartass," replied Colby.

"I'm not joking," said Mendez. "But we are digressing from the topic."

Lieutenant Colby countered, "No, not really; I see significant similarities in how the church and our traditional scholars expect us to accept what they believe to be true. Mainstream scholars criticize ancient-astronaut theorists because many of their conclusions are based upon inadequate evidence and assumption. Where is the evidence to support some of the mainstream scholars' theories or religious claims?"

Mendez asked, "What do you mean?"

Lieutenant Colby replied, "Darwin's theory of evolution, atheism, Christianity, creationism, and intelligent design have very diverse beliefs about creation with little evidence to support them. Some people believe in them; some don't. How is the ancient-astronaut theory any different and less credible than these?"

Mendez responded, "Because these concepts have stood the test of time. More people believe in a God on this planet than not. The ancient-astronaut theory is a relatively new concept and does not have a long-standing track record."

"That's true, Chief, but who is God?"

"What do you mean?"

"Religious scriptures describe God as an all-knowing, powerful being who came from the heavens. God created man, some religions say, in his own image. Could these same scriptures be talking about ancient astronauts?" asked Colby.

"Where's the evidence?"

Colby said, "We aren't close to uncovering all the evidence to support any of these theories. There is so much more to learn. I compare 2012 to the time when man thought the earth was flat and the center of the universe. I believe everything is on the table for debate and discussion. The church, the scientific community, archaeologists, and philosophers ask us to have faith in what they believe to be true, when the evidence in some of these theories is faulty and unproven."

"Lieutenant, I enjoyed this conversation, but I think that is enough learning for me tonight. I better get some shut-eye," said Mendez.

"Yeah, me too; I'm just going to check with the watch duty, and then I'm going to get some rest too," said Colby.

As Lieutenant Colby walked over to check with the duty guard, he thought about he'd also enjoyed the discussion. Being in the military did not offer many opportunities to have a stimulating, thought-provoking discussions.

Lieutenant Colby walked up to Buford, who had just relieved Marshall, and asked, "Buford, how is it going?"

"Good, Lieutenant! Everything's quiet."

"You're in charge; keep your head up. I'm going to get some rest. Wake me if you hear anything."

Buford knew he was in for a boring three hours, sitting there while everyone else was sleeping. However, given the situation of the past three days, he took his assignment seriously and knew he had to stay alert in case anything happened.

CHAPTER 16
The Final Obstacle

July 7, 2012: Mound of Tiamat

As Lucero moved closer to the light illuminating the entrance of the cave, he discovered it was a fire. When he reached a pillar thirty yards from the entrance of the cave, he heard the crackling sound of a campfire and knew that someone was there.

Lucero said to himself, "This shit just keeps getting better all the time."

He took his weapon off his shoulder, grabbed it firmly, and moved quickly to seek cover about five yards to the left side of the cave. As he peeked around the corner, he saw two soldiers sitting around a campfire about fifteen yards inside the cave entrance. One soldier was drinking from a pouch while the other was eating something. Just then, one of the soldiers got up and walked toward Lucero, who was lying down behind a rock prepared for battle. With each step the soldier took, Lucero's heart beat faster. The next fight played out in Lucero's mind. The enemy soldier stopped only a few feet in front of Lucero and just stood there.

Lucero's heart beat even faster than before, pounding against his chest. Lucero thought he was caught. Without warning, a loud noise startled everyone. Rocks and debris fell from the ceiling. Lucero curled into the fetal position and covered his head. The enemy soldier, now only a few feet away, fell to the ground. Hundreds of bats hanging among the stalactites were startled and began to swirl and nose-dive the men. The soldiers shielded their heads. The sound of flapping wings and loud screeching echoed throughout the cave as the flying rats blindly scrambled in all directions and eventually headed out of the cave. Startled, the soldier stood up, looked around, grabbed a small bedroll, and then headed back to the campfire.

Lucero breathed a sigh of relief. He knew from his close encounter that the soldier was wearing the colors of an al-Qaeda terrorist. Lucero brushed the bat dung off his shoulders and arms and grabbed his backpack from under a pile of debris. He opened it and pulled out one explosive.

Although the odds were against him, Lucero thought that he had only one move that could turn this around to his advantage. If he placed a small explosive in the right spot, the cave walls would collapse and hopefully bury the two al-Qaeda soldiers. The walls were weakened and very unstable from the bombing of the F-15s, so it would not take much to get the desired effect. He realized that an explosion could seal the cave and trap everyone inside, including the Navy SEALs. However, the odds were favorable that the blast would be contained to a small area.

Given his position, Lucero had no clear shot at the enemy. Besides, he was concerned that his rifle had been damaged by the fallen rocks. There was no way to test it, and he was running out of time. He needed to contact command quickly and warn them that Recon One was in danger. So using an explosive was his only logical option.

The enemy soldiers were shielded behind a large rock formation, and Lucero could just barely see them through a hole in the large pillar. Hours later, before dawn, both enemy soldiers were finally asleep. It was time for Lucero to take his last shot. Trying desperately to avoid detection, he crawled slowly and carefully on his stomach toward the enemy.

Only yards from the al-Qaeda, Lucero deployed the explosive carefully on the left cavern wall. While placing the bomb, his foot got jammed between two rocks. Out in the open and without cover, he tried to get his foot ajar. He frantically twisted his leg in several directions. He pulled up and pushed down, but his foot remained wedged between two rocks. He tried everything, but it was too late. The enemy soldiers had awakened and spotted Lucero and were reaching for their rifles.

Lucero made one more desperate attempt to escape. He bent down and tried to pull the two rocks apart as he pulled up on his leg. Miraculously, his foot came loose. One of the enemy soldiers came out from behind the pillar and aimed his rifle. Lucero scrambled quickly and then dove for cover, leaping through the air among the barrage of bullets that ricocheted off the walls.

He reached for his pistol and fired a series of bullets that struck one of the al-Qaeda terrorists in the abdomen, leg, and arm. The soldier was brutally injured and fell to the ground. The second soldier crawled and hid behind his comrade for cover.

Lucero crawled to get back to his backpack to detonate the bomb. The second soldier got off several rounds, two of which hit Lucero in the stomach and lower body, tearing his leg to shreds. Wounded, Lucero moved frantically toward the detonator. Another bullet hit him, this time a flesh wound to the arm. Lucero leaped forward, grabbed the wireless detonator, and pressed the button. The bomb went off.

The explosive caused the left side of the cavern wall to crumble, and rocks and dirt fell in all directions. Minutes later, Lucero's arm popped up out of the debris, and he mustered his last bit of energy to look up at his enemy. Both al-Qaeda soldiers were buried alive. Lucero's face smacked hard against the ground, and he lay there completely still. Although the battle was won, his brothers were still in the cave, not knowing the enemy was just a heartbeat away.

Two hours later, Lucero woke and moved his hand slowly through the debris, feeling around for his radio. Although the pain from his wounds was excruciating, he dug his hand deeper into the debris in search for his communicator. The radio was his only lifeline to the outside world and only chance to save his fellow Navy SEALs.

When he pushed through the rubble, Lucero finally found the radio and pulled it close to him. He grabbed the headset and struggled to put it on. He was bleeding badly. Any movement was extremely painful, but he was able to call regional command.

Lucero yelled out, "Bravo Company, come in. Recon One, over ..."

"This is Bravo Company. Come in, Recon One, over."

"Roger that. This is Petty Officer Joel Lucero."

Command responded, "Recon One, the transmission is garbled. You must be close to some interference; please change position."

Recon One had top priority status, and the communication division had orders to advise the colonel if Colby's platoon called, no matter what. The radio operator immediately contacted the colonel.

Minutes later, Colonel Christopher flipped opened the canvas that served as a back entrance to the tent. He looked at the tech sergeant who was now manning the radio and asked, "Who is on the line?"

"Sir, Petty Officer Joel Lucero."

"Did he say anything about the situation yet?"

"Sir, the communication is garbled, but we did hear him say that there is something big happening down there. He was seriously wounded in a firefight with al-Qaeda and is bleeding profusely. There is some serious interference with the transmission, so we asked Lucero to move farther away from the entrance of the cave. But, sir, with his wounds, I'm not sure he can do that."

"This is just great. We need to do something."

———————

Lucero started to crawl to the cave entrance. He dragged his body along the dirt path, inches at a time as he tried to block out the pain. Distressed, he knew he needed to get outside the cave fast.

Lucero somehow picked himself up, flung his radio on his shoulder, and walked. Wobbling and weaving, just trying to keep his balance, Lucero managed to get to the wall for support. His left hand grasping the cave wall, he pressed his other hand firmly against his stomach to stop the bleeding. Finally, he reached the cave entrance and tried frantically to get some distance from the Mound of Tiamat. He fell on his knees and then fell flat on his face. As he lay there unconscious, it appeared he was not breathing.

CHAPTER 17
The FBI Report: "Are We Alone in the Universe?"

July 7, 2012: Headquarters, Central Intelligence Agency, Langley, Virginia

It was three in the afternoon. Patricia Deichert was sitting at her desk thinking about the upcoming evening events. Jack Gordy, an official from the State Department assigned to the Russian embassy, had asked Patricia to go with him to the US president's reception for the Russian president at the White House.

Patricia was daydreaming about the reception until a phone call on the hotline interrupted her. The hotline was one of the two secured phone lines she covered for the director. All hotline calls were top priority, and the CIA director was to take these calls no matter what time.

"Director's office, Patricia Deichert. How can I help you?"

"This is John McNabb, chief of staff. Is the director in?"

"Yes, sir. I'll put you through immediately. Please hold."

John McNabb had been appointed the president's chief of staff just three months ago. John was the third chief of staff appointed in this administration. The trend of the past three administrations was that the chief of staff usually stayed no more than three years.

Although one of the brightest minds in Washington, John was considered the third string chief of staff. He'd gone to Harvard and was a friend and classmate of the previous chief of staff, who had appointed him to be his deputy. The president had promoted John McNabb to become the next chief of staff when the previous chief of staff had resigned to take a position in the lobbyist department at Deichert, Lewes, Gaudy, and Barlow PLLC.

John was more of a manager than a politician, and thus those on the hill viewed him as a liability for the president. He lacked the savvy to work with Congress to implement the administration's agenda, but so did the two others before him. The inability to work with Congress to get things done would most likely become the legacy of this administration.

What happened to those good old days when America's leaders solved problems informally? Presidents like Johnson, Reagan, and Lincoln would meet with the Speaker of the House or others over a late-night bourbon or Scotch to resolve their differences and get the country moving in the right direction. As unorthodox as it seemed, that was how things got done. That was leadership, and those great men had done what they'd needed to do. They had not been afraid to compromise and barter to improve the country.

"John, how are you doing?" asked the director.

"Fine, Nate, just need to pass along some information from the president," said the chief of staff.

"Okay, what's that?"

"The DNI has sent a platoon of Navy SEALs into Sumer, Iraq. Long story short, we bombed the area and killed thirty or so al-Qaedas just outside Basra. We are calling this Operation Sumer, and the Navy SEALs are conducting a recon of the area as we speak. I just spoke to General Hitchens, and I told him to brief you on the situation. Just a heads-up:

there are some strange things going on. The mission is a highly sensitive matter for the White House and our number one priority. Keep me informed so I can brief the president. One more thing, the president has asked that you reconvene MJ-12."

As he hung up the phone, the CIA director wanted to ask the chief of staff why they had waited so long to tell him about Operation Sumer, but he didn't. The director did not want to jump to conclusions without more information. So he decided to be patient, even though he was curious and concerned. The director also found it unusual for a routine recon mission to require a call on the hotline. As Nate Stiles sat there contemplating the politics of it all, Patty anxiously waited to remind the director about his lunch appointment with the FBI director.

"Sir, your lunch is at the Sheraton at one o'clock, the one near Embassy Row," Patricia said. "I briefed the driver on the location and time. He is at the rear of the building waiting for you."

Embassy Row was an extravagant section of Washington, DC, where most of the foreign embassies resided. The buildings were very well maintained, and the area architecture was extremely attractive. The director loved to ride through this area, and he often asked the driver to go past Embassy Row when it was practical.

As he stared out the window, he thought about the president's request to reconvene MJ-12. There were only a few reasons to reconvene the committee, so it must be something big. As he thought through the scenarios, Roswell, New Mexico, first came to mind and then the Kennedy assassination.

The driver pulled into the back entrance of the Sheraton and opened the car door for the director. He escorted the director to the restaurant where FBI Director Bart Smith was sitting at a table near the far wall.

"I hope I didn't keep you waiting," Nate said.

"No, I just got here myself."

"So how is everything on the domestic side of things?"

"Okay, but there is one thing I need to discuss with you and get your advice on."

"Sure, I'm always ready to give advice to the FBI. What do you need?"

"Well, I have a situation. John McNabb told me to contact you to see if you and your people could help."

"Okay."

Bart continued, "There's an archaeologist, Natalie Marie Duval, who is a concern to the White House and the NSC. We were asked to investigate her and her activities. We found out that she is the daughter of computer tycoon Lawrence Duval. She is an instructor and graduate assistant at Stanford University. The White House told us to get with you on this because it is now within the jurisdiction of the State Department and the CIA."

"I thought this was a domestic investigation. Why is she my concern?" Nate asked.

"I'll get to that in a minute, but let me give you the background first. Although a little outspoken, especially about traditional science, we found that Natalie is an excellent law-abiding citizen. The family has great wealth, and they are extremely charitable. The Duvals did support the other guys in the past election, and they seem to be doing the same this time."

"Is that why the White House is interested in her?"

"I thought that at first, but now I'm sure it's something else."

"So no political reasons?" Nate replied.

"I'm sure of that," Bart said. "After reporting the findings of the investigation to the White House, the DNI told us to dig deeper. We've discovered that she is out of the country doing archaeological research, but we don't know where. Although unconfirmed, the report said something of an archaeological expedition somewhere in the Near East."

"I doubt that this is coincidental, but Jim Brown attended an NSC briefing the other day, and they informed him that there is an expedition in Basra, Iraq, funded by Premier Oil and headed by Professor Ashe, a professor at Stanford."

Bart said, "You know, Natalie does work as a graduate assistant to Professor Ashe."

"I bet you a grand that Natalie is on that expedition."

"So what now? Any ideas?" asked Bart.

"Why are they so interested in Natalie Duval?" Nate asked.

Bart replied, "If she's in Basra, I think their interest in Duval is somehow related to Professor Ashe's expedition. Also, our investigation discovered that Natalie is a little radical in her thinking about anthropology and archaeology. As a certified instructor at Stanford, she has taught Ancient-Astronaut Theories, the Gaps in Darwinism, and the Truth about the Origin of Humanity. Her lectures focus on the flaws in many of the mainstream theories on these subjects, both scientific and religious. Additionally, her graduate thesis emphasized that there are many other theories on the origin of humanity that are just as plausible as the more accepted traditional theories. She mentioned the ancient-astronaut theories, intelligent design, and many other less traditional theories."

Nate said, "That wacky theory again!"

Bart asked, "Did you see the FBI special investigative division's report on the growing interest in the ancient-astronaut theory? The report profiled the type of individuals interested in the theory in the United States. A shocking seventy-five percent of the American public believes there is something to these theories. In fact, seventy-seven percent believe that extraterrestrials have visited earth throughout human history."

"The American people are gullible," said Nate.

"I wanted to sack the report. However, it involved so many people I just couldn't let it go. Just the sheer number of people surveyed and interviewed alone would have caused such a stink if I canned the report. Additionally, the hassles with the Freedom of Information Act would have drawn so much attention that my people told me that it could mushroom into something else," Bart said. "The final and most important factor influencing my decision to release the report was the president. He put funding in the budget for the study and requested a copy of the study when completed. So I decided just to release it, making sure it received the least amount of attention from the media and the public."

Nate said, "I can see why the public believes extraterrestrials have visited earth. We spend billions of dollars on Kepler, Hubble, and SETI looking for life. The Kepler Space Telescope searches for habitable zones and earth-size Goldilocks planets that can support life. We spend a significant amount of money on these projects, so it's no wonder so many people feel this way."

"The FBI report has an interesting section entitled 'Are We Alone in the Universe?' Our scientists believe there are billions of stars in the Milky Way alone. The report goes on to say that there are an estimated one hundred billion galaxies in the universe, each one with billions of stars. The report concludes that there is a high probability that at least three planets rotate around each star. If true, there could be well over a trillion, possibly sextillion, planets in the cosmos, and that is a low estimate."

Nate said, "My staff did send me a report from the Kepler project indicating the space telescope has identified twelve hundred planets that could support life."

"True, but some scholars believe the universe is so large it's impossible to travel to these planets even if life did exist on them," said Bart.

"That is all good information, but what does that have to do with Duval? Why is she a threat to national security?" Nate asked.

"She is not a threat according to US or international law," said Bart.

"So what's the point?"

"That is a good question."

"I'll speak to Deputy Director Brown, and we'll look into this matter and pass on what we find out directly to you. We already have some feelers out to our people about the expedition. We will also ask them to find out anything they can on Duval, and I'll get back to you. However, this all must be kept between you and me for now."

"Understood; thanks, Nate!"

"One last thing, the president wants us to reconvene MJ-12."

"I thought MJ-12 was classified and decommissioned," replied Bart.

"Yeah, so did I."

They finished their salads, paid the check, and left in different directions. As the CIA director drove back to his office, he became concerned. He was beginning to sense that Operation Sumer had all the intelligence agencies going in different directions, like a pewee bird, going around and around. After 9/11, a new policy had been implemented to share information among the sixteen intelligence agencies. Some of the activities of the past three days seemed to counter that policy.

Nate Stiles returned directly to his office. He grabbed the phone messages from Patty's desk and reviewed them. One of the messages was from Jim Brown.

"Patty, please see if Deputy Brown has a few minutes to meet with me," Stiles said.

As Patty buzzed Deputy Brown, the CIA director went over the events of the past three days. None of the information fit together. Why was the DNI and the NSC so interested in Sumer? Was it really the return of al-Qaeda to southern Iraq, or was it something else, possibly bigger? He felt that maybe Jim had some information to help fill in the blanks.

Patty interrupted the director's thoughts and said, "Jim is here."

"Send him in."

"What's up?" asked Jim.

"I just had lunch with the FBI director, and you're not going to believe this, but the White House asked the FBI to investigate Natalie Duval."

"Who's Natalie Duval?" asked Jim.

"I'm sorry; I thought you knew who she was."

"No, sir, I don't have a clue."

"We think she is on an expedition in Sumer with Professor Ashe. She is his graduate assistant and teaches undergrad classes at Stanford."

"So what did she do to deserve all this attention?"

"The FBI director says Duval is clean, except she has some very different views on traditional anthropology and archaeology methods and conclusions. She teaches courses in both subjects that mainstream scholars consider extreme. They have labeled her a radical. The FBI believes that Natalie is only trying to get the students to think and question the more accepted methods, especially if those ideas are not supported by concrete evidence."

Jim asked, "So why is that illegal?"

"Bart and I thought the same thing."

"Shit, if that were a national security threat, we would be investigating half the professors in our universities and colleges. It doesn't add up. There must be something else."

"You might be right," said the director. "Operation Sumer and Professor Ashe's expedition have everyone's attentions in Washington, especially the top four intelligence agencies and the White House. No particular intelligence agency has all the information regarding the who, what, and where, except possibly the NSC and the White House. We are all being told that the information is classified as need to know.

"As a result, no one is sharing information or data. No intelligence organization has all the information on this operation. It's like we all are being spoon-fed bits and pieces of information. Someone is playing us all like a violin ... the CIA, FBI, State Department, and even Military Intelligence; we're all instruments in an orchestra that has no music sheet. I think the DNI's the conductor, with the president's approval."

"Why would they do that?" Jim asked.

"There's something big going on down there. The only thing I can surmise is that the White House does not want this information leaked or ending up in the wrong hands."

"I'll stay on top of it and brief you daily," said Jim.

"I need you to contact our agents in the field and see if they can find out anything on Ms. Duval and the expedition. I told the FBI director that we would see what we can find out."

CHAPTER 18
Worried Commander

July 8, 2012: Regional Command
Center, Outskirts of Baghdad, Iraq

Colonel Christopher grew anxious. Thirty minutes had gone by, and there had been no contact with Lucero. Weighing his options, Colonel Christopher thought he needed to brief Central Command.

It was late at Central Command, and everyone was sleeping, including General Hitchens. Lieutenant Colonel Brock was the duty officer and was working on important paperwork for General Hitchens required by the Pentagon and the White House. Two days ago, there had been an atrocious incident involving a drone attack and Afghan civilians. The drone had been deployed to strike a Taliban stronghold but had gone off course and struck a village fifty miles outside of Kabul, killing ten civilians—two children and eight adults.

General Hitchens had to complete several military forms to document civilian casualties. This type of accident was extremely sensitive because the United States had received severe criticism for using drones in combat. The president had taken serious heat from both friendly and nonfriendly nations for using such force. This accident would further strengthen the opposition, and the political fallout would be devastating to the president and the United States.

General Hitchens was upset by the incident since it had occurred during his watch. Although he knew this could adversely affect his career, he was more focused on the devastation to the village, the loss of life, and the families so dramatically touched. He could identify with the families, especially those who had lost children to such a tragic and inexcusable mistake.

Hitchens thought, *What if it was my grandchildren? How would I feel? How much more do these people need to suffer? Year after year, decade after decade, century after century, the Afghan people have experienced so much war, violence, death, human atrocities, and corruption, and for what purpose? None of this makes sense, and we're supposed to be here to help them? Bullshit!*

General Hitchens knew that the United States had invaded and occupied Afghanistan in response to the 9/11 attack and to prevent al-Qaeda from reestablishing a base that could be used to launch terrorist attacks against America. He also knew the official position of the United States was to extinguish any semblance of an alliance between the Taliban and the al-Qaeda in Afghanistan immediately. The reemergence of al-Qaeda must not become a viable threat to America and its allies. Given the Taliban and al-Qaeda's history, close relationship, and similarities in ethics and principles of life, the United States feared that al-Qaeda could use Afghanistan as a base for terrorist activities.

Lieutenant Colonel Brock completed the forms and placed them in the general's inbox. Then he picked up his personal journal and was recording the day's events when a loud voice from the radio filled the room.

"Central Command, this is Bravo Company; come in, please."

Brock took the headset and said, "This is Central Command. Come in. This is Lieutenant Colonel Brock."

"Brock, this is Chris. Well, let me give you the short story. Lieutenant

Colby sent Lucero back to the entrance of the cave so the platoon could contact Bravo Company and provide a status on Operation Sumer. He is severely hurt. We lost contact about forty minutes ago."

"Shit, I better wake the general. Chris, we'll call you back immediately after I brief the general."

———

Colonel Christopher anxiously waited by the radio for Lucero or some direction from the general. Suddenly, there was white noise and a faint call. "Command, come in."

The communication was breaking up like a weak cell phone connection, the voice fading in and out. "Bravo Company, come in; this is Recon One. Command, come in, over ..."

Private Maldonado responded, "This is regional command; read you loud and clear, Recon One."

Maldonado gave the headset to Colonel Christopher and offered him his chair.

Lucero asked, "Who am I speaking with?"

"This is Colonel Christopher. What's your status?"

"Sir, we have big trouble here! We lost communication deep inside the cavern. Lieutenant Colby ordered me to return to the entrance to see if I could establish contact with regional command."

"Are you all right?" asked Colonel Christopher.

"Sir, I don't have much time." Lucero was struggling to get the words out. "I've been shot and am bleeding bad. We lost two men in a battle at the entrance of the cave with an al-Qaeda platoon. It gets worse. On my way back to call you, I ran into a platoon of about twelve al-Qaeda soldiers. I avoided them and remained undiscovered. Unfortunately, they are headed in the exact direction of Recon One, and there's a good chance they could ambush us."

At that moment, the line went dead. There was nothing but white noise. Maldonado's continued attempts to reconnect were futile.

"Shit, why would the enemy send another platoon in there after what happened? They already lost thirty men!" Colonel Christopher said.

"You know, Colonel, they could be on a routine recon patrol and unaware of what has happened the past two days," said Maldonado.

"Private, I doubt that this a routine patrol. You know they are a much-splintered organization. You think we have communication problems? There must be something extremely valuable in the cavern, or they're hiding something," said the colonel.

"You're right, sir."

"Private, please get Central Command on the phone. I need to brief General Hitchens immediately and establish a plan to rescue Lucero and the SEALs."

CHAPTER 19
Government Collaboration

July 8, 2012: Central Command, Kabul, Afghanistan

General Hitchens was troubled that he had no way to warn Recon One of the potential al-Qaeda ambush. It had all the makings of a disaster. He had to make his superiors aware of the danger and get some direction before it bit him in the ass.

General Hitchens bypassed the Joint Chiefs and called the White House directly to brief the president's chief of staff on the situation. McNabb advised Hitchens to contact CIA Director Nathan Stiles. McNabb thought the CIA director could use his field resources in Basra to aid Recon One. He ordered Hitchens to implement the code-red communiqué protocol.

After the conversation with McNabb, General Hitchens knew that this was something more than aiding Recon One. The safety of Recon One was his number one priority, but he was beginning to surmise that wasn't the uppermost concern at the White House. Code-red protocol was used only for the utmost national security matters. Why would the White House use the highest communiqué protocol for a routine recon mission in Iraq?

The code-red communiqué protocol was a set of rules and procedures to communicate and exchange classified information directly with certain high-level government officials. The officials usually were top cabinet members and key intelligence and military personnel. The communications must be carried out in the most secretive manner.

"Two-Way, please contact the CIA director. Proceed with code-red protocol," General Hitchens said.

Two-Way had been in the military for fifteen years and had never had to use the code-red protocol. He had received an orientation in the communiqué protocol at military communication school immediately after basic training. Afterward, he had been provided more intensive training throughout his military career. He also had a classified manual with step-by-step procedures. Two-Way went to the communication locker to retrieve the top-secret manual on communication protocols. He implemented the procedures one at a time and contacted CIA Director Stiles.

Patty quickly buzzed the director's private extension.

"Yes, Patty," the director said.

"Director, you have a code-red communiqué with General Hitchens in Afghanistan."

As part of the protocol, she also buzzed Deputy Director Brown, who was summoned to the director's office. General Hitchens asked Two-Way and all other staff to leave the room.

"General, the director is on the line," Patty said.

The general said, "Nate, this is about Operation Sumer in Iraq. There are a lot of strange things going on there. The White House asked me to contact you and see if you can assist. I get the feeling that the White House is holding all the cards on this one, and they're not filling us in on everything they know. It's similar to how we operated in the past before 9/11, when no one shared information."

"Well, General, we feel the same way," said Nate. "I'm glad to help, but I have a bad feeling about Operation Sumer. The White House and the intelligence community are not working together on this, and I'm just getting bits and pieces of information. Maybe we both can put our information together to make some sense of what's going on. You start."

"We sent a platoon of Navy SEALs into Sumer on direct orders from the White House. Initially, it was the NSC. After that, the DNI and Chief of Staff McNabb got involved, so I assume the president has firsthand knowledge of Recon One's activities."

"Yes," the director said. "I spoke to the president, and he told me he was concerned about al-Qaeda resurfacing in southern Iraq. With the election coming up, he doesn't need bad press."

"I realize that, but I don't give a damn about politics and his reelection. He got himself elected, and I'm sure he can get himself reelected. Shit, I'm here to protect my country and those young soldiers we've sent into this godforsaken hellhole. Now someone better start telling me what the hell is going on here."

"I understand your frustration, General. I'm frustrated too. I'm telling you all I know. So let's work together on this." The CIA director paused and then asked, "Who is Petty Officer Lucero?"

"He's one of the Navy SEALs in Recon One. Lieutenant Colby, the officer in charge, sent Lucero back to the entrance of the cavern to reestablish communication with regional command and here at headquarters."

"Is that it?"

"Hell no. It gets better. There's something down there," said Hitchens. "I can't put my finger on it. I can tell it's something big. During the reconnaissance, the Navy SEALs discovered Sumerian tablets and an unknown gold substance. We have video, and we'll send it over to you on SIPRNet." SIPRNet was the Secret Internet Protocol Router Network.

The director looked up at Jim, pointed to his credenza, and said, "Go to my computer and access SIPRNet and download that video from the FTP site."

"The video is downloading," said Jim.

"General, is there anything else?" the CIA director asked.

"That's all. Do you have anything for me?"

"Yes," the director said. "There's an expedition of archaeologists from Stanford in the area, maybe forty-five minutes from the cave entrance, just south of Sumer. Rocky Savin is heading a team of professional security personal for them, mostly grunts from the military and some mercenaries. We have no idea how they got there. Someone high up in the Iraqi government must be covering for them."

"I know Rocky Savin. He's an excellent soldier, a real professional," Hitchens said.

"So I've been told."

Excited, Hitchens said, "We need to get someone down to the cave quick to help Lucero and to warn the other SEALs. Unfortunately, our closest patrol is eight hours away!"

Nate said, "Shit, that's not quick enough. What about Rocky Savin? He has a security force of eight men only forty-five minutes away with trained mercenaries, real professional soldiers. There are also two CIA operatives, brothers, stationed in the area. We'll need them."

CIA Director Stiles got on the phone with Chief of Staff McNabb to ask for presidential approval for what amounted to deputizing the archaeology security team. It turned out the president was on good terms with Premier Oil's CEO, who had no trouble giving his support since it meant the president would owe him a favor.

After several phone calls the CIA director called Hitchens back with the plan. In less than an hour, the pieces were in place to salvage Operation Sumer. They just needed the president's approval.

As soon as CIA Director Stiles finished his calls, the chief of staff called back and said, "Nate, the president just got off the line with the CEO of Premier Oil. He gave his approval, but he did say we need to get the okay from the security team."

"Any reason why we need their permission?" asked the director.

The chief of staff said, "There are employment contract issues related to liability insurance issues and compensation that require their consent. Also, this necessitates a generous consultant fee. You can take it from the CIA special black budget."

"John, thanks! We'll take it from here," said the director.

"There's one more thing, and this comes directly from the president. He wants Professor Ashe and Natalie Duval part of the group. Their skills are needed to interpret archaeological writings and artifacts."

The CIA director's thoughts quickly turned to his lunch with Bart and the FBI investigation of Duval. That piece of information was now falling into place, but there wasn't enough to make sense or form a conclusion. The chief of staff asked the CIA director to keep him in the loop at all times and told him that was a direct command from the president.

After completing the communication with the chief of staff, the director looked at Jim and just shook his head. "The general is right; whatever is down there is big. When you have the intelligence community, the Joint Chiefs, the president and his chief of staff, Navy SEALs, and the CEO of the largest corporation in the world involved, it must be big."

CHAPTER 20
Operation Rescue Eight

July 8, 2012: Archaeological Site, Basra, Iraq

Frank Corrizo was on guard duty at the archaeological expedition site. His job was to sit on top of a large tower some thirty feet high and stand watch over the camp and the dig site. The security team had three four-hour watch shifts that were rotated equally among the team members.

Frank Corrizo, a retired Green Beret, had the second-most seniority. In the security team, Ed Paradee and Joseph Balachie were also former members of the special forces, both ex–Navy SEALs. Todd Agreen, Basil O'Hara, and Cosmo Cunningham were ex-mercenaries. Jerry McCray was a former CIA operative, and Carlos Trimmer was a former freedom fighter in Africa and South America. They all had code names or nicknames. McCray was called Shooter; Agreen was Turtle; Basil was Mongo; Cunningham was Scoot; Corrizo was Stallion; Paradee was Fast Eddy; Balachie was Joey Bag-o'-Doughnuts.

Joey Balachie was legendary in his neighborhood for always walking around with a bag of doughnuts. Unfortunately for Joey, his brother

Nicky ran into McCray and Agreen at Sugar Daddies, a gentlemen's club in New Orleans. Nicky told them how Joey loved doughnuts and everyone in South Philly called him Joey Bag-o'-Doughnuts. Few knew that Joey was a bagman for a local bookie and that he surely wasn't carrying only doughnuts in that bag. Joey preferred to be called Bags or Joey Bags.

It was a scorching day, and Frank Corrizo was extremely drained from the heat. It was so hot Corrizo's clothes were wet with perspiration. From this location, Corrizo could see in all directions for miles and would have plenty of time to inform the expedition of any oncoming danger.

Using his high-powered binoculars, Corrizo could just make out what looked like something far out across the horizon. The heat waves bouncing off the desert ground reduced visibility, but Corrizo could see that a vehicle of some type was directly approaching the camp. The security team was to call Rocky Savin immediately when anything or anyone approached the expedition's campsite, so Frank quickly grabbed the radio to contact Savin.

"Rocky, there's a truck speeding toward the camp, and I can't ID it. They're about three miles out and moving fast," said Corrizo.

Rocky said, "Okay, I'll be right down. Call the other men, and tell them to report immediately to the tower."

Rocky's first thought was al-Qaeda terrorists finally had discovered the camp. However, he figured the security team would most likely outnumber those in the truck. Nevertheless, any skirmish, no matter how small, would bring attention to the expedition. That would not be good.

Frank Corrizo notified the other members and told them to report immediately to the guard tower. When Rocky Savin arrived, the truck was about two miles out, but they still could not identify the passengers. A minute later, the rest of the security team showed up and began preparing their weapons in case of a battle.

Joey Bags and Carlos Trimmer checked their weapons. Jerry McCray and Cosmo Cunningham reached for more ammo. The rest of the security team were positioned and ready to go.

Frank Corrizo yelled over to Agreen, who was late, "Turtle, for Christ's sake, stop lollygagging, and get your ass in gear! I don't think these are friendlies, so grab a spot, and get you weapons ready."

Within minutes, the vehicle emerged out of the sand, stirring up dust and debris along the road. As the vehicle approached, Corrizo was able to establish that it was a small truck. As the vehicle got yet closer, Corrizo yelled, "There are two passengers."

Savin shouted, "All right, everyone on their toes. Weapons loaded!"

The two men in the vehicle were dressed in traditional Sunni clothing. There was no evidence they were armed. Rocky thought the vehicle might be a car bomb. Terrorists were known for loading a vehicle with explosives and driving it directly into their enemy.

Savin yelled to Corrizo, "Pop those suckers a mile out if they don't slow down." As the vehicle rapidly approached at the same speed, Rocky Savin shouted, "Everyone stand ready to shoot on my command!"

About a mile out, the vehicle slowed down considerably but continued at a moderately rapid speed. Suddenly, the driver slammed on the brakes about a thirty yards out, and the car stopped abruptly, kicking up sand and dust everywhere. The precipitous change in speed jerked both passengers' heads and shoulders forward and then immediately backward, slamming their backs against the seats. The vehicle then proceeded very slowly till it stopped about ten yards from the security team.

One of the men started to get out of the car. Rocky Savin hollered, "Halt immediately! Put your hands above your head now, or I will blow you away." Savin quickly looked at the other passenger in the vehicle and said, "You too; don't move." He nodded to O'Hara and Agreen and said, "Pat them down, and check the vehicle for weapons and explosives."

With his hands still up, the other passenger slowly stepped down from the vehicle and shouted, "My name is Sadit, and this is Raahil. We are CIA, looking for Rocky Savin."

Rocky told his men to stand down. He moved forward and said, "I'm Rocky Savin. What's your business with me?"

Sadit said, "The CIA headquarters in Langley sent us. We have strict orders for you to speak directly with CIA Director Nathan Stiles. Can I approach?"

Rocky, half smiling, said, "Yeah, and my mother is Cleopatra. Do you think we're stupid? Come on; what would the CIA want with me?"

Sadit slowly moved toward Rocky, and Rocky hollered, "Don't move another inch!"

At that moment, Professor Ashe and Natalie Duval showed up.

"I'm Professor Ashe. I'm in charge of this expedition."

"No disrespect, Professor, but we have orders to talk to Rocky Savin first," said Sadit.

"So what is your business with Rocky?" asked the professor.

"There's a situation in Sumer, about forty minutes away, and we need your help. I'm in direct communication with the CIA director, and he will explain the situation. Please, sir, can I grab my radio from the truck?" asked Sadit.

As Sadit reached down to grab the radio, the entire security team cocked their rifles in unison, creating a powerful sound that made Sadit freeze in place. He put his hands up and said, "Rocky, please, the clock is ticking; we're running out of time. With your permission, may I?"

"Real careful, fellow," cautioned Rocky. "My men will gun you down like a mad dog with rabies if you try anything stupid."

Sadit reached into the truck and slowly grabbed the radio and carefully raised it over his head for everyone to see. "Please let me call Langley?"

Rocky Savin looked intensely at the man and said, "This better be good."

Sadit made his phone call and got through to the CIA director's office.

Patty Deichert answered, "CIA director's office."

"This is Operation Rescue Eight with a code-red communiqué for Director Nathan Stiles. This is Field Officer Sadit."

The director was meeting with Deputy Director Brown, but Patty interrupted the meeting and informed the director of the code-red communication from Operation Rescue Eight.

The director told Patty to conference General Hitchens, and then he picked up the phone and said, "This is Director Stiles."

"Sir, this is Sadit. I'm here with Rocky Savin."

Director Stiles responded anxiously, "Good, put him on the line."

Rocky grabbed the phone and said, "Okay, whoever you are, the joke is on me. I don't think this is funny."

"Rocky, CIA Director Nathan Stiles here. No joke, we need your help."

Rocky Savin rolled his eyes and said, "How in the hell do I know you're CIA Director Nathan Stiles?"

The director looked at the deputy director, put his hand over the phone, and said, "He doubts it's me. I think you should talk to him so we can eliminate any trepidation on his part."

"Tell him I'm in the room with you and that we're on a conference line with General Hitchens."

The director said, "Rocky, I'm with Deputy Director James Brown. I'm going to put him on speaker."

The director quickly pressed the speaker button, placed the handset down on the cradle, and nodded to Jim to begin talking.

Jim said, "Hey, Rock, this is Jim Brown."

Rocky quickly quipped, "How in the hell do I know you're Jim Brown? You guys are pissing me off. How do I know this isn't a ploy to ambush us or some foolhardy attempt at corporate sabotage or terrorism?"

The deputy director said, "Rock, remember the time in Nicaragua in September 1982, Operation Cumarandy. You remember. We were on a covert operation to destabilize the Communist Sandinistas. Do you remember the night we were sitting around the campfire, drinking heavily and smoking Cuban cigars that we took off of two guerilla fighters? We talked all night, and you told me about Sarah Banks and the crack house in Philadelphia."

At that moment, Rocky knew it was Brown. First, only he and two other people knew about Operation Cumarandy, and one of them was General Hitchens. More importantly, there was only one person who called him Rock and only a few friends who knew about Sarah, and one of them was Jim Brown.

———————

Sarah had been Rocky's first love, and he did remember telling Jim in detail how Sarah and he had lost their virginity to each other at age sixteen. Just three years later, Sarah and her mother had been killed in an automobile accident caused by an impaired driver drugged up on killer weed and crack. Rocky had loved her very much and had never been able to find anyone else that could come close to her. So Rocky had never married.

What nobody else knew, except for Jim Brown, was that Rocky had hunted that cocaine freak down after he was acquitted due to a technicality. The evidence included cocaine and weed found in the defendant's car, but the breathalyzer test had been inconclusive. The court had dismissed the case because the medical examiner's office had lost the evidence.

Two weeks later, Rocky had found the killer in a crack house in North Philly and shot him up with enough cocaine to kill a dinosaur. Rocky had said, "How could such a piece of shit like you have such a profound impact on so many people's lives?"

Rocky had taken a picture of Sarah out of his pocket. He'd put it up to the junkie's face and said, "Take a look at the last two people you will ever see. Go rot in hell, you son of a bitch!"

The drug addict had been dead in seconds, and Rocky had gotten up and headed for 30th Street Station, where he'd caught a train to North Carolina to join the Marines.

"Hey, good buddy, you're big time now," said Savin. "You and Hitchens moved on up. That is surely a long way from covert operations in Nicaragua. Sorry about the hesitation, but I'm sure you would have done the same thing if someone came out of a remote desert telling you the CIA director was on the phone."

"Hey, Hitchens is also part of this operation. He's on the line too. It's like old home week," said Jim.

"Hey, Rocky, how's it going?" Hitchens asked.

"I'll be damned. Who would have thought we'd all be back together again after all these years?"

"Rocky, I'm going to take you off speaker and give the phone back to the director, who has all the information."

When the director took the phone, Savin apologized and said, "I hope you understand my hesitation, sir."

The director said, "No worry, Rocky; I understand. But I still need your help."

After the director filled Rocky in on the details, he told him that this operation was on orders from the White House and that the CEO at Premier Oil had approved their participation. "According to Premier Oil, it's your decision whether to participate or not. You team will receive a generous consulting fee," said the director.

Lastly, he told Rocky that they wanted Ashe and Duval also to be a part of the operation, strictly as advisors on scientific issues.

The CIA director finished and waited for a response. Rocky Savin was truly surprised and a little taken aback by the request. He turned to his men, Professor Ashe, and Natalie Duval and quickly briefed them. One of the former special ops security team members cocked his rifle and said, "I'm in; let's rock."

Bags asked, "How much is the consulting fee?"

Rocky said, "Two thousand a day."

Bags immediately said, "Count me in."

Four others nodded to signal they were all in.

However, Frank Corrizo could not believe that they were the only armed soldiers in the area. "This is bullshit," he said. "The government wants us to be guinea pigs. I don't like the sound of this. There's no military in this area? I can't believe this."

"Why do they want Natalie and me to go along?" asked Professor Ashe.

"There's a major archaeological find in the caves at the Mound of Tiamat, and they want you and Natalie to go with us to interpret the writings and artifacts," said Savin.

Professor Ashe asked, "What archaeological find?"

Savin looked at Ashe and said, "They mentioned there were Sumerian tablets buried in a cavern. It appears from the initial information that those tablets date back thousands of years."

"I'll be damned," said Ashe.

Natalie said, "I'm in."

"Count me in too," said Ashe. "I also need Charlie Babbitt to come with us to take care of the Finder. We can't leave it behind."

Rocky realized that leaving their most valuable hardware behind was not an option, so he said, "Okay, but Charlie is never to let the Finder out of his sight."

Rocky turned to Frank Corrizo, Todd Agreen, and McCray to find out whether they were joining the operation. All three paused and looked at Rocky and studied the rest of the men's reactions.

Frank said, "Oh shit! I'm in."

McCray replied, "I could use the money for a new car. I'm in."

The other men nodded yes while Agreen looked at the ground.

Frank Corrizo looked over at Agreen and said, "Todd, that's why we call you Turtle; you are always slow to make a friggin' move."

He eventually gave the thumbs-up and said, "I'm in."

Corrizo sarcastically said, "We can all sleep better tonight knowing Turtle is on the team."

Rocky put the radio headset to his ear and said to the CIA director, "Sir, we are all in and ready to go."

"Okay, your code name is Operation Rescue Eight."

The CIA director hung up the phone, looked at his deputy director, and said, "We got us a mission!"

CHAPTER 21
On the Road to Sumer

July 8, 2012: Route 80, Highway of Death, Basra, Iraq

Professor Ashe, Rocky Savin, Sadit, and Raahil were looking at a large map on the hood of their jeep. They also had a Google map of the area and a detailed military drawing downloaded to an iPad. The expedition had state-of-the-art technology and could download maps and images through a wireless satellite provided by Premier Oil.

Ashe pointed to a specific area on the map and said, "This is Recon One's position. Rocky, do you know where this is?"

"I know geographically where it is, but I've never been there."

Abdul interjected, "I know this area. It is the forbidden land of the gods and the great Tiamat. No one is to go near the mound."

Sadit indicated that this area was called the Mound of Tiamat after Tiamat, the goddess in the cosmogonic myth of the Babylonian creation epic called Enuma Elish. Sadit said, "Cosmogony refers to a theory or study of the origin of the universe."

His brother, Raahil, said, "According to Sumerian mythology, Tiamat gave birth to the first generation of deities or gods. Unfortunately, these offspring exercised poor behavior, and she started a war against them. Ancient Mesopotamian texts depict this war as an epic cosmic battle between the gods Marduk and Tiamat.

"Archaeologists from all over the world have wanted to excavate the mound and its surrounding areas. Unfortunately for science, the Iraqi government has declared this area sacred, and it is against both their religion and law to disturb sacred ground."

"My father and mother and all the elders of our tribe forbid us to enter this area," said Abdul. "They told stories of great gods of power and gold."

Rocky Savin looked at the professor curiously and said after a pause, "We'd better get going; we may be too late to help Recon One."

As Natalie passed Joey Bags to get in the truck, Bags smiled and tapped Natalie on the ass. In a condescending manner, he said, "Chop chop, buttercup; you're in the back with the fat man!"

Furious, Natalie turned around and said, "Fuck off, dirtbag."

Bags responded, "Fuck me, buttercup."

Natalie, now extremely upset, said, "You wish!" She grabbed the former Green Beret by the neck from behind and put him in a choke hold that was so paralyzing that Bags was going to pass out.

Savin quickly grabbed Natalie from behind and whispered in her ear, "Let Bags go before you kill him; we need every person here, even if he's a piece of shit."

She slowly released her choke hold, and Bags fell to the ground on his knees, head down, choking and coughing. Natalie looked down at Bags and said, "Up yours, buttercup."

Natalie's strength and quickness shocked the rest of the men. Paradee reached down and helped Bags up and said, "Man, are you crazy or what? I told you to lay off her, and you didn't listen."

Bags didn't want Paradee's help and pushed him away. Humiliated, Bags got up, brushed off his pants, and walked away dejected.

McCray, the ball buster that he was, yelled over to Bags, "Hey, I guess we call you buttercup from here on."

Pissed off, Savin shouted, "Bags, I've had enough of your shit. And the rest of you cut the badgering. We don't have time for this bullshit. Bags, I'll deal with you when we get back. We need to move out. Let's go!"

The fifteen individuals formed a small caravan of three vehicles traveling down Highway 80 toward Basra and then Sumer. Leading the caravan, Rocky Savin, Professor Ashe, Charlie Babbitt, and Natalie Duval were in the small Jeep. A ten-passenger vehicle transported the eight-member security team, while Sadit and Raahil followed in their truck.

Rocky and the professor knew about Highway 80 and realized that traveling on this road could be dangerous. With al-Qaeda in the area, coupled with the poor conditions of the road itself, everyone was on high alert. They knew they did not have much time, so they had to travel fast.

Since 1991, Highway 80 was better known as the Highway of Death. This stretch of road was infamous in the early '90s and during the first Iraq war. Highway 80 was a six-lane highway that went from Kuwait to Baghdad. As a part of the UN resolution of 1991, the Iraqi government had withdrawn from Kuwait using Highway 80.

On February 25, 1991, and continuing to the next day, American aircraft had bombed and destroyed over two thousand military vehicles and killed over ten thousand Iraqis as they returned to their homeland. The military strategy had been to bomb the vehicles at the front and the rear of the withdrawing Iraqi caravan. The bombing had created a bottleneck that made the road look like a parking lot, similar to the traffic on Interstate 95 between Washington, DC, and Virginia at rush hour. The Iraqi army had been sitting ducks, stranded, not able to go anywhere. The US aircraft had a field day. It had been easy pickings, and the resulting carnage had been horrifying. The Highway 80 incident had gone down as one of the worst military massacres in the last two decades.

The caravan traveled on Highway 80 for only ten miles until they turned onto Highway 8. The team was relieved because Highway 8 was less traveled and less dangerous. As they traveled close to fifty miles per hour, a refreshing breeze hit their faces. It was extremely hot, about 115 degrees, and with the vehicle's top down, the hot sun beat on their heads. The breeze generated by the moving vehicles provided some welcome relief.

Operation Rescue Eight's orders were to get to the location as fast as they could and provide backup for Recon One. They were to find Lucero immediately upon arrival. The fifteen members, plus Lucero if he was able, were then to search and destroy anything that was a threat to Recon One.

Seventy-five minutes into the trip, the caravan reached the entrance to the Mound of Tiamat. Rocky Savin contacted Central Command to advise them that they were at the entrance of the cave. Lucero was nowhere in sight. Rocky asked to speak to General Hitchens.

"General, command told us that Lucero would be at the mouth of the cave to guide us to Recon One's location. He's not here, and we've searched the entire area. He's nowhere. We did find two dead, partially buried al-Qaeda rebels."

"Holy balls, Rocky, I wonder if Lucero was captured!"

"Shit, General, if the enemy captured Lucero, that could only mean that there are now more enemy soldiers in the area."

"Knowing Lucero, I wouldn't be surprised if he went back in there," said Hitchens.

"We were told he was wounded pretty badly," replied Savin.

"Regardless, you need to move forward now," said General Hitchens.

Rocky Savin gathered the team around him. "We'll be leaving without Lucero," said Savin. "He probably decided not to wait and moved forward to warn Recon One."

Savin directed the team to inspect their weapons and ordered Frank Corrizo to take a position at the front of the group.

He told the professor, Charlie Babbitt, and Natalie to wait at the entrance until he returned, and he ordered Paradee, McCray, and Sadit to stay back with them.

"I'm going with you," said the professor.

"I can't allow that. I'm responsible for your safety," Savin said.

"I can take care of myself! I've been doing it for over fifty years."

"I would need to call the general and get permission."

"You do that. I'm going forward regardless. Washington asked us to be a part of this mission. Our participation may have an impact on the rest of the mission."

Savin barked at the professor, "We don't have time for this. Christ, Professor, the clock is ticking, and we're wasting precious minutes. Unfortunately, we are at an impasse, good buddy."

"So what does that mean?" asked the professor.

Savin said, "You're staying here as ordered. We are going into battle, and we don't need a bunch of civilians around. I can't waste any more time dealing with this."

Rocky Savin did not feel comfortable leaving Professor Ashe behind, but he knew he did not have much choice. He could not waste any more time. Savin knew any more delays could further jeopardize any rescue attempt of Recon One. It may already be too late.

Standing behind Frank Corrizo at the front of the rescue team, Savin looked backed, raised his rifle over his head, and said, "Let's go kick ass and save our brothers."

Frank Corrizo yelled out, "Pucker up, boys; it's showtime."

CHAPTER 22
The Escape

July 9, 2012: Mound of Tiamat

The Navy SEALs finished their breakfast and started to gather their gear to move out. Lieutenant Colby was worried that he had not heard from Lucero and that he still could not communicate with his superiors. Colby began to fret that he'd lost Lucero to the black hole or the treacherous terrain that characterized this hellhole.

At this point, he didn't know whether to go back or move forward. He agonized over this decision. So Colby asked Mendez to meet him about five yards away from the rest of the men.

"Chief, I'm afraid we've lost Lucero," whispered Colby. "It's been too long. We should have heard something."

"Yeah, I agree, but Lucero is a strong player."

"We have a dilemma. Do we stay here, move forward, or go back?" asked Colby.

"Shit, Lieutenant, we need to do something!"

Colby had already lost several men in this godforsaken place. With his manpower reduced, he worried that he could lose more. But he had to do something.

Colby ordered Casper Pantano and Buford Baily to go back toward the entrance of the cave to get some intelligence. He instructed them not to go any farther than a mile and a half to see if anything was happening and report back.

Tucked away in the dreary depths of the cave, the two men made it about a mile into their mission before coming across anything noteworthy. This part of the cave was gloomy and dusky with sharp, weathered rocks on both the walls and ceilings. Casper pointed to the stalactites, stalagmites, and water flowing down the limestone walls and ceilings. The air was wet and musty and suddenly smelled acidic.

Casper shook his head. "Buford, do you smell that?"

"Yeah, it reminds me of rotten eggs."

Casper and Buford continued to walk carefully through the cave; then something caught Casper's eye.

"Did you see that?" asked Casper.

"What?"

Casper nodded toward the ceiling. "Do you see the reflecting lights?"

"Yes, I see them. They look like flashlights flickering off the cavern walls and ceiling," said Buford.

"Yeah, and they're heading our way," said Casper.

Someone was approaching fast, less than 135 yards away. Casper and Buford had no idea whether it was Lucero or the enemy. But they would soon find out.

"You wait here," Buford said. "I want to see if I can get a glimpse of who it is. See if you can get the lieutenant on the radio."

Buford went slowly toward the lights, hoping to hear some chatter as a clue to who or what was in front of them. He was about fifty yards from the lights. Buford proceeded about twenty more yards and took cover behind a large, wet, dripping stalagmite. He peered around the pointed pillar and noticed that the lights were stationary on the ceiling, indicating the enemy had stopped.

Buford called Casper on the radio and whispered, "Casper come in."
"Yes?"

"Join me, but keep it easy."

Casper cautiously moved forward to join Buford behind the pillar. Casper asked anxiously, "Where are they?"

"They haven't moved for about five minutes," Buford whispered as pointed toward the soldiers. "Did you contact the lieutenant?"

"No, there's nothing but white noise."

"Shit! You know, I've been to Iraq, Afghanistan, Somalia, and just about every shit hole on this globe, and I just got a bad feeling about this," said Buford.

"I hear you, brother."

"Somalia was a real loser, but this takes the cake," said Buford. "Look, we need to find out who they are. You wait here, and I'll go about ten yards to ascertain their identity and strength."

"Dude, be careful," said Casper.

"That's the only way I roll, big guy."

Casper watched as Buford crawled through the murky sludge. Buford's face was full of mud as he clawed his way inch by inch through the muck and grime. His pants were wet from the cold drippings that drizzled down the cone-shaped rocks.

Approaching along the left cave wall, Buford finally reached cover behind a large brown rock laced with gold specks that gave it a subtle glow. Lying on his stomach, Buford peered around the rock to see who was behind the lights. He had an excellent visual of the target and determined that there were at least twelve of them. They were well armed and spoke Arabic, and there was no trace of Lucero. Given all this and the platoon's worn, mismatched uniforms, Buford concluded they were terrorists.

With his pants soaked and hair and face covered with mud, Buford started to feel a chill. The conditions were difficult but no worse than scuba training in the cold waters of the north Atlantic.

When he peeked around the gigantic rock a second time to see what was going down, one of the soldiers started to walk toward him. Buford jerked his head back swiftly. Concealed, he flipped over on his back with his head propped against the rock, prepared for a fight.

Only three yards from Buford, the enemy soldier suddenly stopped, pulled out a cigarette and matches from his top pocket, and lit up. He took three puffs, and the air quickly filled with the strong smell of stale cigarette smoke. He went a few steps, took three more puffs, and then continued to walk in Buford's direction.

Puffing heavily on his cigarette, inhaling every bit of nicotine as if his life depended on it, the soldier stopped five feet past Buford's hiding place. As he turned, he saw Buford hiding there like a trapped animal. Startled, the enemy soldier reached quickly for his pistol, pulled it, and aimed it directly at Buford.

Trapped, Buford said, "Checkmate! I lose."

Now standing directly over Buford, the soldier suddenly had a shocked look on his face, as if someone had just sucker-punched him. With intense fear and pain in his eyes, he desperately reached behind him, trying to grab something from the middle of his back. Standing still and staring straight ahead, the enemy soldier dropped to his knees for five seconds and then fell on top of Buford.

Confused but relieved, Buford didn't know what had happened. Then the Navy SEAL got his answer when he saw a large hunting knife jutting out of the man's back. He covered the soldier's mouth immediately and pushed the knife farther into his back. The enemy soldier died instantly.

Buford realized that his good buddy had his back. He looked over at Casper and nodded his head in thanks as he pushed the enemy soldier off his lap. Buford looked to see if anyone else was coming. Seeing no one, he gave a thumbs-up, signaling Casper to join him.

Casper crawled his way toward Buford and knelt next to him. Buford looked at Casper and said, "Thanks, Casper. I was toast."

"Got your back, bro; what's up?"

"There's no movement. It looks like they didn't hear us."

"So what do we do now?"

"We must hide the body and hope they don't discover it before we get back to the platoon."

"Where do we hide it?" asked Casper.

Buford pointed down the cave to his right and said, "There's a small opening between this rock and the wall that goes down about ten feet."

"That body can't fit through there," said Casper.

"Precisely," replied Buford as he pulled out his bowie knife and held it in front of Casper.

"You're kidding me, right?" Casper said.

"You ever carve a turkey? You take the arms, and I'll take the legs."

Casper pulled out the knife lodged in the enemy's back and just shook his head in disbelief. He knew their options were limited, so they started to cut up the body.

When Buford and Casper finished hiding the body, blood covered their wet uniforms, faces, arms, and hands. Buford pulled a large handkerchief nonchalantly from his back pocket and tried to clean his face and hands. He looked over to Casper and said, "I'd let you use my handkerchief, but as you can see, it's soaked."

"Don't sweat it; I have one," Casper said. "Now what?"

"We have our orders. Go back and tell the lieutenant what's going down. I'll stay here and determine their next move and meet up with you later."

Casper grabbed his gear and started back through the murky, wet mess.

A short time thereafter, the enemy started to pack up to move forward. Buford decided to return to the platoon with needed information on the enemy position. Breathing heavily and covered with blood, he finally reached the Navy SEALs' campsite. Trying to catch his breath, Buford told Colby the al-Qaeda platoon was on its way toward them.

The other men gathered around. One of the SEALs grabbed a small towel and a shirt from his bag and tossed them over to Buford.

Colby asked, "Where is Casper?"

"What do you mean?" asked Buford.

"Where is he? Tell me," said Colby.

Shocked, Buford bellowed, "I sent him back to brief you about thirty minutes ago!"

Colby looked around and then said, "As you can see, he's not here."

It wasn't looking good for Recon One. Various scenarios ran through Colby's mind: How far away was the enemy? What had happened to Casper? Had the enemy captured him? If so, where were they? The Navy SEALs had been in this position before, but for some reason this seemed different and more dangerous.

Colby ordered the platoon to move out swiftly and make sure they covered their tracks. The Navy SEALs were trained and experienced in breaking camp quickly. Each man had a specific task to rid the campsite of any evidence that they had been there.

Buford approached Colby and said, "What about Casper? Do we plan to leave him here?"

"Leave him where?" Colby asked. "I can only do what I can see."

"Shit, Lieutenant, I want to stay here and wait for him," said Buford.

Colby shouted, "I can't allow that! I'm short men as it is. We need to go now!"

Colby knew his back was against the wall, and he had to find a place to make a stand or keep moving.

CHAPTER 23
The Pathway to Heaven or Hell

July 9, 2012: Mound of Tiamat

Rescue Eight was on its way to help the Navy SEALs. Rocky Savin and the expedition team had traveled about five miles into the cave. About five minutes ago, Rocky had sent Blake Marshall to recon fifty yards ahead. He'd just returned to brief Savin.

"Listen up!" yelled Savin. "Marshall tells me that the road ahead is little tricky. We will need to follow the path carefully. According to Marshall, the path becomes very dangerous, especially at the bend. It is narrow and deep, and if you slip, you will plunge into hell. We will proceed in groups of three, two minutes apart. Gather your hardware, and we'll leave in five minutes."

The men assembled. Joey Bags was still brooding over his humiliating encounter with Natalie Duval. He clearly felt isolated and embarrassed. Several of the men were busting his chops in jest, and he took it personally. Bags retaliated by taking a swing at Carlos Trimmer, who struck back. Having had enough of Bags's bullshit, Basil O'Hara went after him too, pushing Bags and raising his fist in preparation of a rumble. Furious, Carlos took a swing at Bags.

Carlos yelled, "You want a piece of me, buttercup? Come and get it. I'll kick your ass."

Four of the security team stepped in between the three men and broke up the fight.

Savin yelled, "That's enough. What's wrong with you shit heads? You want to give our position away? And, Bags, if you don't get your head out of your ass, I'll leave you here."

Within seconds of the commotion, the abyss below started swirling like a black hole spinning in space.

"Now look; you woke this thing up, whatever it is," shouted Corrizo.

The fight had triggered the violent rotating column of air. It had started slow and gathered momentum till it reached an incredible speed. Interestingly enough, the intense vortex resembled a waterspout tornado extending from a thunderstorm funnel cloud near the ceiling to the ground, despite the fact waterspouts usually formed only over a body of water.

The vortex was now moving in a tremendous curvilinear motion, spinning out of control just below the ledge of the cavern directly under the platoon's feet. The black hole phenomenon caused a tremendous suction that made it extremely dangerous to cross to the other side.

Agreen yelled over to Cunningham, "Scoot, we are on the pathway to hell. I knew this mission was a loser."

"I'd say," said Scoot.

"Stop complaining," said Savin.

The first group started to carefully navigate the dangerous path around the sharp bend. Corrizo was at the head of the group, Carlos Trimmer was in the middle, and Basil O'Hara was last. The three men struggled to keep their balance. The earth was loose, and the path crumbled underneath the men. They grabbed desperately onto any part of the smooth wall.

As they approached the bend, the angle of the curve was more perilous than the three had imagined. The drop-off from the ledge was steep and dark. They knew one false step would result in sudden death. The whirling wind pulled the men toward the endless abyss and sure death. All three men pressed their backs against the cavern wall as hard as they could and slowly moved their feet an inch at a time.

As they carefully maneuvered around the bend, Carlos looked down at the dark, endless abyss. The swirling motion made him extremely dizzy, and he suddenly lost his balance and fell forward. Basil tried desperately to grab Carlos's arm to stop his fall. As the gravel crumbled under his feet, Carlos tried to balance himself by grabbing onto the wall. But the wall was too smooth, and there was nothing to grab. It was too late; he fell straight down into the abyss.

Everyone stood there shocked. Corrizo and Basil were afraid to move. Their footing was not stable, and they were afraid to take another step. They stood there frozen in their tracks. No one had yet made it to the other side. Given the danger, Savin had to make a decision whether to continue or retreat.

CHAPTER 24
Sandwiched

July 9, 2012: Mound of Tiamat

After traveling in the cave for a few more miles, the Navy SEALs thought there was sufficient distance between them and the enemy, and they stopped to rest in an open area. Colby ordered Fish and Trash Thompson to stand guard. Fish covered the forward position, while Trash was stationed about fifteen yards in front of the platoon. Their orders were to provide the platoon with a heads-up if the enemy approached while Colby determined their next move.

Two rocks provided Trash needed cover. The angle of his position would allow him to see the flashlights of the enemy as they approached. Out of nowhere, Trash suddenly saw shadows approaching about twenty yards out. The enemy had snuck up on them in the darkness. They weren't using their flashlights, so Trash couldn't determine their distance. The terrorists must have captured Casper and discovered the SEALs were close by.

As the enemy approached swiftly, the Navy SEALs scrambled for cover. Bullets were flying everywhere, and the place lit up like Times

Square on New Year's Eve. Immediately, the Navy SEALs sprayed four enemy soldiers with machine gun fire and dropped and killed them quickly. Jackson Michaels took a bullet in the arm, and Sullivan took one in the buttock, but both were able to run for cover.

The eight remaining al-Qaeda soldiers retreated and took cover behind rocks, cavern coves, and anything that would help shield them from the onslaught of Recon One's fury. About ten minutes into the battle, Colby knew that they would be in for a long dogfight.

Fish Calamari moved to get a better vantage point on the enemy and took bullets in the leg and stomach. Then Buford took a bullet to the thigh, but it was only a flesh wound. They both were alive, but Fish was bleeding profusely. Buford moved quickly to cover Fish. The adrenaline of the fight took over, and he didn't feel a thing. Once he reached Fish, he pulled him to a safe area.

"Where were you hit?" Buford asked.

Fish pointed to his stomach, and Buford pulled bandages and medical tape from his backpack. He laid the bandages across the wounded area and told Fish to apply pressure to slow the bleeding. As Fish did so, blood squirted out all over the place, including on Buford's face. Both Buford and Fish knew it was not good.

Fish looked at Buford with a faint smile and murmured, "I'll be fine; go help the others. Get those bastards!" Knowing that Fish would bleed out in a few minutes, there was nothing more Buford could do. As Buford turned away, Fish grabbed his arm and whispered, "Tell Molly she's the love of my life."

"We'll get out of here, and you'll be able to tell her yourself, Fish," said Buford.

Fish replied, "I'm not sure, good buddy. I don't know where I'll be a few minutes from now. I hope it's not hell."

Just then Fish's eyes shut. He had no expression on his face. Buford frantically shook Fish, but it was too late; he was dead. Clearly upset, Buford placed his hand on Fish's shoulder and tapped slowly three times to signal good-bye to his good friend.

Buford quickly stood up and ran, dodging bullets, to get over to Slick Sullivan. They all now realized that this was not going to be a fifteen-minute battle. They were in for a dogfight, and they were bogged down in a stalemate.

With bullets still coming from all directions, Colby joined Mendez and pointed toward the enemy. "Chief, do you see the bullets coming from behind the enemy?"

"Yeah, looks like some of them are now firing in the other direction," said Mendez.

Colby and Mendez could see two unknown soldiers moving quickly toward the enemy from the other direction. With bullets flying in all directions, the two mysterious soldiers weaved from one side of the cave to the other to take advantage of the best cover available.

As they approached in front of him, Colby could see two groups in battle and knew now that one of them was friendly. Ambushed from the other side, the al-Qaeda were outnumbered. Colby couldn't help but smile.

Still ducking bullets, Colby leaned over to Mendez and said, "I don't know who those guys are, but we owe them big time."

Savin and the rescue team had made it, and they had the enemy bogged done. Rescue Eight had snuck up on the enemy without being noticed and pulled off a surprise attack. Sandwiched like meatballs between two slices of bread, the enemy had nowhere to go. Given the positions of the rescue team and Recon One, the enemy was forced to split up their forces to fight two fronts.

Many of the al-Qaeda soldiers' backs were now to Savin and his platoon. Savin paused for ten seconds, lifted his arm, and pointed toward the enemy, triggering a barrage of gunfire. Corrizo, Cunningham, and Bags fired off numerous rounds and made quick work of several enemy soldiers. Since the start of the dogfight, six al-Qaeda were shot and dead in less than five minutes, and only four remained alive.

Lieutenant Colby ordered his Navy SEALs to attack the remaining enemy. Miguel Mendez, Tex Carter, Michael McDermott, and Jackson Michaels split into two groups and made quick work of two of the four al-Qaeda remaining. Savin yelled to the two remaining enemy soldiers to surrender.

One of them raised his hands and slowly stood up as he uttered something in Arabic. The enemy soldier cautiously approached Colby and his men. Colby said, "Let him approach." With his hands still over his head, the al-Qaeda soldier continued to speak nervously. It sounded like gibberish—loud, incoherent, and incomprehensible. His face covered with fear, his voice got louder and louder, and Colby told him to calm down. Everything started to get out of control. He continued to get louder and louder as he approached the US forces. Abruptly, the other al-Qaeda soldier stood up and shot his fellow soldier directly in the head. In less than ten seconds, ten soldiers in Recon One and Rescue Eight gunned down the last al-Qaeda enemy in a barrage of what seemed like a thousand bullets. The force of the bullets was so ferocious that numerous pieces of flesh tore from his body. It was not pretty.

The cavern was full of smoke, and the air smelled like sulfur. It was the smell of war that they all had grown far too familiar with during their military careers. As the smoke cleared, Lieutenant Colby recognized Savin from their early days in the Marines. Colby approached Savin, shook his hand, and thanked him for helping them fight the enemy.

"Rocky, I thought you retired from the Marines," said Colby.

"You bet I did," responded Savin.

"Then what are you doing here?"

"A special invite from the CIA director and the president."

"What?"

"The short story is that we were on an archaeological expedition with Professor Ashe from Stanford, just a short distance from you. The White House asked us to help out since there was no one else in the immediate area. Given the intelligence provided by Lucero, the White

House thought the al-Qaeda might ambush you. They hired us to get in here fast to either warn you or provide reinforcement."

"Where did you get these soldiers?" asked Colby.

"They are my security team assigned to the expedition for protection."

"Yeah, I recognize several of these ex-grunts—special forces, right?"

"I put this team together several years ago when Premier Oil hired me as their director of security."

Lieutenant Colby took a quick look around and ordered his platoon to start rounding up the bodies. Savin asked Sadit to find his brother, the professor, and Natalie and bring them here. The SEALs lined the enemy bodies in a row on their backs.

Michael McDermott was kneeling next to Fish Calamari, leaning over his best buddy to pay his respects. "You died a hero, with honor and dignity, my good friend. I will make sure you get out of this hellhole and have a proper burial fitting a hero."

McDermott pulled out a body bag and carefully put Fish's body into it. He pulled out a fantasy baseball magazine out of his backpack and put it on Fish's chest. McDermott slowly pulled up the zipper of the body bag and said, "You may not need this where you're going, but I want you to have it. It's the only thing I have with me that you would think has value. I won't need it anymore. It won't be the same without you. Good-bye and God bless, good buddy. You da man!"

Lieutenant Colby walked over to Mike McDermott and knelt next to Fish to pay his respects as well. He looked over at Mike and said, "Fish was a great soldier." He placed his hand firmly on Mike's shoulder for a few seconds, said a short pray, and then got up to join the rest of the platoon.

The men finished collecting the bodies, and Lieutenant Colby told them to gather around. He introduced Rocky Savin and explained how Operation Rescue Eight had gotten there. Tex Carter asked the lieutenant why they'd received such attention from the White House.

"You know, that's a good question, one that I've been asking myself since Rocky Savin arrived," said Colby.

Colby asked Mendez to recon the perimeter. About 150 yards into his assignment, the ancient tablets were everywhere again. However, these tablets were different—more decorative, illuminative, and colorful, with gold framing around the edges. The tablets were more spectacular but also more sophisticated, even benevolent-looking, compared to the other tablets they'd seen.

Mendez went back to inform Colby. The lieutenant ordered his men to move forward. Colby was at the front of the line and stopped to observe several of the tablets when he reached them. These artifacts were magnificent, less coarse and more advanced than any Colby had seen when studying Sumerian culture at Harvard. While Colby studied the tablets, the men passed by him, but the lieutenant eventually caught up to the platoon and resumed his place at the head of the squad alongside Mendez. Colby shook his head in disbelief.

Mendez said, "Hey, Lieutenant, do you believe this? Man, I feel like I should kneel down and worship something. Are you able to interpret anything?"

Colby said, "This is unbelievable, Chief. It's just as I suspected. Something incredible is in this cave."

Mendez asked, "You mean the tablets?"

"Yes, but there's more. I can't make it all out, but each tablet contains a piece of the whole."

"English, Lieutenant!"

"Sorry! What I mean is each tablet talks about an event or provides a piece of knowledge or history like chapters in a book that ultimately tell a complete story with a theme. You cannot just take them one at a time; you have to put it together to tell the whole story."

"So it's a puzzle of some sort?"

"I can tell you this much: there is some physical object. I think it is a cup, a chalice, maybe a vessel of some kind that contains something insightful and profound. I can't tell; this is way over my pay grade."

"What do you mean by insightful?"

"Well, the tablets talks about some spectacular events in our history, but I can't make it out."

"What else do the tablets mean?" asked Mendez.

"There are two tablets that look like instructions to build something. One other interesting observation is that these tablets are easier to understand than the ones we saw a couple of days ago. It's almost like reading something written by F. Scott Fitzgerald as compared to something written by my ten-year-old niece. The overall quality of the writing and the tablets are far superior, thus making the translation easier and less random.

"Regardless, it's beyond my abilities to interpret these writings. Without more time, I can't provide any comprehensive or meaningful interpretation. I know one thing for sure: we must protect these tablets so those skilled in interpreting such writings can make sense of them."

"So what now?" Mendez asked.

"Gather the men together."

"Yes, sir."

As Mendez assembled the men, Lieutenant Colby grabbed his journal and a pen from his backpack. The men quickly convened around Colby and anxiously waited for some logical explanation of what the hell was going on here.

Tex maneuvered his way in front of Lieutenant Colby and said, "Sir, I saw some pretty amazing stuff in my day, but this tops it. It's almost godlike."

"Good observation," replied Colby.

"What's going on here, sir?" asked Tex.

"I do know one thing: we must guard these artifacts and make sure nothing happens to them."

Lieutenant Colby knelt down and started to document the events in his journal.

CHAPTER 25
A Destiny with Hell or Heaven

July 9, 2012: Mound of Tiamat

Professor Ashe, Natalie Duval, Charlie Babbitt, Raahil, McCray, and Paradee had stayed back as Savin and his men went forward to rescue Recon One. However, the professor and his team were about two miles ahead from where Savin had told them to wait because Professor Ashe had kept pushing the group to go forward, anxious to get to the archaeological find in the cave. McCray had tried everything to prevent Ashe from moving ahead, and he had finally been able to convince the professor to stop and set up camp for now.

Paradee and McCray were now conducting a reconnaissance of the area. Paradee went forward about three hundred yards while McCray went back toward the entrance to see if anyone was headed their way. Paradee looked down and noticed that his shoes were covered with glistening gold powder.

"McCray, this is Paradee; come in."

"This is McCray; what's up?"

"Join me," said Paradee. "I'm about three or four hundred yards ahead. Bring the professor, Natalie, and Charlie. There's something you all need to see."

When the three arrived, they noticed the gold substance sparkling all over their shoes and pants.

"Hey, Professor, what's up with this gold powder?" Paradee asked. "Do you have any clue of the substance's composition or origin?"

Professor Ashe knelt down on one knee, scooped up a handful of the gold substance, and rubbed it through his fingers. Then he slowly brought it up to his nose to smell it. He paused for about ten seconds, and as he shook his head, he gave Paradee and Natalie an intense and somewhat-puzzled look. He then took a sample of the substance and placed it in a jar from his backpack.

"Charlie, please take pictures," Ashe said.

Charlie asked, "Do you want me to document the entire area?"

"Yes," replied Ashe. "I've never seen anything like this before. Without a lab, it's difficult to determine the precise makeup or its origin. However, I can tell you the substance appears to be some by-product or derivative of processed gold."

Natalie knelt down to touch the material. She immediately stood up and said, "I saw something similar while at Stanford. This reminds me of a by-product of digestible gold I researched years ago. I had a boyfriend who was a fitness freak. He was always working out, drinking protein shakes, and taking vitamin supplements. You know the type. He would consume close to four thousand calories daily but did not have an ounce of fat on his body. He was fit, healthy, and a major stud."

Paradee interrupted. "What's that got to do with this substance?"

"Let me finish," said Natalie. "He took a supplement called Forever Young. He was always looking for that next wonder product, the one, as he would say, that would take him over the top to live healthier and longer and to be smarter than most people. I did some research for him on the supplement, which was basically colloidal gold—gold particles suspended in a liquid."

"So does this gold substance resemble colloidal gold?" asked the professor.

Rubbing it through her fingers, Natalie said, "It's similar to colloidal gold when it's in the original state, but it's not colloidal gold. Colloidal gold is usually a reddish color and isn't powder."

Paradee said, "I remember reading something about Forever Young in one of those Sunday-newspaper inserts. It claimed to be a miracle pill."

"Yes, I saw those advertisements too," said McCray.

"It's poppycock," said the professor. "There's no such thing as a miracle pill, and the manufacturers of this product haven't produced any evidence to substantiate that claim."

"Maybe so," said Natalie. "When I researched, I discovered that colloidal gold is nanoparticles of pure gold suspended in pure water. When digested, it supposedly increases energy and alertness; improves brain and motor functions, including focus and creativity; and has a calming effect that eases stress. There are many more proclaimed benefits."

"Enough of this; this is an exercise in mental masturbation! Do you have anything else constructive to add?" McCray asked.

"There is one more interesting point," said Natalie. "There's also another form of digestible gold, ionic gold. It's sometimes referred to as monoatomic gold. I'm not sure, but there are claims that this substance is toxic to humans. It contains gold chloride, a substance that can cause peripheral neuropathy, which is associated with nerve damage and symptoms such as numbness. My research indicated that colloidal gold was safer, so he began taking it religiously."

"I can't believe how this substance lights up the area. It's so bright and illuminating," Paradee said.

"Well," said Natalie, "that is one substantial inconsistency. Neither of the substances I researched illuminated like this stuff. My only guess is that this is a substance of gold mixed with some other extraterrestrial substance."

As Paradee moved about ten yards farther into the cave, he turned and asked Natalie, "What do you mean?"

"It's not of this planet!" Natalie said.

"Do you have scientific proof of that?" asked Ashe.

Just then, Paradee pointed to the left wall and said, "Professor Ashe, there are symbols on the wall!"

"Where?" Ashe anxiously replied.

Still pointing, Paradee said, "Do you see them, over here on the wall? There are stone slabs with symbols! They're everywhere!"

As the professor walked toward the tablets, he proclaimed, "They are magnificent!"

Paradee looked at what the professor was staring at and asked, "What are they?"

The professor paused for a moment, trying to regain his composure, and said, "They are pictographs, the basis for cuneiform writing used mostly by the ancient Sumerians and later by the Egyptians. The writing is usually carved on stone tablets."

The professor moved right up to the wall and rubbed his fingers through the grooves in the tablets that formed the symbols of the pictographs. He turned to Natalie and Paradee and said, "This is authentic; it's for real!"

McCray told Paradee and Raahil to set up camp while the archaeology team investigated the tablets. The professor, Natalie, and Charlie quickly busied themselves trying to interpret the cave writings and determine their age.

The two walls of the cavern were each a continuous row of tablets with pictographs. The writing surface was incredibly smooth and flat. He could not believe how they were so perfectly preserved. His carbon testing indicated the writings were at least 4,500 to 6,000 years old.

Ashe asked Charlie to set up the Finder to see if there were any artifacts beneath the ground close to the tablets. Charlie removed the Finder from the custom-made dolly, unwrapping a strap made from a new type of soft but strong plastic, designed to secure and transport the Finder.

When he turned on the Finder, red, green, and blue lights flashed on the front of the square box, flickering like a computer booting up.

As he stood guard, Raahil paced nervously in a circle around the professor. He was afraid for Recon One and the rescue team but, most importantly, his brother, Sadit. Ever since Saddam Hussein's lynch men had killed their parents, he'd always taken care of and protected his brother. Raahil had always been the strong one, the more streetwise and the savvier of the two.

Now that the professor had determined the age and condition of the tablets, he turned his attention to interpreting the writings. He pulled his DELL Latitude laptop out of his bag and turned it on. He'd had this laptop for the past three years and had just recently had the memory and operating system upgraded to 64 bit. He has been pleasantly surprised by how fast the laptop calculated various algorithms and formulas when he was out in the field. It was at least ten times faster after the upgrade.

Stored on the laptop was the professor's language-decoder software. Thanks to the upgrade, he now could use the application in the field to interpret ancient languages and writings quickly. He'd developed the decoder application in cooperation with Professor Forrest Susskind, a linguistics professor at Stanford who headed the computational linguistics department. Susskind and Ashe were married to each other and were one of the first same-sex marriages to be legally performed in California.

Susskind and Ashe had developed a Linux and Java computer application that automated the translation of languages. The program used artificial intelligence and algorithms coupled with new methods in computational linguistics. It took and stored words in various languages and could translate the meaning from one language to the other. They called the computer program ALICOMP, Automated Linguistic Interpreter Computer. The science community had not yet accepted the device, and the program was patent pending.

ALICOMP was designed to interpret Sumerian and other similar languages. Professor Ashe typed in the word *Sumerian* into ALICOMP, and the video screen filled with pictographs. The system was designed to list hundreds of objects. Professor Ashe selected each object that corresponded with the pictograph on the tablet. Ashe and Susskind had collaborated with scientists at the University of Pennsylvania to develop this automated library and dictionary of the Sumerian language.

Interpreting the Sumerian cuneiform writing was like putting together a difficult, complex puzzle, made even more difficult because it was in a foreign language that many people did not totally understand. However, Professor Ashe had done this numerous times. Yet something was significantly different with the pictographs this time. The writing seemed more sophisticated.

He initially focused on the first tablet. He recognized the meaning of some of the pictographs but could not interpret the writing. So he continued to laboriously search and select each comparable pictograph when displayed on the screen. Professor Ashe knew it was going to take some time to get the tablets translated, but he was extremely excited, like a child the night before Christmas.

After several hours, Ashe's preliminary interpretation of the tablets indicated that something in the cavern held great knowledge. The translation kept saying something important was buried in this cavern.

Ashe said to himself, "Archaeologists work their whole lives for a big score like this, the history changer." Professor Ashe's gut told him something huge and historic was in this cave, and he was anxious to proceed.

Professor Ashe said, "Charlie, pack up the hardware, and be ready to move out and see what else this cave has in store for us."

"Do you think this is such a good idea? Savin told us to sit tight until they get back," said Charlie.

"With all due respect to Savin, I don't give a shit. Someone in the White House wants us to provide scientific support for this mission, and that's what we're going to do. Do you realize the importance of this find?"

Natalie, Charlie, Raahil, McCray, and Paradee walked over to the professor. Natalie asked, "What's up?"

"We're moving out," said Charlie.

Now visibly upset, McCray barked, "What are you talking about?

Savin told us not to leave till we hear from him, and we are already over two miles from that spot. Look, this is a military mission, not scientific."

The professor replied sternly, "I'll move forward with you or not. Charlie, let's go."

The professor started to walk, and McCray moved quickly in front of him and confronted him. "Look, we already set up camp. Let's stay here tonight and then see what happens."

The professor looked up at McCray and said, "Excuse me, sir, but get out of my way. I have a professional responsibility to research this find. What's in this cave could be the biggest discovery in human history."

The professor went around McCray, who grabbed him and said, "Sir, we have our orders."

The professor said, "Those are your orders, not mine."

Realizing he was not getting anywhere with this, McCray said, "Give us a minute; we'll go with you."

The professor said, "We don't have a minute; hustle up."

McCray said, "Pack, we're moving out. I'll probably get fired over this!"

Natalie, Charlie, Raahil, McCray, Paradee, and the professor began the journey forward. About two miles into their journey, the cave narrowed and became more treacherous. Paradee was leading the way, and McCray was covering the rear.

Paradee went ahead about twenty yards and then quickly returned and said, "Stay alert; the trail is getting more dangerous and narrower."

As they went farther into the cave, they came upon a narrow pathway about fifteen inches wide with a drop-off so deep they couldn't see the bottom.

"It looks like an endless pit," said Paradee.

Just like before, a swirling vortex appeared out of nowhere. The whirlwind picked up momentum till it reached an incredible speed and was moving in a tremendous circular motion, spinning out of control immediately below their feet. The tornado-like funnel again caused a suction effect that added to the extremely dangerous conditions.

Paradee approached the professor and said, "We need to go back. It's too dangerous."

Irritated, Ashe replied angrily, "I'm not going back. I need to see what else is here. The tablets say that there's something special hidden in a cave, and we must find it. We were asked by Washington to provide scientific support, and I only know one way to do that, so we must move forward."

Unsure and apprehensive, Paradee said, "Okay, but the equipment needs to stay behind."

Upset, the professor became frustrated and said, "This is a scientific expedition, and we will need all of it!"

McCray quickly responded, "Professor, you don't get it; this is a military rescue mission, and I'm in charge!"

"The military mission is miles ahead. This group is scientific, and your job is to provide protection."

McCray yelled, "That's what I'm trying to do! You leave that heavy, awkward hardware, or we stay here. Got it? Do you think you're going to get across that hellhole without our help?"

Natalie touched the professor's arm softly and said, "We should do what he says. We can't get across on our own, and the equipment is just too heavy."

"I guess I have no other option," the professor said. "Charlie, you stay behind with the gear. But I will take the ALICOMP and my instruments."

Paradee organized two groups to cross the hellhole. The first group was McCray and Raahil. The second group was Paradee, Professor Ashe, and Natalie.

The first group carefully navigated the dangerous path around the sharp bend. McCray and Sadit moved extremely slowly. As they maneuvered their way across to the other side, Raahil stooped suddenly, fighting off the force of the wind and suction and trying desperately to maintain his balance. He froze, and McCray went back to help him. McCray reached out and grabbed Raahil's hand, serving as an anchor for Raahil until they reached the other side without any further incident.

The second group cautiously approached the narrow pathway. Paradee was at the head of the line, responsible for getting Ashe and Natalie across to the other side. The professor was second in line behind Paradee, and Natalie was at the rear.

"Do exactly what I do, and slowly take one step at a time," cautioned Paradee.

They slowly moved toward the other side. When they approached the dangerous bend directly above the swirling black hole, McCray gave Professor Ashe two thumbs-up for encouragement. Since Professor Ashe was overweight, not very athletic, and in his fifties, everyone was concerned for his safety.

As they approached the bend, the angle of the curve was more perilous than the three had imagined. The drop-off was extremely steep. The suction created by the swirling wind made it more dangerous and difficult. Professor Ashe's weight provided him with an extra burden as he walked sideways slowly and carefully. He pressed his back against the cavern wall as hard as he could and moved his feet an inch at a time. Ed Paradee moved at the same pace in order to stay close to Ashe.

As dirt and rock crumbled under him, Ashe slipped and lost his balance but quickly recovered. Terror was written all over his face. He was trembling as he took baby steps toward the other side. Ashe was in a trouble, and he knew it. Sensing death, Ashe panicked. Suddenly, he screamed, "I can't make it. I don't want to die!"

Paradee reached over to Ashe and said, "Don't worry; I got you, Professor. I promise I will not let you fall."

"But I can't move!"

"Yes, you can. Trust me," said Paradee confidently.

Ashe took two more tiny steps.

As they slowly maneuvered around the bend, Professor Ashe looked down at the dark, endless abyss and became extremely dizzy from the spinning motion of the vortex. He jerked his head back, catching himself from falling. When he pulled back, his head hit the cavern wall, and his glasses fell off. His instincts took over, and he tried unsuccessfully to grab the falling glasses. The momentum took him forward toward the abyss. Ashe tried desperately to grab the wall with his hand, but there was nothing to grasp. The suction from the black hole pulled him forward, drawing him toward the abyss.

As the professor began falling forward, Paradee forcefully slammed his right arm against Ashe's chest and reversed the professor's motion, pushing him back firmly against the wall. Ashe stumbled but gained control of his body.

The sudden and forceful motion caused the gravel under Paradee's feet to crumble. As he scrambled desperately to grab anything, he swiftly fell straight down into the hole. As he rapidly descended, the others could see his outstretched arms trying to grab onto anything as he plunged down into the abyss of hell. They could see excruciating pain, fear, and agony flash across his face as he tumbled through the swirling black hole. He knew he was going to die. He spun furiously in circles as the abyss swallowed him up.

The fall was dramatic, and everyone stood there shocked. Professor Ashe became hysterical and was paralyzed, unable to move. The fear on his face was intense; his eyes bulged out, and his lips trembled. McCray knew someone had to do something quick, or he could lose one more to this churning vortex. His immediate reaction was to go after Professor Ashe, so he moved sideways as quickly as he could till he reached the professor. He grabbed Ashe's hand while Natalie grabbed his shoulder, and he told the professor to move sideways slowly. Beyond hysteric now, Professor Ashe tried to pull away. McCray knew that a physical approach would not work, so he resorted to quiet persuasion.

McCray whispered, "Professor, the White House needs you to interpret the tablets and the artifacts. Don't you want to be the man who discovers the greatest archaeological find in human history? You've worked all your life for this opportunity; now buck up, and put your big pants on."

The thought of going down in history as the greatest archaeologist of all time provided the incentive Ashe needed to move on and survive.

After ten minutes of coaxing, Professor Ashe calmed down and slowly worked his way to the other side.

Natalie also reached safe ground. She was upset over the loss of Ed Paradee. Natalie had liked him very much. He had always been a gentleman, trying to keep Bags and some other grunts in line. She cautiously approached Professor Ashe, not knowing what to expect. Ashe did not show any resistance, so she put her arms around him to comfort him while Raahil patted him on the back. Ashe eventually gathered his composure.

"I think I'll be okay," Ashe said. "I've never seen anyone fall or die like that. It was a frightening and horrible experience, and I became panic stricken. The man died trying to save my life. I apologize for my behavior. I promise you it will not happen again."

"Professor, it was an accident," said Natalie. "He was doing his job. That is what Ed always did. He protected us; he was protecting you."

McCray said, "That part of the cavern is treacherous. The swirling black hole, the narrow pathway—it was all too dangerous. We're lucky we didn't lose anyone else. Ed was a good soldier, a great man, and the epitome of uncommon valor. We will miss him as a friend and a colleague."

McCray looked down at the swirling abyss in disbelief over his best friend's death. Although McCray was a hard ass and never showed his emotions, he was clearly upset. McCray had known Ed all his life. They had been neighbors growing up, and they'd gone to the same elementary, junior high, and high schools together. McCray had been the best man in Ed's wedding and was godfather to one of his three boys.

Natalie walked over to McCray and tried to console him. "I'm sorry. I know you guys were close, being born two months apart and everything. Ed told me you guys played together as infants and children, dated the same girls in high school, played the same sports, and just did about everything two friends could do together."

"Shit, Natalie, what do I tell his wife? She's only twenty-one years old with three kids; the oldest is four. I hope this mission is worth it. This place is a hellhole. It even smells like death. Why are we even here? Those SEALs are most likely dead, either killed by the al-Qaeda or victims of that pathway to hell that took Ed."

Angry and frustrated, McCray tossed Paradee's rifle into the black hole as a futile sign of retaliation and frustration. He knew it wouldn't serve any purpose, but that was the only thing he could think to do to get some retribution from the pathway to hell.

"I know this is no comfort at this time, but the company will take care of his family," promised Natalie.

"When you say the company, do you mean Premier Oil or the CIA? Because if you mean the CIA, you can forget it. The government only uses people to perpetuate their need for power. The politicians that make these decisions are supposed to be public servants, but we the people have become the public servants of the politicians. It's flat-out bullshit, and we both know it."

"What can I say? It is what it is!" said Natalie. "Sorry, good buddy, but we need to move out! If we don't complete this mission, Ed's death will be for nothing. You know that's not what Ed would want."

"You're right, but what about Ashe? Can he continue?" asked McCray.

"Ashe will recover. He may not seem it, but he's pretty resilient," said Natalie.

"Grab your gear and weapons, and let's move forward," said McCray.

Natalie put her right arm around Professor Ashe to provide support and comfort as they moved forward.

CHAPTER 26
The Discovery

July 9, 2012: Mound of Tiamat

Many of the men from Recon One and Rescue Eight gathered the weapons and bodies of the dead enemy soldiers. Several tended to their own wounded soldiers who were resting after a hard-fought battle. Savin and Colby went forward to find a suitable campsite.

As the men disposed of the dead bodies, McCray arrived with Professor Ashe, Natalie, and Raahil. Raahil walked over to Sadit and hugged his brother, both expressing signs of relief that the other was alive and uninjured. Ashe and Natalie just stared at the bodies. They had never witnessed anything like this—so much death in such a small area. They both headed toward the remaining members of the security team, and the professor asked, "What happened here?"

"What do you think happened?" Corrizo responded.

"What purpose does all this killing serve?" Professor Ashe asked.

"You need to ask the al-Qaeda terrorists that one," said Corrizo.

Natalie pointed over to the Navy SEALs and asked, "Are these the Navy SEALs from Recon One?"

Frank Corrizo said, "Yes, this is what's left of them. We arrived just in time, but it was a bloody battle, and we had causalities."

Ashe asked, "Where's Savin?"

Savin and Lieutenant Colby went forward to find a suitable campsite.

"I need to talk to them ASAP," said Ashe.

Corrizo pointed straight ahead and said, "You should find them about several hundred yards ahead."

As Natalie and Professor Ashe started to walk in the direction Corrizo had pointed, McCray asked, "Professor, where are you going?"

"Natalie and I are going to try to catch up with Savin and Colby."

McCray yelled, "You better wait for me. I have orders not to let you out of my sight."

As the three of them were leaving the area, Corrizo yelled out to McCray, "Where's Paradee?"

With a slight emotional tone in his voice, McCray softly replied, "He's gone!"

Only two hundred yards into their journey, Savin and Colby noticed the cave become lighter. As they progressed forward another hundred yards, the gold substance all over the floor and walls glowed like hundreds of lights. The gold powder lit up the cave and reflected off the tablets hanging from the walls. The scene was breathtaking and more beautiful than the other sights they'd seen earlier.

Rocky Savin turned to Lieutenant Colby and asked, "What are those objects all over the walls?"

Colby replied, "Man, this is incredible! They are Sumerian tablets, and they are very different from what we saw earlier."

"What do they mean?" asked Rocky.

Colby reviewed the writing on the tablets carefully before saying, "I think it is a message."

"I still don't know what you mean, Lieutenant."

"Someone or something is trying to tell us something."

Not getting a specific answer, Rocky changed the subject and asked, "Are we camping here?"

"No, we should go back about twenty yards and camp. It's a better strategic location."

No sooner did Savin and Rocky begin to unpack their gear than along came Professor Ashe, Natalie, and McCray. Ashe had an intense and anxious look on his face and walked purposely toward Savin and Colby.

"Lieutenant, let me introduce you to Professor Ashe, Natalie Duval, and Jerry McCray," said Savin. "The professor and Natalie are the scientists on the expedition. The White House asked that they serve as science advisors for the mission. Jerry is a member of my security team."

"Nice to meet you all," said Colby.

"Same here, Lieutenant," said the professor.

Natalie extended her hand and said, "Nice to meet you too, Lieutenant."

Colby reached out and shook hands with McCray and asked, "CIA, right?"

"Yes, we met in Afghanistan in 2009."

Colby asked Ashe, "And aren't you the famous Professor Ashe from Stanford University?"

"Yes, that's me in the flesh."

"I know this isn't a big deal, but I studied Sumerian culture at Harvard. I read your textbooks and attended a guest lecture you gave called 'Interpreting the Sumerian Culture.' It was fantastic."

"Did you study under Professor Alter?" asked the professor.

"Yes, I did," replied Colby.

The professor said, "His 'Alternative Interpretation of Sumerian and Other Ancient Cultures' paper was groundbreaking. I found it to be one of the most important and interesting theses written in this decade. In fact, Natalie here is a devoted follower of Alter's work."

"I knew Professor Alter well," replied Colby. "We would discuss this subject in detail for hours at Rose's Diner in South Boston. I could not get enough of it. Professor Alter would always say that you were the guru of ancient archaeological theory. Coming from him, I say that is pretty significant recognition. I must say, sir; I admire you and your work."

"You SEALs must be pretty important too," said Professor Ashe.

Lieutenant Colby asked, "What do you mean?"

"To get the White House's attention like this," replied Ashe.

"Yeah," said Colby. "I've been wondering about that. The assignment was supposed to be a simple recon mission but has evolved into something way beyond the simple task of gathering intelligence."

"What do you mean?" asked the professor.

"Professor, there's something very significant in this cave. The findings may be of great magnitude to science."

"Are you talking about the tablets and the gold substance?"

"Yes. Look, I don't know a tenth of what you know about this culture, but these tablets are different from the ones I saw earlier."

"What, there are more?" asked Ashe.

"Yes, over there," said Colby. He pointed to the area with the new tablets. Professor Ashe had a curious look on his face that quickly turned anxious as he walked over to the new set of tablets. He inspected each of the fifteen tablets slowly and carefully while Duval, Colby, and Savin stood to the side.

The area was covered with the gold substance, and there were gold artifacts everywhere, including gold statues of winged giants, some with human heads and some with bird or snake heads. One artifact depicted three humanoid figures with elongated heads holding the tree of life and another humanoid with a long, braided beard holding an image of the DNA double helix. Other artifacts depicted humanlike beings in winged vehicles; some looked like spaceships.

Just then many of the men from Recon One and Rescue Eight joined the group. Lieutenant Colby signaled to Sullivan to videotape everything. Recording every move, Sullivan focused the video camera on Ashe as the professor approached the tablets.

Ashe slowly walked about ten feet to the back of the cave. The back wall was about thirty feet by one hundred feet. The tablets with the pictographs were in the center of the wall, and each one covered a five-by-ten-foot area. Overwhelmed by what he saw, Professor Ashe fell to his knees and stayed there for a long time, looking up at the tablets. Ashe finally got up slowly, grabbed his camera, and started to take pictures. As he went from one tablet to the other, the professor's face flashed with excitement, like a child on his birthday. He went to the last tablet, then turned, walked back to the first one, and inspected each one again.

At that point, the professor walked past each tablet again, taking more snapshots. He pointed to them and said, "These pictographs tell a story of our beginning. They outline the origin and history of humanity and the mysteries of the universe. I cannot believe how much clearer and easier to translate this cuneiform writing is than the writing discovered in Nineveh in the 1800s and the tablets we discovered about a few miles back."

These new tablets had more form and a gold trim on the borders. Each tablet glowed, as if sunrays were reflecting off each one. They were breathtaking. The professor was amazed at how the tablets were etched perfectly on lapis lazuli slabs, like layers of quartz crystal, and not carved like the others. The writing was fused to the tablets.

The professor turned to everyone and said, "It's important to understand the properties of lapis lazuli and its place in history. Natalie, please explain to the group what it means."

"Yes, Professor," Natalie said. "In ancient time, lapis lazuli was a favorite stone of the Egyptians, Greeks, Romans, Sumerians, and Islamic nations. Some ancient cultures valued it as much as gold. It's used in some cultures to provide enhanced focus and uncommon clarity of thought. More importantly, it is said to enhance intellectual ability and memory and to stimulate the desire for knowledge, truth, and understanding. Lapis lazuli is associated with all forms of spiritual communication, and it is said to have healing properties for the mind and body. Considered the universal symbol of gods, power, spirit, vision, and wisdom, it is often referred to as the stone or symbol of truth."

Colby asked, "So what is the significance? Does the lapis lazuli provide some additional clue to the meaning of the tablets?"

"I'm not sure," replied Natalie. However, ancient cultures believed it provided protection from evil and darkness, and it was associated with the stars and the universe and was said to resemble the color of the heavens. Holy garments were dyed with lapis lazuli because that was the color the gods supposedly wore."

Finishing his initial investigation of the new tablets, the professor looked up at Savin, Colby, and Natalie and said, "There's so much here; I need some more time to interpret it."

Lieutenant Colby said, "Look, everyone's had a rough day. We will need rest and food. Professor, why don't you and your team take all the time you need to study the tablets, and we can sort this out tomorrow."

Colby ordered the men to set up camp for the night and asked Mendez to sort out the guard duty.

The professor yelled over to Natalie, "Let's get to work!"

CHAPTER 27
The Interpretation
of the Tablets

July 10, 2012: Mound of Tiamat

Lieutenant Colby and three of the Navy SEALs were up at five o'clock. Professor Ashe and Natalie Duval were still sleeping after a long night. They both had stayed up most of the night analyzing and interpreting the tablets.

As Lieutenant Colby made his breakfast, the cavern filled with the aroma of dark-roasted Colombian coffee. Within the next fifteen minutes, everyone else awoke, including Professor Ashe and Natalie Duval. Feeling extremely exhausted, Professor Ashe and Natalie went directly over to Lieutenant Colby and asked him for a cup of coffee. They both needed a kick of caffeine to function after ten hours of reviewing and analyzing the tablets.

The professor took a big sip of the coffee and complimented Colby on a great cup of java. Just then Rocky joined the group. Colby and Savin were anxious to hear the results of last night's work. After the third sip, the professor looked at Colby and Savin and said, "Gentlemen, we need to talk. Natalie and I worked through the night interpreting the tablets."

"Did you find out anything?" asked Colby.

"We could not decipher all the tablets but could determine some of the message."

"Okay," said Colby.

Rocky Savin asked, "What message, and who left it?"

"I'll get to that. Can we meet in private and go over the findings?" asked the professor.

Natalie, Savin, Colby, and the professor agreed to gather at the location of the first tablet. The professor got up and headed toward the tablets. He turned slightly, looking back over his shoulder at those following him, and said, "We've just scratched the surface of this archaeological find. This find is amazing, just remarkable!"

When they stopped at the first tablet, Rocky asked, "So what did you find out specifically?"

The professor said, "According to these writings, intelligent beings on earth date back to when the earth was at the beginning of the Cenozoic Era and Quaternary Period, called the time of the mammals and humans. The Quaternary is the most recent period of earth history and is viewed as the end of *Homo erectus* and the beginning of *Homo sapiens*."

"So how is this different from what we've been discussing the last few days?" Rocky asked.

"The tablets in these caves provide more concrete evidence than any others," replied Ashe. "The writing is very precise and the meaning very clear. Based upon my initial translation, whatever is in this cave could rewrite history; it could be a genuine and impactful history changer."

"Can you be more specific? How did you arrive at these conclusions?" asked Lieutenant Colby.

"I inputted the pictographs into my translator. Several of the tablets mention a vessel of life, the knowledge and truth of life in the universe."

"What does that mean?" asked Savin.

"According to the translation, this vessel contains the absolute knowledge of all life in the universe. The tablets say that this vessel is located in the heart of the cave, placed here by the bearers of knowledge. The vessel contains the necessary knowledge for us to survive as a species and save our planet from destruction."

"Who are the bearers of knowledge?" asked Rocky.

The professor responded, "I think the Anunnaki."

Rocky asked, "Who are the Anunnaki?"

Ashe said, "I'll get to that in a minute."

Anxious to hear the rest of the story, Colby said, "Okay, go on."

"First, I need to sit down. Does anyone have water?" asked Professor Ashe. "I'm parched."

Savin reached into his backpack and offered the professor a bottle of water. While Ashe guzzled most of the bottles in five seconds, Duval found a spot to sit next to the others.

Colby and Savin were eager to learn what the professor had discovered during his analysis of the pictograph writings.

"What did you learn about the tablets?" asked Colby.

"I'll try not to cover old ground, but it may be difficult not to, so bear with me," said Ashe.

They all gathered around the tablets. Ashe said, "What I have to tell you may seem incredible and implausible, but I can assure you it will change our history. So just listen carefully and keep an open mind. Let's start at the beginning with the first tablet and work our way in sequence to the last one.

"According to the pictographs displayed on the tablets, alien species colonized earth over 450,000 years ago. The first extraterrestrial species to settle and occupy the earth was called the Anunnaki. The Anunnaki originated from a star system in the Milky Way galaxy filled with planets with intelligent life, some like humans and some not.

"According to my translation, the Anunnaki came to earth on a mineral expedition and later colonized our planet. They were from the constellation Orion and a planet called Heaven that means 'Good.' The writings say the Anunnaki were holy and kind beings whose only goal was to continue their species and to share their knowledge and culture to all those who were godlike.

"Initially, the Anunnaki were the first to colonize earth and mine its valuable resources. According to the tablets, the earth was one of the most valuable planets in the galaxy due to its rich deposits of gold, copper, oil, platinum, and water. Our oxygen-rich atmosphere and close distance to the sun made it a favorable habitat for those in the Orion and Canis constellations.

"The Anunnaki desperately needed gold, which they refined with a mixture of earth's spring water and a chemical substance from their planet called *pataah*, which means 'sustainer of life.' Even their greatest technology could not replace the resources required to sustain their life. The earth was the only planet that had the exact materials and favorable conditions to create a chemical reaction to produce the substance they desperately needed."

"So this explains the gold substance," Colby said.

"Yes, some of it," said Ashe.

"Did they digest it?" asked Colby.

"Yes, but sometimes they had to take it intravenously. My translation, although preliminary, is that the Anunnaki exhausted their planet's most important resources. The substance extended their life centuries longer, and thus, the demand for gold increased as their population grew. Their supply of gold substance was exhausted, so they came to earth.

"The tablets indicate that the extraterrestrials' technology was far superior to ours and goes beyond our comprehension even today. The Anunnaki traveled swiftly through portals from one constellation to another and one planet to another in huge spaceships.

"In this next tablet, it talks about how they were able to travel freely through space across vast distances. It goes on to say that wormholes were used as superhighways to travel light-years in seconds. It was just as Einstein and Rosen theorized—space bends, shortening the distance between two points."

"That's impossible," said Savin.

The professor looked at Savin and said, "Let me show you; right here it clearly states, 'We the Anunnaki have perfected passageways between worlds.' They can create wormholes and use them as superhighways."

"I think that's impossible," said Savin.

"Well, I think it is possible," said Colby. "Go on, Professor."

"The Anunnaki could journey between parallel dimensions, which turned light-years into weeks, jumping from one celestial body to another, traveling in what they called interstellar lifeboats. A lifeboat was like an artificial planet. It was spherical, self-contained, and protected by an artificial ozone and atmosphere. They used a sophisticated form of terraforming to provide oxygen and a sustaining living habitat. A lifeboat resembled a planet like earth but half the size. The main difference between earth and an interstellar lifeboat was that the planet spaceship could control its direction and speed.

"According to the writings, the Anunnaki traveled to earth on an interstellar lifeboat called Nibiru. This planet spaceship was parked directly behind Jupiter on the far side of the Galilean moon Europa and was the twelfth planet in our solar system. In our terms, it can best be described as a mother ship. It is interesting to note that Europa is one the four Galilean moons of Jupiter and derives its name from a lover of Zeus."

Ashe pointed to one of the tablets and said, "This tablet depicts an interstellar lifeboat. See how the vehicle is shaped like a planet. See how blue it is. It looks like earth.

"As I told Rocky just recently, ancient-astronaut theorist Zecharia Sitchin referred to a twelfth planet called Nibiru that circled our sun once every three thousand six hundred years. Ironically, it appears he was partly right, but little did he know it was an artificial planet made by the Anunnaki."

Ashe pointed to another line on the tablet. "Look here; the interstellar lifeboat was carbon and iron based. Its core was comprised of a hydrogen-fueled engine that served both as a propulsion system and life-sustaining device. The surface was made of artificial dirt material consisting of rocks, crushed lava, stardust, gold, copper, processed waste, and other raw materials. As nature took over, rocks mixed with decaying leaves, roots, waste, vegetation, dead bugs, and animals, creating a sustaining soil.

"Similar to earth, the surface was used to grow food, cultivate flowers and plants, and feed livestock, as well as several other purposes. Rivers, lakes, streams, and oceans were strategically located close to life zones to provide habitat for aquatic life and the drinkable water all living species needed. Food and water were abundant."

Colby asked, "The Anunnaki traveled through wormholes in an artificial-planet spaceship called Nibiru? Is that your translation?" Colby pointed to the tablets and asked, "Is that what this group of tablets means?"

"Yes, I am sure," said Ashe.

"Unbelievable! Could your translation be incorrect?" asked Rocky.

"No!" Ashe said. "The writing is so clear I can translate it without the assistance of the ALICOMP. I just used the device to validate my findings."

The professor continued, "I cannot believe how alike our civilization is to theirs in many ways. See this picture here of a living pod. There were regions on Nibiru where the Anunnaki lived and worked called life zones. They were perfectly planned communities with work complexes, living pods with sustenance marketplaces for food, clothing, and everything anyone would need to exist comfortably. Nibiru had it all; it was the Garden of Eden."

Rocky Savin asked, "What do you mean by Garden of Eden?"

The professor said, "The Garden of Eden existed, but it wasn't on earth. The Garden of Eden was on the interstellar lifeboat. Nibiru was a paradise, just like the description in the Bible and in scriptures and poems in other cultures."

Rocky asked, "Can we go back and talk about space travel? My understanding is that the distance between Orion and earth is about fifteen hundred light-years. If that's correct, how could Nibiru travel through the cosmos and reach earth in weeks, days even, and sustain life?"

Ashe turned to the group again and said, "Why not? Earth does. We travel through the cosmos and have sustained life for thousands of years. As I said earlier, the only difference is they could control where they went, and we are on autopilot, per se. Nevertheless, space travel to them was conceived from another dimension we know nothing about."

Rocky said, "Another dimension? Are you making this up as you go along?"

"Okay, can we please continue?" said Colby.

"Look here; these two tablets are dedicated to explaining their civilization and social structure. It's fascinating stuff," said Ashe. "Life zones were democratic with organized governments and were clustered cultural centers, conveniently located for easy access to everything. They were the heart of all activates on the planet. Life zones were centers for courts, art, music, education, religion, commerce, and medicine.

"Nobody ever wanted for anything," said the professor, "but every Anunnaki was required to contribute to the existence and operation of the life zone. Everyone had a specific work function and responsibility to perform. Each Anunnaki was evaluated and made accountable. The reward structure was based upon performance and productivity levels.

"The social structure of the Anunnaki is unique. Their society can best be described as a democratic, socialistic, capitalistic, communal, and work-based social structure. Sounds almost like a contradiction, but according to the tablets, this societal structure worked perfectly for millions of years."

Ashe pointed to a line at the bottom of the sixth tablet. "Here, I find this fascinating. Those that did not contribute or work were incubated and gestated for a specified time. Subsequently, they were given another chance to become productive Anunnaki. If they failed again, they returned to incubation until their normal life cycle expired. The Anunnaki did not tolerate those who didn't work or were unproductive. Deviant and criminal behavior was not tolerated and was dealt with swiftly by permanent incubation."

Colby asked, "What is permanent incubation?"

"It's a state of unconsciousness—unable to taste, hear, touch, smell, and see," replied Ashe. "You exist in an unconscious state until your organs cease to function."

"We should try this method of behavior modification," Rocky said sarcastically. "Our society could use some more-productive citizens. Maybe we can eliminate the word *entitlement*."

"Come on, Rocky; get serious," said Colby. "Please go on, Professor."

Ashe moved to the next tablet and said, "Now it gets even more interesting. Although the Anunnaki were the first extraterrestrials to colonize earth, they were not the only alien species to visit or settle here. According to the writings, several extraterrestrials visited earth, not just one. The tablets refer to many different alien species from nearby stars that also needed gold and other minerals that were so abundant and plentiful on earth."

"So it wasn't just the Anunnaki who colonized earth," Colby said.

"Where did these other extraterrestrials originate initially?" asked Colby.

"They came from star systems in the Orion and Canis constellations. Some, like the Anunnaki, were from Orion. Other came from Sirius, a binary star in the Canis Major constellation. Orion's Belt was abundant with planets with intelligent life-forms."

The professor continued, "The Orion and Canis constellations are intergalactic nurseries where stars are frequently born. Orion's Belt consists of three primary stars: Alnitak, Alnilam, and Mintaka. Two of the three stars have planets that are in a zone conducive for intelligent life-forms, many of whom have visited earth for thousands of years.

"It's interesting to note that humans were taught how to group these stars into particular constellations so they eventually could determine where the various extraterrestrials originated."

Colby asked, "Where did they settle on earth?"

"Over time, a variety of species settled in various places on earth. They came to earth with different agendas, some good and some evil. Some came in peace, some in war. They divided the earth up into colonies, each species carving out their little piece of earth. Continents we now refer to as Africa, Europe, Asia, Australia, Antarctica, Atlantis, North America, and South America became sovereign, independent, self-governing colonies, each ruled by different species."

Ashe pointed to the middle section of the tablet and said, "According to this line here, Atlantis was a continent in the north Pacific Ocean between Japan and North America. The continent was submerged during the great flood and an earthquake that followed.

"Extraterrestrial species came in many sizes, skin colors, and varied characteristics that distinguished one species from another. The extraterrestrials include the Anunnaki, Nordics, Pleiadians, Grigori, Grays, Nephilim, Reptilians, Nagas, Sirians, Mayans, Zeus, and Poseidon. They colonized various parts of the earth. The Anunnaki settled in Iraq, the Grigori in the Middle East, and the Reptilians in Asia. The Nagas laid claim to India, the Nephilim settled the Near East, and the Sirians colonized Africa and Australia. The Mayans inhabited Mexico, and the Star People settled North and South America. The Nordics and Pleiadians thrived in Scandinavia and Eastern Europe, and the Zeus and Poseidon inhabited Western Europe and Atlantis. There is also some reference to a group called the Watchers, but it refers to several different extraterrestrial species, not just one."

"Did the aliens get along with each other?" asked Rocky.

The professor paused for a moment and then said, "That's not totally clear yet. However, there was another extraterrestrial alien species called the Saturnians. The Saturnians were a cruel, evil, immoral species who were very powerful and wreaked havoc and destruction everywhere. The species were a rogue, outlaw species that waged war against everyone, abducted humans for many purposes, and wanted man to follow their violent and sinful ways.

"The next tablets go on to say that all the alien species competed for limited resources required for sustaining life. The extraterrestrials fought between different species and among their own. In fact, there appears to have been a final galactic battle on earth for power and control of the planet. The tablets detail a scene of smaller spacecraft resembling fiery chariots being launched from interstellar lifeboats, mother ships, and ground bases on earth. These space vehicles discharged fiery and glowing weapons that resembled blue lightning at each other. There's also mention of a highly destructive weapon that only the Saturnians would use. The other extraterrestrials possessed such weapons but had pledged not to use them."

"Yeah, so they are just like humans: violent, warlike, and hungry for power and wealth," said Rocky.

"The Anunnaki had no choice but to wage war with other less benevolent species to maintain some semblance of order on earth and in the universe. The Anunnaki fought against the evil ones to protect themselves and their way of life, and they protected humanity from extraterrestrials who perpetrated atrocities against the human race."

Professor Ashe paused for a moment and turned to Colby, Rocky, and Natalie and said, "There's something very important that I have not yet been able to translate." Ashe pointed to an important section of the tablets. "This explains why they chose and colonized earth. It is puzzling because there are other carbon-based, terrestrial planets composed of rock all over the universe."

"So why did they come to earth?" asked Colby.

"The tablets indicate that they came to earth in need of earth's minerals. My intuition tells me there's something else, but I can't put my figure on it."

"Do the tablets say why they left and if they are coming back?" asked Savin.

"These are important questions," replied the professor.

Colby asked, "Does it say who won the great battle?"

"I don't know," Professor Ashe said. "I told you there are many sections of the tablets that I cannot interpret." Ashe pointed to the third, fourth, and fifth tablets from the end. "I'm having trouble translating these three tablets."

Ashe walked over to the last two remaining tablets: tablets fourteen and fifteen. "These tablets are a set of instructions of some sort, but notice that these don't have any of the gold substance on them like the others. They look new."

"So these artifacts were just recently placed here?" asked Rocky.

"It looks that way," answered Ashe. "But here is the most interesting section of the tablets. There is a golden vessel that contains knowledge of the universe and our place in it. According to the tablets, the vessel was enclosed in the back wall of the cavern, and the instructions written on these two tablets hold the key to accessing them."

Ashe stood in front of the back wall of the cave for about five minutes reviewing his notes. His eyes focused intensely on every inch of the two tablets. Colby, Rocky, and Natalie watched, impatiently waiting for the next extraordinary piece of information.

Savin turned to Colby and asked, "Do you believe this? I don't."

"I know there's more evidence. We just need to be patient."

Last night, the professor had taken meticulous, detailed notes in his journal, documenting everything. His notes indicated that the instructions included three different possible sequences of codes that must be entered in a specific order to open the wall and gain access to the inner chamber. But they were not codes as he knew them. They were small pictographs that need to be touched in an exact sequence. The professor was a little nervous about what might be behind the wall, so he had waited until now, when everyone was there, before he tried to open it. The professor tried the first sequence, and it did not work. He tried the second sequence, and it did not work either. Everyone, especially the professor, became frustrated and disappointed that they could not uncover an important key to the riddle of the mystery of human life.

"This is impossible," said Ashe. "The instructions are vague when it comes to the exact order the pictographs are to be executed."

"You'll get it; think positive," said Natalie.

Focusing on the last possible sequence, Ashe ran his fingers over the symbols, pressing his palms softly over the surface of certain pictographs on the tablets. He then touched the corners of the last two tablets in a clockwise manner. Ashe looked back at his notes, and he touched five more pictographs counterclockwise.

All of sudden, one of the tablets opened slowly, swinging outward from the center of the wall toward the professor. Then a digital system of some type on a shelf slid out from the inside of the quartz wall. The device was a large, transparent touch screen with sixty small, colorful pictographs stationary in the air. The crystal clear screen served as an interface with Sumerian-like hieroglyphs used to instruct the apparatus. The tablet instructions indicated that commands were executed by voice or touch. The digital device was the gateway to something behind the cave.

Ashe again looked at his notes in his journal. He touched three pictographs in a specific order. Nothing happened. Thinking that he'd entered them in the wrong sequence, Ashe carefully changed the order he'd touched the pictographs.

Everyone was now getting even more anxious. The professor was becoming very impatient and said, "I am out of options."

Natalie asked the professor if she could try.

"Sure," said the professor as he passed his notebook to her.

Natalie said, "Professor, it says here that the device is touch and voice activated."

"How can you voice activate it if you don't know the right words?" Ashe asked.

"There have been clues since we got here," said Natalie. "I know it's a wild guess, but I see a common thread."

"Go on," said the professor.

"Who's pertinent in the creation story?

"According to the clues from the artifacts, Enki, Adam, and Tiamat," said the professor.

"Yes, but let's substitute the name Adama for Adam," said Natalie.

"Why?" asked the professor.

"According to Genesis, God created Adam as the first man. The Torah explains the name Adam. According to Judaism's scripture, the Hebrew word for earth is *adama*. Adama is a variant of Adam. God formed man from the dust of the earth, and that connection with Adama, earth, is the basis for man's name."

Natalie went through and touched the pictographs on the tablet in the same sequence as the professor did, but said, "Eniki, Adama, and Tiamat."

With the ancient pronunciation of the names, there was a sudden loud resonance. The sound was piercing, intense, and deafening. The high-pitched, earsplitting frequency put tremendous pressure on everyone's eardrums. Everyone initially covered their ears, and many bent over in pain. After a few moments, the high-pitched sound quickly passed. Without warning, a large crystal slab opened gradually into a large interior room.

The door was enormous and made of pure gold and crystal. It gleamed brightly and had an aura surrounding the metallic frame. Cuneiform carvings were etched all over it, along with statue-type artifacts of large, winged humanoids and drawings of constellations.

When the door opened just an inch, a bright, almost-blinding gold light illuminated the entire cavern. At first, it was so concentrated they could not see what was behind the door. The intensity of the light slowly diminished as the door opened completely, and they could see more clearly.

In the background, there was an altar made of quartz. Behind the altar were quartz tubes resembling organ pipes. Rubies and emeralds sparkled on a gold vessel, resembling a chalice, that sat in the center of the altar. Gray, clay, earthlike material lined the vessel.

When Professor Ashe approached the altar, a shining light reflected off the vessel and crystals and enhanced the sparkle emanating from the gold and jewels. The professor became engulfed in the bright glow of the light, and it created a halo effect around his body. The scene was spiritual, resembling depictions of gods in scriptures and religious paintings.

As the professor moved closer, beautiful, transcendent voices began humming harmoniously. The humming got louder and louder, and then out of nowhere, a bright light burst out of the vessel. Trumpets roared, announcing something that had to be truly amazing. At that moment, a three-dimensional hologram image of the Ark of the Covenant sprung out of the chalice. The picture was radiant and clear and had no backdrop except thin air.

The four-foot-long, two-foot-wide ark looked to be made of quartz overlaid with pure gold. It glowed and looked magnificent. Four gold rings were fastened to the two sides of the ark. Two poles were placed through the rings to carry the ark. A cherubim was sitting on the top cover of the ark.

When the professor and Natalie approached the object, the cover of the ark opened slowly. An image appeared of four humanoids huddled together in a circle around a surgical station in a space vehicle. There was no mistaking that they were extraterrestrials.

They were performing a medical procedure on two beings lying in separate gurneys next to each other. One being was hairless with womanlike features. She was a female extraterrestrial with large eyes, thin lips, a small nose, very fine skin, and an elongated skull and pointed head. About eight feet tall with large, feathery wings, she looked similar to the other four extraterrestrials in the circle. However, the body on the other gurney looked prehistoric with features similar to *Homo erectus* and *Pithecanthropus erectus.*

One of the four extraterrestrials held a vessel that resembled a chalice, while a second one held a long syringe. The extraterrestrial inserted a huge, long needle directly into the rib of the prehistoric being and slowly removed fluid from the body and then performed the same procedure on the female extraterrestrial. The extraterrestrial then injected the two DNA samples into the clay-lined chalice and mixed them together. The third extraterrestrial, using a second, larger syringe, withdrew the

DNA fluid from the chalice and inserted it into the womb of the female extraterrestrial. As he inserted the fluid, the female looked over at the prehistoric being with a proud, benign, and companionate smile. At that moment, the video became static and ended.

Everyone in the cave was mesmerized and speechless. They stood there stunned as they tried to make sense of the content of the video. Savin looked up with a confused expression. He slowly moved his eyes to focus on Professor Ashe and asked, "What was that, Professor?"

The professor turned and stared at the group, trying to formulate the correct words to describe the video. Everyone was silent, waiting for the professor to explain the remarkable event they had just witnessed. He glanced down at his journal and slowly turned to the page that contained his notes on tablets ten and eleven.

He concentrated on his notes for a while before he said, "Tablets ten and eleven address the Sumerian creation story. According to these tablets, the Anunnaki upgraded humans, making us more intelligent, humanoid, and in their image. The DNA of extraterrestrials was mixed with the DNA from prehistoric man. The Anunnaki and other extraterrestrials seeded mankind and subsequently bore hybrids, part human and part alien. This offspring inherited alien traits such as skin color, facial features, body type, height, and other physical attributes."

Rocky Savin looked at Professor Ashe intensely and asked, "What the hell does that mean?"

Professor Ashe quickly looked over at Rocky and said, "This is how we were created. We were reengineered by extraterrestrials. This is our beginning!"

CHAPTER 28

MJ-12

July 11, 2012: Washington, DC

CIA Director Nathan Stiles had been given the responsibility of reassembling MJ-12. A secret government/military/private organization, MJ-12 was a subcommittee of a larger group called Rapture. Rapture had been established during the Great Depression to implement government and economic policies to turn the economy around and maintain order.

Rapture committee members were responsible for defusing anything that could potentially disrupt the status quo or humans' way of life. The members reviewed and analyzed events that could disrupt world order, like climate change, epidemics, meltdown of the financial market, terrorism, and alien encounters of the first, second, third, fourth, and fifth kinds. A close encounter of the first kind was a visual sighting of an unidentified flying object (UFO). A close encounter of the second kind was a UFO that caused a physical effect or trace, like an impression on the ground such as scorched earth or chemical evidence. A third kind was a UFO encounter where creatures such as humanoids, robots, or humans were present. The fourth type was an alien abduction, and a close encounter of the fifth kind was the exchange of information, a knowledge transfer of technology, culture, religion, or so on, between extraterrestrials and humans.

MJ-12 was a spinoff of Rapture established to focus more attention on encounters with extraterrestrials after the Roswell incident. Their mission was to investigate incidents involving a close encounter of any kind and discredit these encounters with disinformation. For over sixty years, MJ-12 had covered up any evidence of UFOs or extraterrestrials by invoking MAD, misinform and deny.

If the encounter was credible, MJ-12's job was to determine the extraterrestrial's intentions and capabilities. If there was any physical evidence, such as alien technology or bodies, MJ-12 would take it to a Nevada military installation for study and reengineering. MJ-12 often employed black operations to discredit and cover up extraterrestrial encounters and dealt only with problems classified as "social changers."

Corporate and banking money funded MJ-12, but these institutions had no idea how the money was used. Contributors thought it was a secret commerce fund responsible for perpetuating their prominence in business. Corporate sponsors were carefully selected and provided with special tax exemptions and given favorable consideration for federal contracts. The money had to come from somewhere other than the US budget in order to avoid disclosure. Scrutiny from ambitious congresspersons, newspaper reporters, or federal employees from the office of the inspector general could disclose MJ-12, so a secret, private fund was set up.

The day after the president ordered the reassembling of MJ-12, CIA Director Stiles had arranged an emergency meeting to be held in Washington. Military and government escorts were immediately assembled and dispatched to provide transportation to MJ-12 members so they could be in Washington in the morning. Since most of the government and military members of MJ-12 were already in Washington, only a few scientists and two CEOs from private corporations had to be flown in for the meeting.

The 10:00 a.m. meeting was held in the White House Cabinet Room. Usually, MJ-12 meetings were held in a secret government compound donated by a wealthy banking family that could be accessed only by air. However, since the incident was ranked as critical on the high-impact scale, it was imperative that the president be close to all the military and logistic resources at the White House.

All the committee members were present except one, the committee's chairman, who also happened to be the CEO of the largest corporation in the world. Most of the members knew each other through business or government activities, so not many introductions were necessary. CIA Director Nathan Stiles gave a short ninety-minute briefing, and then the president entered the conference room and welcomed the group as he sat at the head of the table.

The president said, "Thank you all for coming on such short notice. As members of MJ-12, you were chosen for your expertise in specific areas. You're responsible for analyzing information gathered by a special top-secret agency. Congress and the public do not know this agency exist, so I trust that you will never acknowledge or discuss this secret operation.

"I want to reemphasize the importance of this work and the oath of secrecy you took. For those of you who are new, you cannot tell your wife, husband, girlfriend, boyfriend, mother, anyone. Any leak will be a breach of national security and will result in serious consequences. Is that clear? All present nodded yes.

"So let us begin. For those who may not know, let me provide you with some background. It appears we have a possible situation in Sumer, Iraq. Several days ago, our satellites picked up extraordinary heat signatures from this area followed by an extraterrestrial encounter also witnessed by two young shepherds. There are several sites with heat signatures all over the world but no others with this level of intensity.

"As you would expect, our government has been keeping close encounters with extraterrestrials under wraps for national security reasons. Over time, there have been various discoveries like what we discovered this week. In the past, we've found tablets, artifacts, art, and monoliths, but we've also recovered WMDs at certain sites.

"People like Elizabeth Harris, the head of the special interagency team, and other secret agents have investigated, destroyed, or confiscated the evidence and reverse engineered the technology when possible. The stealth bombers and drones are reverse-engineered alien technology, which, I might add, companies in this room have benefited from. No one wants the WMDs getting in the wrong hands, and so far, we've been lucky to contain the technology. However, there have been some close calls over the years.

"So where does all this take us, and where do we go from here? In response to the heat signatures, our government immediately sent a top-secret team to Sumer to investigate and gather information. Due to the presence of al-Qaeda soldiers and limited alternatives to further investigate the matter, the top-secret team left Sumer and returned to Andrews Air Force Base two days later to analyze the evidence they'd discovered."

One of the members of the committee politely interrupted the president and asked, "Does this mean the extraterrestrials have returned?"

"That's a good question," replied the president. "I'm not sure yet, but it appears so."

The president continued, "Four Navy F-15 fighter jets completed a bombing mission of the same site. In the process, the bombs unintentionally killed thirty al-Qaeda enemy soldiers, burying them alive. After a heavy and intensive bombardment of the cave, however, the mission failed to destroy the evidence, creating an even larger entrance to the cave.

"We could not let this information get back to our enemies or the public, so we immediately deployed a platoon of fourteen of our best Navy SEALs to recon the cave. Due to national security, the Navy SEALs received minimal information. Their orders were to investigate the insurgence of al-Qaeda in the area, period, nothing else. These same Navy SEALs stumbled over Sumerian tablets and other artifacts providing evidence of a superior civilization that resided in this area thousands of years ago.

"Your task over the next few days is to review the evidence gathered at Sumer and analyze the findings, develop possible scenarios, and make recommendations. In the meantime, we've implemented MAD. CIA Director Nathan Stiles briefed you on the goals and objectives of your tasks. So let's get to work, and we will reconvene in a few days. Thank you."

CHAPTER 29
The Vessel

July 11, 2012: Central Command, Kabul, Afghanistan

It was night at Central Command. The communications unit had been given specific orders to try to contact Recon One. After several failed attempts and nothing but white noise, they miraculously got through.

Two-Way turned quickly to someone in the room and told him to get General Hitchens immediately. Hitchens walked through the door into Central Command's headquarters building and said, "No need; I'm here. What's up?"

"We got through to Recon One," replied Two-Way.

"Well, don't just stand there; get on with it," barked Hitchens.

Two-Way blurted, "Recon One, provide your position, over."

"Roger that. This is Recon One; we are inside the cave about seven miles from the entrance where the Chinook birds initially air-dropped us several days ago."

The general moved hastily toward the communication workstation and grabbed a headset. He looked at Two-Way and said, "Boy, don't just stand there; call the White House, and let's see if we can get a three-way video link."

"Lieutenant Colby, what's your status?" asked General Hitchens.

"We are good, thanks to Rocky Savin and his team," said Lieutenant Colby. "We engaged in a skirmish with an al-Qaeda platoon and were pinned down. It was a stalemate. The battle would have gone on for days if it weren't for the reinforcements. Savin and his men ambushed the enemy from the rear. If it weren't for their help, we wouldn't be talking right now. Thank you for sending reinforcements, General. However, sir, there is one more thing. We lost four good men."

"Who?"

"Jacobs, Collins, Calamari, and Paradee," Colby said.

"Do you mean Ed Paradee?"

"Yes, General."

"Damn-good man; I knew his father, great soldier. Four soldiers, what a waste; I hope this is worth it."

Colby went on and informed the general of the gold substance, the tablets, and the holographic video. He finished his overview and turned the briefing over to Professor Ashe for more detail on the meaning of the tablets and what they had seen on the video.

Once Professor Ashe finished the briefing, General Hitchens asked, "Is this authentic, or could this possibly be a hoax perpetrated by the enemy?"

The professor said, "In all due respect, General, that is absurd. I can assure you that this is genuine and that beings not from this earth purposely left all this evidence here."

Colby strongly interjected, "General, the professor's interpretation is very credible and backed by a video displayed on technology we've never seen before."

Savin added, "I had my doubts, but it is definitely real."

"General, we are all positive that this was a message from extraterrestrial beings," said Colby.

"Will the aliens return?" General Hitchens asked.

The professor replied, "I'm not sure!"

After the debriefing, Hitchens's mind started racing. He realized the importance of this discovery and the possible consequences on mankind and society. He knew he needed to brief the president.

"Sir, I have the White House on the line," Two-Way said.

"Great. Set up that video link ASAP; we will need it later."

"General, are we on a secure line?" asked the president.

"Yes, we are, Mr. President. We are the only two on the line."

General Hitchens briefed the president on the situation. The president did not seem surprised, and it seemed that maybe he had already known something about the situation and the current state of affairs.

The president said, "This is quite a story, General. If it's true, this encounter is the biggest discovery in the history of mankind and will most likely change our civilization forever."

General Hitchens said, "According to Lieutenant Colby, Rocky Savin, and Professor Ashe, the writing on the tablets is authentic."

"Do you believe it?" asked the president.

"I believe in Lieutenant Colby and Rocky Savin, Mr. President, and if they say it is legit, it is so."

"Could al-Qaeda have planted all the tablets and all the other items found in the cavern?"

"I wondered that too," said General Hitchens. "However, Colby and Savin indicated that neither al-Qaeda nor their allies could have pulled off such an elaborate hoax. Professor Ashe also supported that conclusion and went as far as to say that no one on this planet has the knowledge to pull off such an extravagant ruse."

"General, I don't care about their opinions regarding this matter," said the president. "We cannot rule out any possibility."

"As you say, Mr. President," replied Hitchens.

"General, we cannot let Recon One and Rescue Eight out of the cave with that vessel. If what you are telling me is true, we could have a major meltdown of institutions all over the world. The possible chaos could be devastating. The impact to our economy, military, religions, world markets, law, and order would be beyond comprehension. To put it bluntly, it will all go to hell! Do you want to be responsible for that? If the White House hadn't acted quickly in 1947 in New Mexico, the shit would have hit the fan back then, and who knows what America would be like now."

"What do you mean?" asked General Hitchens.

"I am talking about Roswell, New Mexico."

General Hitchens said, "I thought the Air Force concluded that to be a weather balloon, and that was later confirmed by Project Blue Book."

"That was public disinformation, what we call MAD, misinform and deny."

"Mr. President, sir, no disrespect, but are you selling the American people short?"

The president said, "Since that incident in 1947, every president has been briefed on the Roswell incident and the possible repercussions of extraterrestrial encounters. We were all told about the alien beings, called Grays, that crashed in the desert. The Grays were part of an alien Alliance of Angels. We retrieved their spaceship, and we been trying to reverse engineer their technology for over sixty years. The spaceship and the bodies have been hidden two thousand feet below in a secret military facility in the Nevada desert.

"All throughout history, presidents have been dealing with the dilemma of trying to maintain order in our society versus disclosing the truth. In the 1960s, President Kennedy had to deal with a rouge alien species that tried to start a war between the United States and the Soviet Union by creating a delusion that both governments were launching a nuclear attack.

"By some unknown miracle, both governments determined that neither had such intentions and that extraterrestrial forces were making it look like both were launching nuclear weapons. Both governments then entertained the idea of joining forces, but somehow that got derailed quickly. The president intended to tell the American people, but that too was sabotaged by someone or something.

"President Ronald Reagan did try to warn world leaders at the United Nations in 1980s. He said, 'How quickly our differences world-wide would vanish, if we were facing an alien threat from outside this world.' He repeated this several times in other speeches and even one with President Gorbachev. He also attempted to build a weapon system in space to defend ourselves, but it was too expensive, and there was no real support for it.

"Unfortunately, only a few knew the truth, and President Reagan could not divulge his real reasons for those statements. Reagan, like the past ten or so president, took an oath never to say a word about it. They probably would have assassinated him if he'd said anything—you know, make it look like an accident, a lone gunman, or a conspiracy."

General Hitchens asked, "Who is 'they'?"

"They're a secret government organization called MJ-12, which is comprised of CEOs of large corporations, scientists, military leaders, and government officials. They are responsible for defusing anything that can potentially disrupt the status quo, our way of life, world order, or our financial markets. Their job is to discredit all encounters and deny them with disinformation.

"The organization has big money and uses clandestine operators. Due to national security concerns, their activities are classified. MJ-12 controls a significant amount of top-secret information, most of which is in the Beginning file."

"What is the Beginning file?" asked Hitchens.

"Without going into too much detail, the Beginning is a top-secret file that outlines the existence of extraterrestrial species and how they reengineered our race. The file includes close encounters of the third and fourth kinds, including the recovery of extraterrestrial humanoid bodies at Roswell. The file also documents abductions, like the Hills in New Hampshire and that lumberjack in Arizona. The file records numerous authentic encounters from all over the world, including several

Russian and Mexican encounters, the one involving the military at the Rendlesham Forrest in England, and the ones at various nuclear weapon launch facilities."

"Additionally, the Beginning file contains the discoveries of an ancient, secret, high-tech Sumerian library that the US military found in the Retezat Mountains in Romania in 2006 that also records the origin of humankind. The Sumerians settled this area after leaving Iraq. The Beginning file also includes a list of technology we created from the efforts to reverse engineer alien technology and those corporations who benefited. I've only heard of and have never seen the files related to the alien experiments and their efforts to reengineer our DNA. We have been using some of the same procedures to artificially inseminate humans."

General Hitchens asked sarcastically, "So this is about money, the disruption of the economy and our financial systems?"

"I will not honor that question with a response, General."

The president told General Hitchens that the only reason he'd shared this information was to make sure Hitchens understood the importance of keeping the Sumer encounter top secret. Hitchens was never to divulge what the president had told him, and he could not let any of the evidence leave the cave. If he did, it would be a breach of national security, and he and his family would be in grave danger. At the conclusion of the briefing, the president paused and said, "General, I think you get the drift. Let's bring the others into the conversation."

Two-Way established a three-way videoconference between Central Command, the White House, and Recon One. Two-Way looked up at General Hitchens and said, "Sir, we are streaming video." Seconds later, the White House, Recon One, and Hitchens came online in a split screen showing all parties.

"Mr. President," General Hitchens said.

"Are Lieutenant Colby and Professor Ashe there?" asked the president.

"Yes, Mr. President, we're here," responded Lieutenant Colby.

The president said, "I'm here with the director of national intelligence and the chairman of the Joint Chiefs of Staff. Elizabeth Harris from the National Geospatial Intelligence Agency is on a conference line from Iraq. I am glad you and most of your men are alive and well, Lieutenant; great job, son! And Rocky Savin, you and your men are a credit to your country. I want to thank you all for a job well done."

Professor Ashe said, "Mr. President, I am Professor Ashe from Stanford."

"Yes, Professor Ashe, I know your work well."

"Sir, I can assure you this is a legitimate find and will change science forever."

"I have many questions," said the president. "How do we know that this is authentic?"

Colby quickly responded, "Sir, the tablets and a vessel provide real substantial evidence. It is genuine."

Elizabeth Harris interjected, "Lieutenant Colby, we met in Afghanistan two years ago."

"Sure, hi, Elizabeth, I remember you."

She asked, "Lieutenant, regarding the gold substance, can you give me any more details on it?"

"I've never seen anything like this before. The substance is smooth, soft, and granular in nature. There is no smell; however, it has an interesting aurora-like quality about it."

"We have reports that there is a material in that vicinity that is a nuclear by-product."

"Nuclear, do you mean radioactive?"

Harris responded, "No, let's not get crazy. It is neither toxic nor radioactive. Everyone is safe from any contamination."

"Are we sure that the vessel is not a WMD of some kind?" asked the president.

"I don't think so, sir," said Colby. "The tablets indicate that it contains only knowledge and technology designed to help humanity understand the truth of life and to improve our civilization. This message was constructive, not destructive."

"No disrespect intended, Lieutenant, but could this be a hoax of some kind?" asked the president.

"Mr. President, I can assure you this is no hoax."

"I can't take that chance, Lieutenant. There is too much at stake."

The president told Lieutenant Colby and the rest of the group to sit tight and he would get right back to them with their orders. The video link ended. However, the president instructed General Hitchens to stay on the line, and then he politely asked the chairman of the Joint Chiefs of Staff and the director of intelligence to leave the room, informing them it was a personal matter. At the same time, the conference call with Elizabeth Harris was terminated.

As the three-way satellite video link ended, the president and General Hitchens remained on the line.

"Are you there, General?" asked the president.

"Yes, Mr. President."

"We have a problem on our hands. We cannot let them leave with that vessel," ordered the president. "I need you to contact Lieutenant Colby and order him to secure the area and keep the archaeologists from tampering with anything. We got what we need from Ashe."

"So what are you suggesting we do, sir?"

"We must leave the vessel there and seal the cave up with explosives. We need to bury or destroy any evidence of this encounter. When everyone is out of the cave, we will send in the drones and seal it forever. We cannot take a chance."

"So I understand, sir. You want us to blow up this cave twice—once with our ground troops and then with drones?"

"Look, General, I saw what they saw. We had Natalie Duval secretly record the entire incident, both the tablets and the video communication. She uploaded the video to a special satellite we'd positioned over the area. We reviewed the recording while everyone waited for the connection to the three-way video link."

Confused, General Hitchens said, "I thought Natalie was a graduate student at Stanford?"

"Yes," said the president, "but Natalie Duval is also a special under-cover secret agent assigned to the division of external technology (ET) at the Defense Intelligence Agency. Since the professor is a leading expert in Sumerian culture and there is a close link between extraterrestrials and the Sumerians, Natalie was to provide us with intelligence. Any major find in the field will most likely come to Professor Ashe's attention, so we needed someone inside to get close to him. She was our mole. Additionally, Professor Ashe's inventions are revolutionary in his field, and we needed someone to make sure the technology did not get into the wrong hands."

"Do you mean the Finder and his language-interpreting devise?" asked General Hitchens.

"Yes, we need to make sure this technology does not get into the wrong hands."

"Now I understand why you wanted her to be a part of the rescue team."

"Natalie has been with us for fourteen years. She was recruited out of high school and educated in various sciences, including archaeology and anthropology. Natalie's grandfather's computer company was a benefactor of alien technology, so they obviously supported her joining the program. We originally planted her at Stanford as an undergrad and eventually as an intern for Professor Ashe. Professor Ashe then hired Natalie as a grad assistant. She now has her master's and is finishing her thesis for a doctorate. That is her cover."

The president continued, "Elizabeth Harris and Natalie are part of a secret government agency whose mission is to investigate unusual phenomena, especially extraterrestrial events like sightings and abductions. Only a handful of people know this organization exists. The agency was created in 1947 in response to the Roswell incident."

General Hitchens said, "I'm confused. The CIA director informed me that the White House was investigating Natalie Duval."

"That is true," said the president. "We recently received some counterintelligence on her activities, so we needed to determine if it was true. It was not."

"Sir, if you don't mind me asking, how could you obtain a video recording from within the cave? No wireless signal could get through because of interference we experienced."

"The whole time we had the NSA special ops technology unit jamming the signal with a new device Tomorrow Technology, out of San Jose, California, had developed for us. We had to control the information and could not let it leak out to the public, so we made it look like something in the cave was causing interference with the communication."

"I understand your concern about this information getting out to the public or to our enemy. But, sir, the people can handle this. It could be a ray of hope for everyone."

"A ray of hope for what?" asked the president. "You want everyone in the world to put their faith and hope into an alien intervention? We can't even get the Iraqis, Syrians, and Afghans to stop fighting among themselves, so how are we going to convince the world that this is a real thing? Christ, there is so much mistrust between their own people, so why would they put their trust in an unknown alien species we know nothing about? That's ridiculous!"

"What if the aliens mean what they say?" said General Hitchens. "Knowledge transfer could result in a better life for everyone and could be a positive world changer—no hunger, new medical cures, technology we never dreamed off, no more wars. An encounter does not have to be a negative experience."

"Come on, General; you're being naive," the president said laughingly.

"No disrespect, Mr. President, but look around you. There is hunger, disease, war, suffering, corruption, and crime all over earth. We are on the verge of destruction. It gets worse every day. Right this minute, I am sitting on a powder keg, and it is ready to drop some heavy shit on us. Pardon my expression, sir."

"General, I am going to tell you something that only a few know, but you must promise me never to mention this information to anyone. Understood?"

"Mr. President, you have my word."

"Well, we've found similar heat signatures with tablets, artifacts, and art all over the world. WMDs were usually also present at these sites."

"Why did the extraterrestrials leave the weapons behind?" asked General Hitchens.

"I don't know. But I do know that special agents like Elizabeth Harris and Natalie Duval have investigated and destroyed evidence of various encounters over the past decades. In a situation like the second Iraq War, we invaded that country because their government found an alien site with WMDs close to Baghdad. Our special ops were able to find and destroy the weapons extraterrestrials had left behind. According to the documentation we've found, the various species fought constantly."

"What did they fight over?"

The president said, "They fought over the same things we fight over—power, wealth, and land. Also, there is some evidence that certain species frowned upon extraterrestrials taking earth women and having hybrid children. The benevolent extraterrestrials did not tolerate how the malevolent ones raped, pillaged, and made slaves of humans."

"Mr. President, I'm flattered you have such trust in me, but why are you telling me all this?"

"I need you to know the gravity of all this, so you will understand why we need to destroy this evidence to protect our way of life."

"So you want me to order my men to blow up the cavern with the vessel in it."

"Yes, and shortly afterward, we will send in the drones. We need to put closure to this immediately."

"I will make sure the orders are carried out precisely, sir."

CHAPTER 30
The Tomb of Human History

July 11, 2012: Mound of Tiamat

General Hitchens hung up from his conversation with the president. Then, carrying out the president's directive, he contacted Lieutenant Colby.

"Lieutenant, everyone is to leave the cave immediately," ordered Hitchens. "I have orders to blow it up ASAP. Your job is to carry out these orders. The tablets and vessel must be sealed tight in the cave. Also, son, no one can know we're blowing up the cave except for those absolutely essential to the mission."

Hitchens directed Colby to deploy and detonate the explosives the expedition team had brought once everyone had cleared the area. He outlined specific instructions even down to the placement of the explosives. The orders were precise, as if command had a blueprint, a map of the inside of the cave.

Lieutenant Colby was shocked and confused. He needed assurance he had heard the orders correctly and asked the General to repeat himself.

General Hitchens said, "Yes, Lieutenant, I am ordering you to blow up the cave and destroy the evidence. I expect you to carry out these orders."

Lieutenant Colby said, "But, sir!"

Now irritated, the general barked, "Damn it, Lieutenant, I don't like this either! It sucks, son, but orders come directly from the president of the United States! The president wants the contents of this cave sealed forever. He has his reasons, and since he is the commander in chief, well ..."

"Sir, no disrespect, but what reasons?"

"Listen, Lieutenant, your behavior is out of line. The president doesn't think the people can handle the truth about aliens and human history. He's also afraid that this encounter could severely alter our way of life if it gets out. No more needs to be said. Also, once you get out of the cavern, you must immediately get everyone one hundred yards away from the entrance of the cave. We've ordered a drone attack."

The lieutenant said, "Yes, sir. I will take care of it."

Little did Lieutenant Colby know that Natalie Duval was gathering samples behind the rocks and had overheard the conversation.

Natalie Duval walked over to Professor Ashe and said, "Professor, we need to take possession of the vessel."

"Shit, Natalie, we can't. The president's involved. You heard what he said. He probably knows something that we don't."

"Please pick up the vessel, and put it in your backpack now," Natalie whispered firmly.

The professor gave Natalie an irritated look and said, "I don't think I can do that."

Natalie said, "If you don't, I will."

With a puzzled, indecisive look, the professor said, "No, this is now a military and national-security matter."

Natalie looked at the professor with astonishment and said, "No, it is a scientific matter. This site may be the most important scientific discovery of our time, and we have a responsibility to science."

At that second, Natalie quickly but discreetly walked over to the altar, grabbed the vessel, and put it in the bag without being noticed.

Professor Ashe said anxiously, "I don't know what you think you're doing, but they are not going to let you walk out of here with that vessel."

"At least I won't be a chickenshit like you, Professor! The people have a right to know."

Lieutenant Colby walked over to Mendez and told him to prepare the men to move out immediately.

"I'll brief Savin and his group," said Colby. "One more thing, meet me at the east side of the cavern about ten yards from the altar as soon as everyone begins leaving the cave."

Lieutenant Colby approached Savin and told him to instruct his team to proceed immediately to the cave entrance and asked him and Natalie to stay behind. Natalie thought Colby knew she had the vessel; why else would he ask her to stay back? Different scenarios went through her mind as she prepared for a confrontation with Colby.

About ten minutes later the professor, Colby's, and Savin's men were well on their journey back to the cave entrance. Rocky came over to Colby and asked him what was up.

Colby said, "I need the explosives you brought from the expedition campsite."

Rocky gave Colby a surprised and concerned look and asked, "Why do you need the explosives?"

"I cannot divulge that information."

"That's bullshit!"

"I have orders!" yelled Lieutenant Colby.

"What, to blow up the cave? Who in their right mind would order that?" asked Rocky.

"The president of the United States," Colby said.

"Maybe the extraterrestrials can show us a better way to live," said Rocky. "This could be good for everyone."

"Maybe, but I have my orders," said Colby.

"Lieutenant, you're going to have to go through me to blow up this cave!" yelled Rocky.

"We don't have time for this!" Colby said.

"Oh, yes we do. I am not going to let this happen!"

"Well, I guess you leave me no option," said Lieutenant Colby.

"Looks that way!" bellowed Rocky.

Rocky swiftly moved to the right and spun around and kicked Colby in the side, crushing his ribs. Colby fell to his knees, and Savin quickly spun around again and kicked him in the face. Startled, Colby remained on his knees, in agony, trying desperately not to fall flat on his face.

Torn between finishing off a fellow soldier he respected and preventing Colby from destroying what possibly could be man's greatest discovery, Rocky decided to spare him any additional pain and embarrassment. Rocky grabbed Colby by his shirt, shook him, and hollered, "Why are you doing this?"

Colby looked at Savin in anguish and in a distressed voice said, "It's not me. I have my orders! Nondisclosure!"

Rocky asked, "Why?"

Trying to sit up, Colby said, "The president of the United States does not want the contents of this cave disclosed; that's why! The president believes this discovery could be devastating to our way of life."

Rocky sarcastically said, "So what they're really concerned about is money and power and who controls it."

Still struggling and holding his side, Colby mustered enough strength to say, "They are worried about the chaos it would cause; the impact of this knowledge would be overwhelming. The president thinks the public can't handle the truth!"

Rocky snapped, "The president can't handle the truth! I'm begging you, Dan; don't do this."

Rocky slowly reached out, offering his hand to help Colby up. With a defeated look on his face, Colby pushed Savin's hand away and said, "I don't need your help!"

Rocky grabbed his weapon and said, "I can't allow it! Destroying this knowledge is the most horrific mistake in human history."

Colby slowly got up and looked directly at Savin. "You think anyone would believe you? You're a fool, Rocky! Do you really think those in power will let you jeopardize their desire to control this thing?"

Rocky pointed his rifle at Colby and said, "I don't care what you think. I'm in control now."

Hiding behind a large rock, waiting patiently for the right opportunity, Mendez stood up, pointed his AK-47 at Savin, and shouted, "No, Rocky, we're in control. Stand down, and drop the weapon now!"

Colby cautiously grabbed Savin's weapons and his backpack containing the explosives and said, "Now get the hell out of here."

Rocky said angrily, "This better be legit, or I will blow the whistle on this so quickly heads will turn!"

Rocky and Natalie were slow to move. Natalie, still possessing the vessel, was relieved she hadn't gotten caught. She knew their only chance of securing the truth about the origin of humanity was to get out of the cave with the vessel.

Colby winced, still hurting from the blows he'd sustained. He yelled, "What don't you understand? Move your asses now, or we will blow your friggin' heads off!"

Frightened, Natalie looked over to Rocky and said, "We better do what he says. We don't know the reasons for their actions; maybe they're legit."

Rocky leaned down, brushed his pants off, and looked up at Colby. "You better be right, Colby, or I will be your worst nightmare for the rest of your life. Understood?"

As Rocky and Natalie walked toward the cave entrance, Rocky said, "This better not be another government cover-up. I don't trust them; they're in way over their heads. You know how the government works: if they don't understand it, they just make it go away by sweeping it under the rug. For their sake, this better be a huge rug. The people have a right to know, and they can handle the truth."

Natalie looked up at Rocky and said, "This may be the greatest government cover-up of all time, and we won't be able to stop it. Those crazy bastards even have a name for it: MAD. Well, they're the ones that are mad."

Rocky shook his head said, "The people have a right to know! It's their birthright."

CHAPTER 31
Run like the Wind

July 11, 2012: Mound of Tiamat

Colby grabbed the backpack of explosives and placed them as planned. The explosives were extremely powerful and could move a mountain. The expedition team had used them to remove boulders and other large objects so they could search for tombs and other artifacts in hard-to-reach places. There were fifteen explosive devices, enough to blow up at least a five-mile area.

Colby put three explosives two yards from the first tablet and two by the altar. He looked over to inspect the vessel, and it was gone.

"Shit, where's the vessel?" yelled Colby.

Mendez quickly walked over to Colby and said, "What? You're shitting me!"

Colby looked at Mendez and said with a raised voice, "Someone took the friggin' vessel!"

Mendez quickly said, "Who? Savin?"

Upset, Colby said anxiously, "We need to get out of here now and get back with the others to secure the vessel! Whoever took the vessel has put us all in danger. Chief, this is now a life-and-death situation for all of us. The people making these decisions don't play around."

Colby grabbed the backpack, and they hurried toward the cave entrance.

Mendez asked, "Do you have the detonator?"

"It's in the bag; let's move out!"

Noticing Colby's limp, Mendez asked, "Lieutenant, are you okay?"

"Don't worry about me; I'll be fine," said Colby.

Colby and Mendez jogged slowly toward the entrance with the remaining explosives. Along the way, Colby positioned several explosives in the cave to make sure there was enough force to seal it tight.

The plan required Colby and Mendez to be precise in the placement of the explosives and their exit strategy. The entrance of the cave was seven miles from the altar, and the range of the wireless detonator was five miles. The detonator had a twenty-minute delay before the bombs would go off, so Colby and Mendez would have enough time to get far away from the explosives before they went off.

Moving quickly, Colby placed each explosive carefully, as command had directed. There was an eerie silence as they journeyed from one predetermined bomb location to the next, and the soldiers could not overcome the feeling of gloom and doom.

The silence was suddenly interrupted as rocks crashed all around them. Something was trying to stop them from carrying out their mission. A large spear-like stalactite almost pierced Mendez as he dodged large rocks and limestone columns falling everywhere. Both men zigzagged from left to right trying to avoid the debris that rained from the roof of the cave.

Colby stopped, trying to gauge the best possible path, but he knew it was hopeless. A rock ricocheted off a column and just nicked Colby, forcing him to the ground and aggravating his wound sustained earlier. Mendez ran over and helped him up, and both weaved and dodged the onslaught of rubble.

When they had traveled about a mile, the avalanche of rocks stopped as quickly as it had started. Both men were breathing heavy.

Mendez shouted, "What the hell was that?"

Colby replied, "I don't know, Chief; it's like something is trying to stop us. We got our orders; let's go."

Colby and Mendez finally reached the five-mile marker to detonate the explosives. Placing the last bomb, Colby yelled over to Mendez, "There are enough explosives to blow this gift of the gods to kingdom come!"

Mendez said, "Lieutenant, we only have a few minutes to get this done. The drones aren't going to wait."

Colby knelt down, pulled the detonator out of the bag, and looked at Mendez. "You know, I don't like being put in this position. We could go down in history as the two soldiers who buried human history and ruined our chances of solving the mystery of human life."

Mendez said, "Look, we could be saving the human race from oblivion! The fact is we don't know, but we have our orders; it's not our call. Let's blow this sucker and run like hell!"

"What about the vessel?" Colby asked.

Mendez replied, "We'll have to address that later. For all we know, it still could be in this cave."

Still unsure, Colby paused a minute to reconsider his options. He didn't want to bury the answers to the most prolific questions involving humanity. But even if he didn't detonate the explosives, the bombs from the drones surely would. Regardless, he had his orders, and since he was a loyal Navy SEAL, he would do as instructed.

Colby held the wireless detonator in his hand and asked, "You ready, Chief?"

Mendez replied, "Light this candle, big guy!"

Colby slowly raised his arm and pressed hard on the red button of the detonator. Conflicting thoughts raced through his mind as he contemplated how these events would affect everyone on the planet. He knew that his life would never be the same.

Colby and Mendez took off jogging fast toward the entrance of the cave. They only had twenty minutes to run two miles before the bomb would blow. Both men monitored their speed to make sure they had enough stamina to get to the entrance in time.

As Lieutenant Colby jogged, his bruised ribs began hurting. Regardless of how excruciating the pain was, he couldn't stop thinking about the enormous responsibility that had been placed on him and his soldiers. It was a no-win situation, and he'd most likely be a loser either way. Colby had his orders, and he was convinced this was the right thing to do at this time.

A mile in, Colby was running about three yards behind Mendez. He could hardly breathe and was running in a bent-over position, struggling to stay on his feet. Unfortunately, he could no longer tolerate the piercing pain and the difficulty breathing. He quickly slowed to a staggered walk. He dropped to the ground, holding his side and grimacing in pain.

No longer sensing Colby's presence, Mendez looked back and saw the lieutenant lying on the ground rolling side to side on his back in agony about twenty yards behind him. Mendez stopped and quickly returned to Colby, knelt next to him, and asked if he was okay.

Breathing laboriously, Colby pointed to his ribs. Mendez leaned down, grabbed both of Colby's shoulders tightly, looked him square in the eyes, and said, "We do not want to die here, buried alive in the tomb of man's history. Get up, sir; the clock is ticking." Mendez firmly grabbed Colby's wrists and pulled him up. "I got you, sir. Let's run; let's run like the wind!"

Running side by side, Mendez provided support for Colby as they headed toward the cave entrance. It took them about seventeen minutes to run the two miles. As they reached the entrance of the cave, Colby and Mendez ran an additional forty yards and stopped. Bent over, the two men put their hands on their knees as they tried desperately to catch their breath.

Colby fell to his knees, holding his side, and he almost passed out. A few minutes later, he raised his head and saw that everyone was about one hundred yards from the entrance of the cave. Three Navy SEALs were standing guard. Several of them trotted over to help Colby. Curious, the men wanted to learn what was happening.

Colby looked at his watch. There was one minute left till the bombs donated. Trying to catch his breath and still in severe pain, Colby told his men to clear the area. He blurted out, "The cave will blow in forty seconds! Move away from the entrance now!"

Surprised and puzzled, some of the Navy SEALs walked quickly back to where Savin and his team were standing, while Buford and Tex remained at Colby's side. As they walked to safer ground, they looked back every five seconds at the huge mound, anticipating the explosion.

Confused, Tex said, "Tell me, Lieutenant; we're not really blowing this up, are we?"

Colby, still breathless, said, "We have our orders. Get the hell out of here now."

Tex turned to Mendez and said, "Chief, tell me this is not true."

"You heard the lieutenant; we have our orders, and they're from the top."

"But, sir!"

Ignoring his concern, Mendez changed the subject and asked, "Tex, did we find out what happened to Lucero?"

Tex replied, "We found him in the cave on our way back. He was badly injured, but he is okay. He is over by those vehicles with the rest of the men getting medical treatment."

Colby limped to safer ground toward the others. Noticing that the lieutenant's injuries were serious, Buford walked toward Colby and helped him. Colby put his arm around Buford's shoulders as they walked back toward the others. Colby was still looking at his watch. As the watch struck the magic moment, Colby shouted, "Fire in the hole!"

Looking toward the cave in anticipation of the pending devastation, Colby whispered to Buford, "We are robbing mankind of his beginning."

As they stood there, thirty seconds passed, and there was no explosion. Three minutes more passed, and again, no explosion. Five minutes more passed, and still there was nothing.

Awaiting the detonation, everyone became noticeably confused, looking at each other and then back at the mound, trying to get some understanding of what was transpiring. The only thing they saw were three white owls circling directly over the mound like buzzards.

Colby and Lucero were lying next to each other receiving medical attention for their injuries. Lucero asked Colby, "Sir, is it typical for white owls to fly around a barren desert like this, in broad daylight?"

"No, it's not," said Colby.

Colby looked at Mendez. Both were concerned and puzzled. Colby tried visually to trace the steps he'd taken to deploy and detonate the bombs. He continued to look at his watch, and when five minutes more passed, he said, "Shit, we have a serious problem. Please get Central Command on the line now."

Everyone else stood there, anticipating something to happen. There was no explosion, nothing.

As Buford was getting Central Command on the line, Colby's mind raced through various scenarios of how the White House would react to news of the failed detonation and of the missing vessel. Colby thought, *What if the White House thinks we disobeyed their orders and sabotaged the mission? Would they send a second drone attack directed at us?*

Colby took the headset of the satellite radio and told the general the bad news. "General, the explosives didn't detonate."

"What! You're shitting me, son. What went wrong?" asked Hitchens.

Colby said, "It has to be the same electrical interference that blocked our earlier communications in the cave. I have no other explanation. I can assure you we double-checked everything and carried out your orders precisely."

General Hitchens said, "Okay, what's your status?"

"General, to prepare you, there's one more piece of shit news."

"What could be worse than this?"

"The vessel, sir, it's gone!"

The general went ballistic. "This is a cluster fuck! If someone sabotaged this mission, I can assure you that they will not be long for this world."

"What do you mean?"

"What do I mean? Shit, Lieutenant, let me say it another way. Everyone will sleep with the fishes. Understand? These guys don't play, and I'm not going to be able to run interference for you and the group. You need to find the person who took the vessel and get them to turn it over ASAP. If you don't, I think there will be extreme consequences. You tell them they won't leave this godforsaken desert with that vessel, and if they try, they will be eliminated so fast they won't know what hit them."

"Got it, General," Colby said.

"Lieutenant, our only chance to salvage this mission now rests with the drone attack to seal off the cave. The bombs from the drones should also detonate the explosives you deployed. They should be there any minute. Get everyone a safe distance from the entrance of the cave!"

"Yes, sir!"

"I will authorize the drones' final approach to strike the cave. If the drone attack successfully seals the cave, there will be less collateral damage for everyone. At that time, I will talk to the White House and get a sense for what they are thinking. Now go find that vessel!" the general said. "Colby, one last thing, check the archaeologists first."

Colby yelled over to Mendez to join him. "Chief, I need you to search the archaeologists. They have the vessel. I just know it. We must do something to find it, or we will all be dead."

"What do you mean, Lieutenant?"

"These people don't play. I mean lethal. Now move fast."

CHAPTER 32
The Messenger: A Close Encounter of the Fifth Kind

July 11, 2012: Mound of Tiamat

Colby was very anxious about the vessel and extremely puzzled about why the bombs did not detonate. He knew he had to find the vessel immediately. Colby looked around to see if everyone was there. He thought for a minute that maybe someone had stayed behind in the cave and deactivated the bombs as he had deployed them.

Confused and unaware of the missing vessel, everyone gathered around Colby expressing their concern about the failed detonation.

Colby yelled, "Who took the vessel?"

Shocked, everybody looked at each other to see if someone would admit to taking the vessel. The group became apprehensive and more confused.

Corrizo asked, "What's going on here, Lieutenant? We need to know now."

Just then, a loud rumbling and cracking noise originated from the sky above the Mound of Tiamat. Everyone looked up and saw thick, fluffy clouds churning directly above them. It resembled the start of a storm system when clouds swiftly rolled in and covered the entire sky. The weather event was in a confined area centered directly above the Mound of Tiamat. Oddly enough, the outer edges around the mound were bright and sunny, while the sky directly above the mound looked like a severe summer thunderstorm.

All of a sudden, fiery lightning illuminated the sky. The flash looked unnatural, almost like a man-made electrical discharge striking out of the cloud. The dark sky spun in a circle, like a massive tornado swirling recklessly at tremendous speeds.

In a few minutes, the sky began to resemble a black hole whirling through space, just like the one they had seen in the cave. The funnel spun violently out of control, rotating rapidly around its axis. In some ways, it resembled a waterspout, spinning ferociously about one thousand feet directly above them, covering the entire sky.

There was no wind or the usual howling sound that accompanied an extraordinary weather system of this type. It was quite the opposite—calm and silent. But at the same time, the sky above was spinning fast and furiously. Remarkably, it was tranquil inside the phenomenon, like the eye of the storm.

Out of nowhere, the sky burned brightly. Colorful sunrays vibrantly lit up the sky, piercing through the clearing clouds and reflecting off the ground. The blinding light was more intense than the sun. The incident was incredible and breathtaking but also peaceful and almost spiritual.

Suddenly, an enormous pyramid-shaped object appeared in the funnel, as if the black hole had given birth to the enormous object. The pyramid slid through the spinning and twirling clouds.

Corrizo yelled, "It's some sort of pyramid-shaped space vehicle."

Bags said, "It can't be; spaceships are cigar or saucer shaped."

Rocky replied, "Maybe that's what we sought in the past, but this is definably a pyramid-shaped craft descending from the sky."

"Spectacular," said Professor Ashe. "Natalie, do you believe this?"

"Absolutely beautiful," said Natalie smiling.

The space vehicle descended slowly toward earth and then hovered about two miles above the Mound of Tiamat. It did not look like the kind of space ship traditionally portrayed in popular science fiction films. It looked exactly like the pyramids located all over the earth but had a sharper, shiny, metallic form. The ship looked more like the pyramids of Giza than those of Chichen Itza, Teotihuacan, and Tenochtitlan. It had smooth, sloping sides as compared to the pyramids in Mexico and Central America whose sides resembled steps.

The spaceship was huge, perfectly geometric, and at least five city blocks across and approximately twenty-five stories high. The pyramid was pitch black except for a crystal point at the tip and a gold insignia. Given the angle of its descent, no one could see it well enough to determine the meaning of the inscription.

When the spaceship moved down out of the tunnel, it was upside down with the point of the pyramid facing the earth and the base facing the sky. The tip of the pyramid seemed to be made of clear quartz and sparkled like a bright star.

The spaceship stopped and remained stationary, hovering about a mile above everyone. Minutes later, the vehicle rotated slowly, flipping itself around, right side up, so the point of the pyramid now faced the sky and the base was parallel to the ground. As it turned, Colby, Savin, Professor Ashe, and their teams could see the base and the sides of the spacecraft more clearly. It was enormous but flawlessly shaped.

The insignia on the one side of the spaceship was more visible now as the object came closer and repositioned itself. Once the pyramid stabilized, they could clearly see that the insignia was an identical replication of the all-seeing eye.

Mendez leaned toward Colby and whispered, "Is that insignia the symbol on our dollar bill?"

Colby replied in a soft voice, "Yes, it is the Masonic representation of the Great Architect of the Universe. It's also referred to as the Eye of Providence, God watching over humanity."

Seconds later, a large panel in the bottom of the pyramid opened up slowly, and without warning, a life-form appeared from the spaceship. It stood stationary, hovering quietly in the sky about seventy-five yards above. Suddenly, the being slid down the beaming light, gliding effortlessly toward earth and slowly becoming clearly visible.

The extraterrestrial life-form had humanoid features but at the same time was different in many ways. The celestial being was very tall, about ten feet in height, and had dark eyes; a pointed, elongated head; and pure-white hair. The alien visitor also had tan, smooth skin; thin lips; very small ears; a jagged cleft chin; a long neck; and broad shoulders. He was extremely fit, muscular, and handsome.

Attached to the visitor's back were large, gold, metallic wings with images of feathers etched throughout. The interstellar visitor could be described only as benevolent and distinguished looking, almost biblical and godlike. He had a halo around him that glowed as brightly as the sun.

He wore a gold-colored robe with two emblems displayed on the front at each side of his chest. On the right side was a picture of four winged horsemen, and on the left was a replica of a pyramid with the symbol of the all-seeing eye, exactly like the emblem on the spacecraft.

Everyone was stunned and mesmerized as they looked at the sky in disbelief. Charlie Babbitt and Slick Sullivan fell to their knees, still looking straight up. Tears rolled down McCray's face, and he wished Paradee was there to see this magnificent event. Corrizo just stared, showing no emotion. Mendez knelt and bowed his head. Natalie smiled.

After the being landed to earth, he said with a strong voice, "I am the Messenger! I traveled a long distance that you call light-years. This planet you call earth was once our home.

"We call this mound the Sacred Knowledge of Life. Those who walked on the earth a thousand years ago put this holy site here. It contains some of the greatest knowledge of the universe, which we call the Library of Life. It was left here to teach you, the human race, about your beginning and to prepare you for your future destiny. The destruction of this holy and reverend site will not be allowed."

Seconds later, the drones soared directly overhead toward the mound on their bombing run as planned. A shiny, almost blinding beam of light appeared from the all-seeing eye on the top of the pyramid and took control of the drones, effortlessly redirecting them about four miles from the expected bomb site. The humans could see, but not hear, the explosion of the drones in the far distance over the desert sky.

Colby was standing next to Tex. He looked at him and said softly, "Are we videotaping this?"

Tex nodded and whispered, "Washington and command are both receiving the transmission."

Out of the blue, Natalie Duval handed Rocky Savin the vessel and walked toward the visitor. Shocked by Natalie's actions, Professor Ashe reached out to try to stop her, but she shrugged him off and continued till she stopped alongside the Messenger and turned to face the extraterrestrial. She bowed reverently for three seconds as she gently touched her chest with her fist three times. The Messenger bowed his head in return and touched his chest three times. Natalie then turned and stood next to the Messenger.

Buford whispered to Bags, "Holy shit, she's one of them. You shouldn't feel so bad now about getting your ass kicked by a woman."

Colby blurted out, "She must be some sort of hybrid."

A moment later, all eyes were again focused on the Messenger. The professor stepped forward and asked the Messenger, "Who are you, and why are you here?"

"I come from a species called the Anunnaki. We came here thousands of years ago and lived among you. Our sun was dying, and thus our planet and species were in danger of extinction. Some of us left our planet in search of a similar carbon-based planet that contained certain minerals we need to sustain life.

"Earth and Mars were the only planets that had an atmosphere, breathable air, and water we needed to live and flourish. Earth and Mars were similar to our planet and had everything we needed. Thousands of years ago, there was a war between our Alliance of Angels and the

Saturnians. In an act of desperation, the Saturnians launched a massive nuclear attack on Mars. The blasts devastated the planet and threw Mars off its axis, resulting in the loss of the planet's ability to sustain life. So we came to earth.

"When we came here, our species reengineered the human primate genera. We mixed our DNA with yours to create you in our image and likeness. As you evolved, your intellect grew. We taught you our culture, science, institutions, and technology. If it weren't for our intervention, you would still be uncivilized primates today.

"Our species has a genetic disorder in our DNA that causes our genes to mutate into a rare disease. The disorder distresses our organs and accelerates the aging process. We required earth's gold to engineer a medicine to cure the disease and extend our lifespan several hundred years. We applied a solution of your minerals and water mixed with a chemical from our planet. It worked so well we made earth our home."

Colby took two steps forward and asked, "Why did you reengineer us?"

"We needed help mining," said the Messenger. "The work to extract the gold was laborious, and our people grew tired of it. So we reengineered your DNA to make a versatile hybrid with advanced intelligence, an upgrade of your *Homo erectus*. We could not teach your primitive species to function in a controlled, productive matter, so we mixed your DNA with ours."

"That's against all rules of nature," said Colby.

The Messenger responded, "Your scientists manipulate DNA every day in your labs."

The professor took a small step forward and asked, "Why did you not leave us any specific knowledge of your existence?"

The Messenger replied, "It's all around you. Your scriptures are full of accounts of encounters with supernatural beings. However, you misinterpreted these stories to support your various religious doctrines and to create your gods. During the time we were here, your species were in awe of our advanced technology and power, often referring to us as gods and higher beings."

Ashe asked, "Are you gods?"

The Messenger replied, "There is only one god in the universe who made the stars, heavens, and all creatures, and that is the sky-god Anu, the god of heaven, lord of the constellations, and architect of the universe. Anu is god of all universes and species, not just humans."

The Messenger paused for a moment and then said, "You are a confused and insecure species, misled and too trusting in your institutions that have deceived you for centuries. Many of your political and religious leaders have known of our existence but kept the truth from you. They place religion, politics, and their self-interest and desire for power and wealth before what is best for humanity."

"Why did you leave us?" asked Rocky.

The Messenger said, "All will become clear in time."

Annoyed by all the interruptions, the Messenger continued, "In the past, we wanted to help you, but your species has not grown enough in order to establish direct contact with us. We provided you with so many clues. We even entrusted great knowledge to some of your best and brightest, including Abraham, Moses, Huldah, Noah, Mohamed, Joan of Arc, Einstein, Leonardo da Vinci, and countless others. We also gave you our grand leader's son, but you were threatened by his powers and fearful of his intentions.

"Throughout time, we have tested you periodically, and you have failed miserably. Your institutions are corrupt and much of your science flawed. You are capable of much violence, and you have such a great propensity for war. Your species continues to pollute the planet and destroy your environment and our ability to sustain life.

"We, the Anunnaki and the Alliance of Angels, are very concerned about your use and stockpile of nuclear weapons. We want the use of nuclear fuel and weapons halted immediately. The destruction of the earth could cause a ripple effect in time and space that would be disruptive to our existence. Such destruction serves no purpose and will not be allowed. If humanity doesn't achieve nuclear disarmament in the next two years, there will be corollaries, an Armageddon caused by a rogue asteroid or another great flood, just like before. But this time, we will not save your species. We will take over the planet and eliminate any trace of your existence.

"We want the human race on earth to succeed. In that spirit, the Anunnaki bequeathed you this vessel that contains knowledge and technology to further your civilization. One of the many technologies in this vessel will replace your current energy resources. The vessel contains technology for an energy source that will cause no harm to earth's environment and can power anything you need. This free energy will make you more prosperous and even the economic playing field on earth. It will improve your way of life. We hope you use it wisely.

"To answer your earlier question, we will return soon for your day of reckoning, your final test. In the past, there were two other tests, but they were just warnings. We used those events to cleanse the earth of the wicked and evil ones and their hybrid ancestry and to protect and perpetuate the pure heredity we bequeathed you. We will return again, and hopefully you will use the knowledge in this vessel to join us and take your place in the universe peacefully.

"Before I leave you, it is important you understand that it is no coincidence you are here together to witness this encounter of the fifth kind. We selected you before your conception, and the Watchers you call grays have guided you throughout your lives. Your destiny is to play a major role in the future of humanity, and we will define your responsibilities later in more detail."

The Messenger looked toward the heavens and ascended effortlessly as the base of the spaceship opened. A few seconds later, Natalie followed, and they both entered the craft. The door closed, and the spaceship moved upward toward the twirling black hole and suddenly disappeared.

Everyone stared expressionlessly at the spinning tunnel. No one uttered a word. Tears were running down the professor's face. Buford fell to his knees and blessed himself with the sign of the cross.

The professor looked over to Rocky and finally broke the silence. "I think we just got our answer."

Rocky said, "Yeah, we are definitely not alone; that's for sure. This is incredible. I never could have conceived of this in my wildest dreams."

The professor smiled and had a satisfied, knowing look on his face. The professor leaned over to Rocky and whispered, "I hate to say it, Rocky, but I told you so."

"Yeah, Professor, looks like you're right. Man, I would not believe this if I didn't see it with my own eyes," replied Rocky.

Bags shouted, "No one is going to believe any of this! We have no proof. Everybody thinks extraterrestrials are bullshit."

Holding up the vessel, Rocky said, "We have the vessel!"

Colby quickly grabbed the vessel out of Rocky's hands and said, "No, we don't; the president has the vessel."

Ashe said, "We have a video recording."

Colby replied, "No, the military controls the recordings."

Rocky said, "We have the contents of the cave."

"Believe me when I tell you the government is not going to let anyone near that cave," said Colby.

Without warning, a call from Central Command interrupted the discussion.

Colby turned to Tex and asked, "Did the video link remain connected to the White House and Central Command?"

Tex turned to Colby and said, "Yes, sir."

Colby went over to the front of the video link and said, "Mr. President, did you see that?"

"Yes, I did, Lieutenant."

"What's next? Do you have a plan, sir?" asked Colby.

"Yes, we are sending in Elizabeth Harris and the special interagency team. Protect the vessel till they get there, and do not let it out of your possession. Lieutenant, that's an order."

"But, sir," said Colby.

"Like I said, Lieutenant, we are sending in the special interagency team. In the meantime, advise your team that they are under Executive Order 32. They are not to say anything about what they witnessed. If they do, there will be consequences. Understand?"

"Yes, Mr. President."

As the video link disconnected, Colby walked over to the group to brief them. "Look, the president asked us to keep this under wraps for now."

Savin asked, "Does he think we are all going to be quiet about this?"

Professor Ashe looked at Colby and said, "I have a professional responsibility to report this remarkable discovery!"

Lieutenant Colby fired back, "We are all under Executive Order 32 until this is sorted out! Understand?"

Professor Ashe asked, "What does that mean?"

"What do you think it means?" asked Rocky. "We either keep our mouth shut, or lights out, amigo."

Lieutenant Colby asked, "Do you want to disobey an executive order from the president of the United States and the leader of the free world?"

Rocky Savin reluctantly asked, "So what is next?"

Colby said, "The president needs time to develop a plan, and once he does, he will direct us on what to do."

"Sure, do you expect us to believe that?" Rocky asked.

"We can only wait and see what happens. Hopefully, they will do the right thing," said Colby.

Three helicopters suddenly appeared on the horizon. As the first helicopter descended, seven armed soldiers appeared at the opened door of the aircraft. The blades of the helicopters caused a small sandstorm as they maneuvered to land. Everyone covered their eyes to shield them from the blowing sand.

Once they landed, six soldiers stepped down from one of the helicopters. Three of the six lined up on the left side of the aircraft door and the other three on the right to create a path. The seventh soldier was tall and dressed in blackoveralls. He jumped out onto the ground and walked between the two lines of soldiers.

"Who is Lieutenant Colby?" he asked.

The lieutenant limped over to the helicopter and said, "That's me; I'm Lieutenant Colby."

The man in the black overalls asked, "Do you have the vessel?"

"Yes, I do."

"Good; that makes things much easier." The soldier pointed to the chopper and said, "Please come with me, sir."

Colby got in the helicopter, and the six soldiers followed him. The tall soldier with the black overalls motioned the other choppers hovering above to land, and then he entered the helicopter behind the six soldiers and Colby. The chopper blades started to spin, and the aircraft steadily lifted off the ground about fifty feet and quickly veered off to the left.

Immediately after, the second and third helicopters landed. Elizabeth Harris got out of the second helicopter followed by four others from the special interagency team. Harris put her hand upon her forehead, shielding her eyes from the sand, and yelled out over the loud ruffling noise of the idling helicopters, "Professor Ashe, please step forward."

Hesitant, Professor Ashe slowly raised his hand, almost afraid. Harris walked over to him and whispered in his ear, "The president would like you to stay with the special interagency team."

Two other soldiers dressed in black jumpsuits exited the second helicopter just deplaned by Harris and the special interagency team and asked the Navy SEALs to board the chopper. A group of two men and one woman exited the third helicopter, greeted the others, and escorted them to the third aircraft.

Except for the special interagency team and Professor Ashe, everyone else boarded the two remaining helicopters, and the aircraft took off, blowing sand everywhere as they went off into the horizon and quickly disappeared. Those who stayed behind gathered their gear and headed for the entrance to the Mound of Tiamat.

CHAPTER 33
The Cover-Up

July 12, 2012: Washington, DC

At the end of the videoconference with the Messenger, the president remained in the White House Situation Room for four hours before he met with MJ-12 in the West Wing's Cabinet Conference Room.

The makeup of the committee had changed some. One of the MJ-12 members who had attended yesterday's meeting was absent. An elderly gentleman sitting at the head of the table had replaced him. Everyone referred to him as chairman, and he had called MJ-12 into special session.

The president walked into the meeting, and everybody greeted him. "Good morning, Mr. President."

He replied, "Good morning, everyone."

The president took his seat at the head of the table to the right of the distinguished-looking chairman.

The president turned to the elderly man and said, "Mr. Chairman, may I begin the briefing?" The chairman nodded yes.

The chairman, now in his eighties, looked more like he was fifty. He was handsome and dressed impeccably, with a white shirt and a red power tie that looked good against his blue suit. Amazingly, he did not have a single gray hair in his dark-brown, well-groomed mane, nor did he have any wrinkles on his tan face. His blue eyes sparkled almost hypnotically. He was very tall, an intimidating six-feet-eleven strong man who always towered over others. His height and his intense eyes had always given him an advantage in business and his personal life.

After getting the chairman's approval, the president began his remarks. "Yesterday, we had an extraterrestrial encounter of the fifth kind. As directed by protocol sixty-nine of the MJ-12 bylaws, I am required to call a meeting of this committee and brief you about events that fall within your jurisdiction of authority.

"The encounter was between an alien messenger and a platoon of Navy SEALs, CIA operatives, and civilians. This group of twenty-three credible witnesses uncovered an archaeological site that includes tablets and artifacts never seen before and provides additional evidence and support of the extraterrestrials' intent to aid humans. At this site, they also discovered a vessel that is capable of transmitting a video containing incredible knowledge of technology, medicine, the universe, the key to unlocking the mystery of human life, and so much more. The transfer of knowledge includes a new free hydrogen energy source that will replace all our existing energy resources.

"We tried to blow up the cave to bury the vessel and the artifacts using ground explosives and an air strike. Unfortunately, we ran into several problems, and all efforts failed to conceal the evidence. Our immediate task is to determine a path forward."

The chairman turned to the president and asked him if there was a breach of protocol 69. The president nodded in the affirmative.

The chairman said, "This is a very simple matter; protocol sixty-nine calls for immediate implementation of Operation Dragon Killer."

The president said abruptly, "So what do you plan to do, Mr. Chairman, destroy the evidence, including the twenty-three witnesses?"

The chairman said, "Yes, we will make it look like both groups were ambushed by the al-Qaeda or some other terrorist group." Without warning, the chairman pounded his fist on the conference room table and shouted, "There is no deviation from MJ-12 preset protocols. We must implement Operation Dragon Killer. There is no other choice."

The president said, "This is not like Roswell or those other encounters of the lesser kind. We have an encounter of the fifth kind involving twenty-three credible witnesses."

The chairman looked up at the president and said, "Sir, may I remind you that we all took an oath to follow and enforce protocol sixty-nine. Operation Dragon Killer will also provide the cover we need to go in there, seal off the area, and dispose of all evidence."

The president, now visually upset, blurted, "Henry, how can you be so cavalier about killing twenty-three people? You act so nonchalantly about the whole thing."

"This is a very unfortunate situation," said the chairman, "but we must not let this information get out. We must destroy any evidence and all witnesses immediately. I insist we invoke protocol sixty-nine and Operation Dragon Killer now!"

"So you are going to kill a platoon of Navy SEALs, two CIA operatives, two scientists, and eight members of your security team," said the president. "What about the fallout? I can bet you there will be an independent investigation that could expose MJ-12 and this conspiracy to kill twenty-three innocent people."

"They're expendable, unfortunate collateral damage," said the chairman. "We've done it before."

"Yes, that is true, and I am ashamed I was a part of it," said the president.

The president paused and quickly scanned the room, looking at each committee member and stopping at the chairman. He looked directly into the chairman's eyes and said, "We've been deceiving the American people and the world too long; I'm no longer associated with this conspiracy and cover-up."

"Wilbur, you are a hypocrite," said the chairman.

"I don't give a damn about what you think. I am the president, and it looks like I will be here for another four years, so I suggest you listen to me."

"There are several ways to skin a cat," said the chairman.

"What do you mean by that?"

"You know what I mean ... 1963."

"We need to tell the American people the truth," replied the president.

"The American public can't handle the truth. I order you to carry out Operation Dragon Killer immediately while time permits."

"No, that's not going to happen."

"Do you forget who I am, Mr. President?"

"Quite frankly, I don't give a shit. You might be Henry Topaz, the most powerful oil tycoon in the world, but I'm the president of the United States and leader of the free world."

With a silly grin on his face, the chairman said, "Now hold on, Wilbur; don't forget who put you in the White House."

The president said, "The American people voted me into office, Henry, not you."

"Don't go there. We poured millions into your campaign. The political strategists we hired worked behind the scenes to show your campaign how demographics could get you elected. We used this information to rally the poor, minorities, and historically nonvoting majority. My marketing gurus could get anyone elected with the right strategy and packaging."

"This discussion is not appropriate or relevant to this meeting. Let's concentrate on how we are going to disclose an over-sixty-year conspiracy," said the president.

The chairman asked, "How can you sit there and tell me that you are going to disclose over sixty years of deceit, lies, and assassinations and not expect any fallout? You can't just wash your hands of all this and any participation you've had in MJ-12 the past four years."

"I will just have to take my licks," the president said.

The chairman looked at the president and asked, "What do you suggest we do?"

"I'm getting to that."

The president looked down at the audio-video control panel on the conference table in front of him and pushed the green button. Everyone's eyes were on him. He lifted his head slowly as a projector and screen descended from the ceiling.

Seconds later, a PowerPoint presentation appeared on the screen. The first slide was titled "The Beginning File: A Response to an Encounter of the Fifth Kind." The president got up from his chair, grabbed a pointer from the table, and began his presentation.

"As part of the protocols for an encounter of the fifth kind, my responsibilities require me to open the file we call the Beginning. As you know, this top-secret file contains documentation on many of the past extraterrestrial encounters and our attempts to reverse engineer alien technology. However, there is more. The file also includes a set of procedures in response to an encounter of the fifth kind that we did not know existed.

"It is important that every member of this committee understands there are options in response to an encounter of the fifth kind other than Operation Dragon Killer. The Beginning file outlines three response scenarios. The first scenario is similar to what you propose, Henry, which is to rid the earth of any possible evidence no matter how grave or at what price. The second response is to acknowledge contact and invoke martial law, turning the majority of power away from Congress and the executive branch over to the military and MJ-12. The third and final scenario is full disclosure of the truth. The first two scenarios are unacceptable and not practical. The third scenario is our best option."

The chairman interrupted the presentation and said, "Are you out of your mind? We have spent decades and billions of dollars to cover up the truth. Do you think we are going to give up our power and wealth to the likes of aliens who will change our way of life, our institutions, and the world economy? Go ahead, Mr. President; I want to hear the rest of this ridiculous plan. Please continue to amuse me."

Sarcastically, the president said, "Thank you for allowing me to continue. I am proposing we disclose the truth in five phases over fifteen months. In the first phase, we tell the public that we've received a communication from an extraterrestrial alien civilization via a SETI Allen Telescope Array, the ATA. Our ambassadors to each country will notify every world leader personally. We will announce the message is friendly and from Orion's Belt. Since the ATA is part of a large array formed in cooperation with Australia and South Africa, it will add worldwide credibility. We will also indicate that we verified our findings with our telescopes in Puerto Rico and New Mexico."

The president continued, "About three months later, we initiate the sighting phase. In this phase, we report that the *Voyager I* space probe has recorded a sighting in deep space. We will provide NASA with evidence of previous footage of alien encounters, and we will mix it with recent footage we recorded of the pyramid-shaped vehicle. At this time, we will notify the United Nations and call a meeting of world leaders to brief them on the encounters and develop a strategy that we will control.

"In six months, we initiate the third phase, physical contact. During this phase, we announce that we've made contact with a benevolent alien race called the Anunnaki. We will release the footage of the vessel video and the Messenger.

"The next phase is full disclosure. About twelve months from now, I will address the nation and the world and disclose the contents of the Beginning file. I'll explain that the government covered this information up to maintain order and our way of life. We tell the world that it was not in our best interest at the time to disclose this information and that our best strategy was to keep this information secret until we had enough intelligence to determine who we are dealing with, what their intentions are, and how it will impact our world. I'll explain that we now know their intentions are friendly. We will indicate that everyone in the government feels strongly that the aliens mean no harm and that the exchange of information will be unquestionably essential to our survival as a species in the universe.

"The fifth and final phase is apocalypse."

The chairman interrupted. "Apocalypse is the full destruction of the world. Is that your plan, to create a catastrophic event?"

"No! I mean knowledge transfer," responded the president. "Apocalypse translated literally from Greek means 'disclosure of knowledge,' i.e., a lifting of the veil or revelation—not destruction. Many words have various meaning. It depends on who is interpreting and in what context. Can I continue?"

The chairman said, "Please go on."

The president turned back to his PowerPoint presentation and continued, "About fifteen months from now, we will announce that the extraterrestrials have offered to share their technology and knowledge of medicine, science, and the universe. The White House will put the vessel and the Ark of the Covenant on public exhibition from a secret and secure location.

"We will publically unveil the technology for the new energy source. Such a display of generosity will show the world that the extraterrestrials' intentions are peaceful and that world acceptance would be beneficial for our civilization. We convince everyone that the aliens only want to help us and enhance our way of life. We will ensure the world the encounter is a positive one and will result in tremendous advancements to our civilization. Their actions will exhibit a ray of hope for all of mankind. Everyone is looking for some miracle to improve their lives, and this hope will be enough to maintain order."

"That all sounds great," said the chairman. "In the meantime, how do you plan to deal with the twenty-three or so people who know what happened here, and how will you keep them quiet for fifteen months?"

"I've been giving that a lot of thought," replied the president. "Our best option is to make them part of the plan and involve them in the implementation of the five phases."

"How?"

"I have established an executive order to create a secret project team under the special interagency team to be headed by General Hitchens, Elizabeth Harris, and Lieutenant Colby."

"So what do we do about Savin and the rest of the witnesses?" asked the chairman.

"That is where you come in, Henry, but I will get to that in a minute."

The president continued, "I've airlifted twenty-two of the twenty-three witnesses out of Sumer to the aircraft carrier USS *John C. Stennis* in the Persian Gulf. From there, they will be flown to Germany, and within a few hours, a 747 will fly them to Andrews Air Force Base. We'll brief them, commend them on their bravery, and compensate them generously with your help."

"So we are just going to let them live to tell their story?" asked the chairman.

"At the right time, this can work to our advantage," replied the president. "It is important that we assure them that we have no intention of covering this up but that we need fifteen months to implement the phases. Hopefully, everyone will understand this is the best approach.

"My plan is to fly the group from Andrews Air Force Base to a secret underground base in Dulce, New Mexico. Dulce Base has hundreds of underground chambers that house top-secret projects. We will use these chambers to secure all the artifacts and evidence from the encounter, including the vessel.

"As most of you know from your briefings, numerous top-secret classified activities take place at Dulce. Many of the activities are outlined in the Beginning file. This facility is in a remote detachment similar to Area 51 in Nevada. Dulce has a small population of forty-four hundred people, and most of them are Native Americans."

"Who's going to oversee this plan of yours?" asked the chairman.

"The project team will be under the direct supervision of General Hitchens, who will handle the daily operations. Colby will assist Hitchens, and Professor Ashe will work with Elizabeth Harris. Hitchens will report directly to me.

"Stanford University has already granted Ashe a sabbatical, and he has remained at the site with Harris and her group. I informed the president of Stanford University that the government needs Ashe in connection with an urgent national security matter. That is all they have been told. The university will receive a big grant that will assure their cooperation.

"Elizabeth Harris and Professor Ashe will coordinate all aspects of scientific research. However, Harris will head up the special interagency team. She will have the final say on all major scientific decisions before they go to Hitchens and me for approval.

"The project team will be responsible for planning and implementing all activities to carry out the five phases of our plan. They will also study and interpret all the artifacts and tablets found at the archaeological site. The objective is to learn as much as possible about our extraterrestrial ancestors and the knowledge and technology they plan to share with us.

"Savin and his team will be responsible for airlifting equipment, supplies, and food into Sumer for the project team. They will remain there to provide security at the site. The Navy SEALs will be responsible for transporting the artifacts and tablets back to Dulce Base after they have been reviewed, catalogued, and analyzed. The SEALs will also help Savin with security at the site. Sadit and Raahil will provide intelligence that's required to seal the site off. We deployed a Navy destroyer to the Persian Gulf and redeployed Bravo Company to a secure area closer to Sumer."

"What about their families? What do you plan to tell them?" asked the chairman.

The president said, "We will contact the projects team's families today and explain that they are on a special top-secret mission. Under our supervision, the project team members will be allowed to contact their families once to assure them that everything is okay. However, they will not be allowed to talk to them for six months thereafter. As we implement the various phases of our plan, their participation and contribution will be recognized, and they will be allowed to have more contact with their families. I believe this approach will secure the cooperation and silence of all participants. I've also invoked Executive Order 32, and I will use it if necessary."

The chairman looked around the room to get a sense of the group.

He paused for a second and said, "You present a well-thought-out plan, but you forgot one thing, the aliens. There are a lot of unknowns regarding how the aliens will eventually respond. Are they really what they say they are? What are their intentions? Are they hostile? Will they attack us?"

The president thought for a minute and said, "Henry, sometimes you just need to have faith."

Henry Topaz shouted, "Faith! You're willing to put our culture, our way of life, and possibly our freedom at risk, on faith. If I relied on faith, I would not be the richest man in the world."

The president looked at Topaz and said, "Throughout human history, we relied on faith when evidence is either nonexistence or inconclusive.…..for example, religion, government and science."

"Yeah, and look what it got him," said Topaz.

"What do you mean by "got him," asked the president?

"Just what I said."

"Nevertheless, I have a plan in case things do not go as expected."

Topaz quickly responded, "And what might that be, sir?"

The president looked around the room and said, "Operation AP, as my aides like to call it."

Topaz laughed and asked, "What in the hell is AP?"

"Armageddon Prevention," replied the president.

"Who is in charge of this operation?" asked the chairman.

"General Hitchens will review the existing top-secret contingency plan developed to counter a hostile alien invasion. He has been directed to revise the 1963 plan where necessary and establish recommendations that more appropriately address today's issues.

"Immediately after the second phase, my administration will put funds in the next budget and announce that it is for preparation and accommodation of the Anunnaki's peaceful arrival. By that time, we will have enough support in the public and Congress to fund it. In the meantime, we will tap the secret emergency fund that we use for these types of activities. Of course, Henry, you and the corporate members of Rapture and MJ-12 will increase your financial support for rights to some of the technology."

Henry asked, "Is that it, sir? Is that your entire plan?"

The president said, "Yes, it is. Do you have a better one?"

Topaz quickly responded, "Yes, I do. We implement the first response scenario and Operation Dragon Killer. We will send jet fighters to blow the three helicopters out of the sky. No more problem!"

The president shouted, "I will not stand for this! I am the president."

Topaz quickly responded, "You've overstated your power, Wilbur. Protocol sixty-nine requires a vote if there is disagreement among the group."

"How dare you talk to me in that tone and order me? I am the president! Enough, this conspiracy must stop now."

At that moment, the president pushed a red button on the conference table. Immediately, ten armed soldiers entered the conference room, marching in unison. The president said, "Sorry, Henry, but that is not happening on my watch."

Topaz countered, "No, Mr. President, I am sorry! As chairman of MJ-12, I have power over you and the authority to assume control of the government. You have forced me to invoke protocol sixty-nine."

The secretary of state stood up and said, "Unfortunately, Mr. President, the chairman is correct. When there is disagreement among members of the committee, protocol sixty-nine takes precedence over everything. According to the bylaws of MJ-12, the chairman takes over the government in situations involving encounters of the fifth kind if the committee is at an impasse."

The soldiers walked over to the president and stood directly behind him. As the two lead soldiers reached down and grabbed the president's arms to escort him away, Topaz barked, "Do you really think we will let you replace our energy and our trillion-dollar industry with some no-cost fuel substitute provided by some unknown alien species? We know nothing about them. They can use it against us later. I cannot let that happen. Take him away."

As he was being escorted away, the president turned around and shouted, "Watch your back, Henry. We'll see who has the final say, and I can assure you, it will not be you."

The soldiers escorted the president out of the room to a secure locked facility. Topaz stood up and took his place at the head of the table previously occupied by the president and said, "With the powers invested in me, I invoke the first response scenario. Now where were we?"

The Beginning

Afterword

For centuries, the human race has asked, "What is the origin of human-kind? Where do we come from? How did all this begin? Are we alone in the universe?"

Even though the earth is 4.5 billion years old, the origin of humanity can be traced back only 250,000 years. Most ancient religious and cultural writings profess that we come from a benevolent supreme being from the heavens. The sciences of evolutionary biology, anthropology, primatology, archaeology, linguistics, embryology, and genetics have been applied to explain the origin of humanity, but the majority of the human race still prefers faith in one God over science.

Darwinism explains our origin through the study of human evolution from organisms, hominids to *Homo sapiens* and modern man of today. The majority of the mainstream scientific community accepts the theory of evolution. However, the debate continues as to whether evolutionism holds the answer to our beginning.

Darwin's *Origin of Species* theorized that humanity's beginning can be traced to closely linked species that evolved over millions of years. According to Darwin, the best of a species would survive and reproduce, and so humans evolved through the process of natural selection. Evolutionary biologists believe that commonly joined species, beginning with unicellular organisms, have been able to adapt, survive, and breed over millions of years to produce humans.

The chain of evolution has been well documented, accepted by respected biologists and scholars, and nurtured over the years. However, some scholars believe there is an evolutionary gap in the chain of fossil evidence between primitive species and modern humans. Although credible in most scientific communities, Darwin's theory of evolution is subject to examination and opposing opinions still today. As a result, we continue to search for answers to the true origin of the human race.

There is now evidence to support unconventional theories about the origin of humanity. It is amazing how many stories, paintings, and artifacts are so similar among different ancient cultures on every continent on earth. Paintings, wall carvings, and other artifacts in various cultures worldwide depict gods and winged angels. Extraterrestrials—like Sky Beings, Nephilim, Grigori, and Star People—are depicted in fiery sky boats and chariots in different cultures around the world.

Mayan, Aztec, Incan, Sumerian, Babylonian, Egyptian, Norse, Greek, and Indian cultures have similar stories of powerful gods who came down from the stars to influence human history. Many of these same cultures describe their gods as spiritual beings that came from the heavens. The Judeo-Christian Bible, the book of Enoch, the Quran, the Sumerian and Babylonian tablets, the Hindu holy books the Bhagavad Gita and Ramayana, and the codices have similar flood and creation stories.

Mountains, seas, and oceans separate these cultures from one another, but their stories are so similar we can no longer disregard the likeness as coincidence. Accordingly, how could so many cultures share some of the same beliefs without any contact between them?

Answers to these questions may be found in the stars. During the past two hundred years, we've learned that the universe is exceedingly enormous. The Milky Way galaxy alone contains billions of stars, and we may eventually learn that at least three planets rotate around each star. Credible evidence supports the claim that there are an estimated one hundred billion galaxies in the universe, each one with billions of stars. Thus, the probability of extraterrestrial life is high.

Some astronomers estimate that there are between one septillion and ten septillion stars in the universe. A septillion is one million to the seventh power or 1,000,000,000,000,000,000,000,000. Given these estimates and the fact that multiple planets revolve around most stars, the number of planets might be somewhere around fifty septillion—a number so large it is incomprehensible.

So how many planets are there, and how many can sustain intelligent life? Recent research confirms that life may exist in habitable zones called Goldilocks planets, where conditions might support life. NASA and SETI have spent billions of dollars exploring answers regarding life on other planets. SETI concentrates its radio telescopes upward from various radio astronomy observatories, searching for messages from other planets.

Kepler's main mission is to help scientists determine how many earth-size planets may be in the universe. According to a March 2012 article in the *Daily Galaxy*, 68 of the first 1,235 planets studied are roughly the same size as earth. Fifty-four appear to orbit in their stars' habitable zones. These findings are just the beginning, and the further we look, the more we will find. One can logically postulate that there is a real possibility we are not alone.

Recent polls indicate that over 55 percent of all Americans and 75 percent of young adults, from eighteen to twenty-four, believe that there is intelligent life on other planets. Moreover, a *National Geographic* survey indicated that 77 percent of Americans believe there are signs that aliens have visited earth. Over 35 percent of adult Americans believe that extraterrestrial beings have visited our planet during earth's history. If more than one-third of adult Americans believes that aliens have visited us, isn't the possibility worth exploring?

Even more surprising is the lack of public trust in the government on the subject of aliens. According to a CNN poll taken in 1997, 80 percent of Americans believe that the government is hiding evidence about the existence of extraterrestrial life-forms. The government may think the American public cannot handle the truth about extraterrestrials.

The existence of other intelligent life somewhere in the universe is probable. Some of these extraterrestrials may be similar to humans and some not. Institutions cannot dismiss the evidence for religious or political reasons. Even the Vatican has just recently acknowledged the possible existence of alien life on other planets.

We are not alone in the universe, and to a large extent, we never were. Given the age of the earth and that *Homo sapiens* have existed for only 250,000 years, there were 4.48 billion years when intelligent life was absent on earth. Or was there? How did intelligent man so quickly emerge on earth after billions of years?

The Beginning seeks answers to these questions, providing another viewpoint on the mystery of human life, the existence of extraterrestrials, and their connection to the earth and the origin of man. One of the primary purposes of this book is to broaden our perspective on the origin and history of the human race on earth.

About the Author

Born in Wilmington, Delaware, Michael R. Nardo has lived in the Wilmington-Hockessin area his entire life. He and his wife, Mary, have been married for thirty-eight years. They have three daughters and five grandchildren.

Michael graduated with a bachelor's degree of science from the University of Delaware in 1975. He served for twenty-one years as a government administrator, mainly as the director of administration and operations in the Delaware attorney general's office. In 1996, he started his own IT company, FuturTech Consulting, which he successfully managed and nurtured for almost twenty years as CEO/owner. Michael is recognized as a technology expert and advisor, and he has received numerous awards for achievement in government, business, and personal life.

In 2013, he started to pursue his lifelong dream of writing a book, and *The Beginning* was born, the first installment of a trilogy.

CPSIA information can be obtained at www.ICGtesting.com
Printed in the USA
LVOW11s0237181016

509215LV00001B/37/P